M000194989

resisting
the rebel

LISA BROWN ROBERTS

Entangled Publishing, LLC
2614 South Timberline Road
Suite 109
Fort Collins, CO 80525
Visit our website at www.entangledpublishing.com.

Crush is an imprint of Entangled Publishing, LLC.

Edited by Liz Pelletier
Cover design by Heather Howland
Cover art from iStock

Manufactured in the United States of America

First Edition June 2016

For heroes and sidekicks, archenemies and villains, best friends and boyfriends...and for Warren and Layla, forever.

Chapter One
Shake Your Groove Thing

Friday, September 16

Mandy Pennington took a deep breath and surveyed the dimly lit room full of entwined couples sprawled across couches and groping each other in dark corners. Music pounded so loudly that her plastic cup vibrated in her hand. Drunken parties weren't her usual scene, but when Gus had casually asked her after school if she wanted to go with him, of course she'd said yes.

Even though it was her birthday and she'd had plans with her best friends to go dancing at an all-ages club.

Even though the party was at Kay's house, the den of her archenemy.

Even though her annoying stoner brother had warned her it wasn't her type of party.

Whatever. Gus had asked her and that was what mattered, because she and Gus were destined for each other, even if Gus didn't realize it yet. But maybe tonight was the night he'd finally—

"Yo, Mandy. Wassup?"

She blinked, focusing on the guy standing in front of her. She couldn't remember his name, but she knew he was on the lacrosse team with Gus, so she gave him her best "I totally should be Gus's girlfriend, right?" smile.

"Not much," she said. "How are you?"

His eyes were glazed, but they focused in on her chest. "I'd be better if you'd let me do a body shot from your—"

"As if." Mandy took a step back. She'd heard the lacrosse guys were horndogs, but seriously? She glanced behind him, looking for Gus to come to her rescue, because he totally would. He was awesome like that.

A prince among frogs.

The guy shrugged, looking bored rather than disappointed. "Whatever. Shoulda known you were too chicken."

Mandy suddenly wished she were with her best friends J.T. and Cammie practicing disco moves at the dance club. That's where she should be, not at this low-life party with jerks like this guy who was still staring at her chest.

She rolled her eyes and turned away, determined to find Gus so they could kick her birthday celebration into second gear. She fired off a quick text, asking him where he was.

Pushing through the crowd, she scanned the room for signs of Gus's curly brown hair and blue hoodie, but it was hard to make out actual faces in the semidarkness.

She kept moving, knowing he had to be around somewhere, but after she'd done a full circuit of the room and even been brave enough to peek into the dark bedrooms, she still hadn't found him.

Crud.

She took a deep breath and recited one of her go-to mantras in her mind: *The universe doesn't give us more than we can handle.* It was kind of a cliché, but she still believed it.

She took another breath, headed upstairs, pushed through the crowded kitchen where all the Jell-O shots were happening, then finally escaped through the sliding door onto the dark patio. The rush of cold air felt good for a few seconds, until she started shivering. She rubbed her hands up and down her bare arms. Maybe her retro minidress hadn't been such a great idea.

Beckoned by the faraway sound of laughter, she leaned over the deck railing, straining to see if Gus might be one of the people standing around the fire pit in the far corner of the vast backyard.

"Great. Just great," she muttered aloud. Why had Gus abandoned her so quickly? She'd assumed they'd hang out together. Maybe dance. Maybe…more.

"Lose someone?"

Startled, she whirled around, coming face-to-face with a shadowed figure leaning against the far edge of the deck railing. She heard the unmistakable *click* of a lighter, and a tiny orange glow illuminated his face.

Caleb Torrs.

Suddenly she wasn't cold anymore because Caleb was… well…not the kind of guy she felt cold around. He was the exact opposite in fact, the kind of guy who stirred up an internal bonfire with just one glance.

Not that he ever noticed *her*. He was into bad girls, which made sense because he was totally a bad boy. Black leather jacket and motorcycle boots. Black jeans with the knees ripped out. Tangled dark hair and a stony face. Dark eyes watched her in the glow of the flame from his lighter.

She cleared her throat nervously and glanced toward the fire pit again. "Um, maybe…I don't…know."

He doused the lighter, shrouding himself in darkness again. "Maybe I've seen him." His disembodied voice curled around her like smoke. "Who are you looking for?"

"Why do you think it's a him?" The words tumbled out before she could stop them.

His responding laugh was low, sending a tingle up her spine.

She bit her lip, trying to make out his features, but all she saw was the faint glint of light from his eyes and the curve of his mouth, curled in a smirk.

She might as well ask him since she'd looked everywhere else. "Gus. Lacrosse guy?"

The lighter flicked and she noticed his smirk morph into a grimace. Then he doused the flame, shrouding them in darkness again.

"What are you, a pyro or something?"

"Maybe." He shifted against the railing, running a hand through his tangled hair. His hair was the stuff of legends and fantasies at Sky Ridge High. Maybe even a few of *her* fantasies, but that was pointless because a) he had a girlfriend and b) Mandy was in love with Gus.

"Whatever." She stepped toward the door, frustrated with his bad-boy act and the way she was distracted by his rock star hair. "I don't have time for games. Have fun torching Kay's house." She wanted to get out of here. This definitely wasn't how her birthday was supposed to turn out.

Caleb stepped away from the railing, moving into the light spilling from the kitchen onto the deck. God he was…

She took a breath. *Whatever.* Yeah, he was hot, but he was also a jerk, based on all the rumors she'd heard, and she didn't have time for that. Guys like Caleb were the reason she liked Gus—sweet, adorable Gus who definitely didn't own a lighter.

"I saw him," Caleb said, taking another step toward her. His hair shadowed his face, but she still felt the heat of his gaze. "He and Kay headed for the fire pit a while ago."

Gus and…Kay? He was with the most evil girl in school? Mandy swallowed, telling herself Caleb had to be mistaken.

He glanced toward the dark yard. "Not sure if they're still out there."

Now what? Should she try to find Gus to ask him to take her home? But what if he really was with Kay doing... whatever. She definitely didn't want to interrupt that.

But he wouldn't. Not with Kay.

It was *her* he was supposed to be with tonight. She was the one he was supposed to be dragging away to the bonfire, not Kay.

Trust the signs, she told herself, though she wasn't sure exactly what the signs were, other than badass Caleb flicking his lighter and telling her something she didn't want to hear.

She glanced at her mood ring. Brown, for confused and restless.

"Well, thanks, I guess," she said, turning toward the deck steps. She'd head out to the fire pit and see if Gus was there. He still hadn't replied to her text, and she didn't want to think too hard about what that might mean.

As she reached the first step the wind kicked up, lifting the skirt of her dress. She tugged it down, and the sudden flick of Caleb's lighter made her flinch. She swore she could feel his eyes boring into her back as she clattered down the deck, hugging herself and wishing for a coat.

. . .

Caleb watched Mandy stumble down the steps, her crazy red hair swirling in the wind.

This party sucked, and his brief interchange with the queen of school spirit had the potential to entertain him, but she was obviously too focused on Gus to stick around and make his night more interesting.

Too bad, because even though she was everything he hated about high school wrapped up in one sparkly package, she was still…intriguing.

He flicked his lighter again, watching the flame dance in the wind. It was an old Zippo, etched with a skull and crossbones. He smirked as he thought of Mandy calling him a pyro. Hardly; he didn't even smoke. But he'd had this lighter for years, ever since he'd found it in his brother Mike's room after he left for college. Caleb held on to it as a weird sort of memento since he didn't see much of Mike these days.

Caleb sighed and shoved the lighter back in his jacket pocket, his fingers brushing against a worn notebook. He watched Mandy pick her way across the grass toward the clumps of laughing people gathered around the fire pit.

Gus wasn't there. He had been, briefly, before Kay had dragged him into the dark bushes. Caleb could only imagine what was going down right now…or who.

He tensed as he imagined Mandy stumbling onto the scene. She was obviously into the guy, but she was about to get a rude awakening. Gus might have shown up with Mandy, but he definitely wasn't leaving with her.

Why was he wasting time thinking about this? Why was he even here? This party was a waste of time and energy. He still wasn't sure why he'd come. Maybe because his dad was home and he'd needed to escape.

Sighing, he turned away from the fire pit and the crazy redhead who looked as out of place at this stupid party as he felt.

He didn't have time for her, or anyone else.

• • •

Mandy approached the edge of the fire pit, stomach twisting with anxiety. She searched the crowd for Gus but didn't see him…until she did.

He leaned against a tree, Kay wrapped around him like a

second skin, her mouth locked on his, his hands…everywhere.

Stunned, Mandy stumbled back from the fire pit.

No. This couldn't be happening. But it *was* happening, right in front of her eyes, and she couldn't un-see it.

Heart pounding against her ribs, she stumbled across the grass, up the deck steps, through the kitchen and living room, and out the front door. Feeling like she might throw up, she stood in the driveway, wondering what to do.

How would she get home? Her brother was out with his stoner friends. Her dad was on the road, hauling Walmart junk in his semi, so he couldn't come get her. She fumbled with her phone to text J.T. and Cammie, hoping they'd come to her rescue, even though she sort of didn't deserve it after abandoning them tonight.

Mayday! Mayday! Rescue needed asap! Can you guys come get me at Kay's?

She fired off the text and waited, shivering, as the wind kicked up and light snowflakes glittered in the streetlight.

Times like this, there was only one way to cope. She fished her earbuds out of her leather fringed bag, crammed them in her ears, and cranked up her Seventies Greatest Hits playlist. Closing her eyes, she took a deep, meditative breath and let the music wash over her.

Chapter Two
I Will Survive

Friday, September 16

Caleb had just started his car when Mandy rushed out of the house. She stopped when she reached the driveway, glancing anxiously up and down the cul-de-sac, but the only people around were the group of guys on the lawn, laughing as they shared hits off a joint.

From his spot at the far end of the cul-de-sac, he watched her shove in her earbuds and lift her face to the sky like a weird snow worshipper. He groaned, leaning back against his car's headrest. He should leave. He'd managed to escape the party after being cornered by his stalker ex-girlfriend, who was still confused about her ex status.

He revved his engine, his gaze tracking the stoner wobbling toward Mandy, now followed by the rest of his posse. He didn't recognize these guys from school, and a sliver of apprehension slid through him as they closed in on Mandy.

Crap.

He flashed his headlights to warn her about the stoner stalkers. She bounced up and down, rubbing her arms, obviously freezing because she didn't have a coat, but she was oblivious to his attempts at headlight Morse code. Knowing her, she probably thought the flashing headlights were a disco ball.

He ran a hand through his hair. Had he pissed off the big guy in the sky somehow? It sure felt like a supernatural punishment, having to rescue this girl who flitted around school like a butterfly mascot, actively involved in everything he avoided like the plague.

"Damn it," he muttered, killing the engine. He stepped out of the car and slammed the door shut. He stalked down the street, his black motorcycle boots pounding the pavement, keenly aware of the mocking laughter from the weed-heads.

He reached her at the same time the first stoner did, reeking of skunk weed.

"Dude." Caleb narrowed his eyes. "Back off."

Skunk-Weed tilted his head as if struggling to tune in to the right frequency. "I'm not gonna bother her."

"Right," Caleb said. "You're not. So get lost." He glared at the rest of the stoner posse. "All of you. Beat it." The stragglers backed away, but the first guy didn't move.

"Pennington," he snapped, but she ignored him, her eyes closed. He could hear the tinny sound of music through her earbuds. Sighing in exasperation, he reached over and yanked the earbuds out of her ears.

• • •

Mandy stumbled as her earbuds fell out of her ears. Her eyes flew open, and she gasped as her startled gaze landed on the last person she expected to see.

"Go," Caleb growled at some guy she'd never seen before.

"Don't make me hurt you."

"Caleb." Mandy found her voice, even though she was still surprised to see him. "Violence is never the answer."

Caleb spun toward her, his dark eyes glittering in the moonlight, and she caught her breath. *I am safe in the womb of the universe,* she told herself, calling up another favorite mantra. *No harm will come to me.*

"Drop it, Pennington," he growled, making the hair on her arms stand up.

Hadn't Caleb caused enough trouble tonight, sending her after Gus and Kay? It took all her self-control not to let loose the tears that had been threatening to fall since she'd seen them kissing.

"What are you doing here, anyway?" she asked.

"Chasing off assholes," Caleb said, shooting a glare at the guy she didn't recognize, who reeked of pot.

"Hey," the guy said. "The lady looked like she needed company."

Caleb snorted. "*The lady*"—she winced at the mocking tone in his voice—"is leaving." He glanced at her. "Right?"

She blinked against the glare of the headlights pointed right at her, wishing she could shove her earbuds back in and tune him out. Wishing she'd never come to this stupid party.

"I'd like to leave," she said with a sigh, "but I don't have a ride." She'd been so full of giddy expectation that maybe tonight Gus would finally realize how she felt about him, and tell her that he felt exactly the same way. But instead Kay had woven her evil spell, and Gus had forgotten her existence.

Caleb muttered something she couldn't quite catch, other than an f-bomb. She glanced at her phone, desperate to escape, but J.T. and Cammie still hadn't responded to her SOS text.

"Let's go, hippie," Caleb said.

She glanced up from her phone, surprised to realize he

was talking to her, not the stoner guy.

"Technically, I'm more disco than hippie," she corrected.

Caleb rolled his eyes. "Whatever. Let's go, Disco." He reached out to grab her arm.

She flinched at his touch, which felt like fire shooting up her freezing arm. He stalked away from the stoners, towing her like a rubber raft bouncing behind a determined steamship.

"What are you doing?"

He opened the passenger door and impatiently gestured her inside, then slammed the door closed, making her jump.

"Geez, Caleb," she muttered to his shadowy figure as he walked around the car, "don't ever go into the limo business. You'll go broke."

But when he slid into the car, his musky scent mixing with the clean smell of snow and completely shutting down her brain cells, she forgot to be indignant.

"I assume you need a ride somewhere."

"Umm." Mandy tried to focus. She needed another mantra, stat, but her mind was blank. It was startling to find herself alone in a car with a guy she'd ogled from afar—*secretly* ogled, the same way she did celebrities and other unattainables.

Caleb started the car and cranked up music that sounded like angry yelling, not at all like the old disco she usually listened to. She darted a quick look at his unsmiling face and took a breath. Maybe a joke would make him crack a smile and help her refocus. "So is this a rescue or a kidnapping?"

His answering eye roll made her wish she'd kept her mouth shut. She swallowed and fidgeted with her necklace. Okay, so he might win the *looks* category of a Mr. Badass America contest, but he'd definitely lose the personality competition.

"Uh, I mean, um," she stammered, grasping for something else to lighten the mood. "I get to ride in the hearse." She flashed him a fake grin so he'd know she was joking about calling his vintage car a hearse. "It's my lucky night."

He shot her a smirk. "Lucky night?"

She squirmed on her seat, because that smirk of his did something tingly to her insides.

"Well, yeah," she said. "I mean, it's awesome of you to give me a ride and…" Her voice trailed away as she panicked, realizing he might have totally misinterpreted her "lucky night" comment. "I didn't mean *that* kind of lucky—God!" She felt herself blush as he laughed softly next to her.

"Your car's awesome. Really, um, shiny. And black." She patted the seat. "Very clean." She knew she was rambling, but she had to do something to make him stop thinking she wanted to get lucky with him.

Because she didn't want that. Well…maybe in an alternate universe she might—

"Are you drunk?" He cocked an eyebrow, and his smirk made another appearance.

"No!" she protested. "I'm the only person *not* drunk tonight."

"Really? That makes two of us."

Caleb's unnerving gaze shifted from her face to the rest of her, skimming down her body. She swallowed and twirled her hair nervously. The minidress had definitely been a bad idea.

"You're cold," he said, surprising her by shrugging out of his leather jacket and tossing it to her. "Put this on."

She touched the warm leather, running her fingers down the worn material, then tucked it around her like a blanket.

"Thanks," she whispered, secretly inhaling the spicy Caleb scent emanating from the jacket.

"Sure." His gaze swept over her again, then he turned away and put the car into gear. "Where to, Disco?" He pulled out of the cul-de-sac, waiting to turn right or left.

"Do you know where the Cheap Seats theater is? I'm just a few blocks from there." She cleared her throat. "And my name is Mandy."

"Short for Amanda?" he asked as he accelerated. She assumed he knew where he was going, even though he probably never went to the dollar movies since his family was loaded.

"No," she said. "Just Mandy. I'm named after an old seventies song."

He shot her a puzzled glance. "Never heard of it."

She shrugged. Most people hadn't. She burrowed deeper into his jacket, closing her eyes, and searching for a mantra to calm her. *Everything happens for a reason.*

They drove in silence for a while as she pondered her situation. There was no such thing as coincidence. Maybe this was a bonus gift from the universe: a sorry-you-saw-Gus-and-Kay-kissing-but-you-get-to-ride-home-with-a-hot-guy-you've-always-secretly-crushed-on consolation prize.

"I was just kidding about the hearse thing," she said, deciding to show the universe she appreciated the gift. "Maybe we should call it...I don't know. A Batmobile?" She paused. "I bet you have a secret cave somewhere. An underground lair full of, um...I don't know, death metal posters?" She forced an interested smile. "What is this music, anyway?"

She heard him take a long breath, then exhale slowly. So maybe he already knew how to meditate? Excellent. He totally needed an outlet for the waves of unsettled energy rolling off him. Maybe it would help if she kept engaging him.

"That's great deep breathing, Caleb. It'll help you relax. That stoner guy was weird, wasn't he? Did you see some of the other guys at the party? Total lowlifes. No wait! I don't mean that. What I mean is, um, fellow travelers trying to find their way. Because there's always hope, right? People can always turn their lives around if they just believe." She punctuated her words with a firm nod. "Always."

He gunned the engine, and she noticed his breathing came quicker now. Uh-oh. Maybe he wasn't relaxing. Fast breathing might mean he was in danger of losing whatever equilibrium he had. *Think, Mandy, think.*

"So how's Elle?" She searched for a compliment, something to flatter him. "You two are, um, cute together. Okay, maybe not cute. More like...imposing. You with your big towering demon thing and her with—"

"My towering *what*?" He took a corner way too fast, then slammed on the brakes, fishtailing slightly on the slick road. He put the car in park and glared at her.

Mandy bit her lip, pulling his jacket tight to protect her neck because now he reminded her of an extremely annoyed vampire. Cammie kept telling her to stop watching old *Buffy* reruns; maybe she was right.

Caleb ran a hand through his tangle of black hair, and she bit her lip harder. She wondered if his hair was as silky to the touch as it looked.

Simmer down, girl, she told herself. *You don't like bad boys—remember?*

She was supposed to be with Gus. Stupid, Kay-kissing Gus, who didn't even remember today was her birthday.

• • •

Towering demon thing? What the hell? Mandy didn't smell like skunk weed, but she sounded like she was on something. She shot him a nervous sideways glance, her huge doe eyes blinking in the glare of the streetlight as her crazy red hair partially hid her face.

"I'm not a demon. I'm your Good Samaritan, doing you a solid and driving you home."

She cocked an eyebrow. "A solid? Seriously?"

He rolled his eyes. "I'm trying to speak the language of your people. Gus-speak."

"Don't even. Gus is dead to me." Her eyes flashed with a spark of anger, then her expression morphed to shock, as if she were horrified by what she'd said. "Not really dead!" She gasped. "That's super bad karma."

He studied her under the glow of the streetlight, assembling the limited facts to try to make sense of the situation. She was pissed at Gus. She didn't have a ride home from the party. After she'd left him on the deck, she'd probably seen Gus and freaky student council president Kay doing...whatever.

Poor butterfly had just had her heart crushed. Sucked for her, but she might as well figure out now that most guys were jerks.

"What do you see in that loser, anyway?"

She blinked, looking slightly stunned. "H-he's not a loser. I've known him since kindergarten and it's just...I've always...he and I, we're *meant* to be together."

Caleb smirked. "Puppy love isn't real, Disco."

She tensed, taut with indignation. "Don't mock me, Caleb."

"Or what? You'll suffocate me with patchouli oil?"

"I do *not* wear patchouli." She lifted his jacket to sniff her arm. "Maybe it's my incense from earlier today. But I definitely don't wear it. Actually, I like this old perfume called Baby Soft. I order it online. I mean, you can get it at Walmart, but online has a better selection, plus the powder and... um..." Her voice trailed away.

Damn. Dealing with her was like watching a subtitled anime — weird to look at, and hard to follow the story. He blew out a long sigh, wishing he'd never left his house tonight. "Whatever. I'm just making conversation, which is challenging with you, Disco. Sort of like talking to a kindergartner on crack."

She gasped and leaned forward. "What is *that* supposed to mean? Are you saying I'm stupid? I'm trying very hard to make conversation with *you*, Caleb. Maybe you're the one making it difficult."

Caleb wondered if his grip would break the steering wheel as he pulled away from the curb. It was about a twenty-minute drive to Mandy's house, longer now that the roads were icing up.

"What are you doing?" She sounded panicked when he turned into the 7-Eleven parking lot, like he was an ax murderer in disguise just waiting for his opportunity.

"Getting a Red Bull. You want anything?"

She shook her head, eyes wide. "You don't want to see me on Red Bull."

Caleb stared, not sure whether to laugh or hit something.

If there was even a speck of truth to Mandy's karma thing, he was earning enough tonight to escape the nine circles of hell.

• • •

Mandy sat in the car scanning social media postings while Caleb got his caffeine fix. She texted J.T. and Cammie that she had a ride home. They replied, saying they hoped she'd survive the ride with her scary driver, and they'd meet her at her house.

She'd texted Gus three times to tell him she'd left without him, but he hadn't replied. She closed her eyes and repeated one of her favorite mantras: *I am right where I'm supposed to be. The universe has a reason, even if I don't see it.* She stroked Caleb's jacket with her fingers, then cautiously put her hand into one of the pockets. Totally snooping and probably bad karma, but she couldn't resist. Her fingers closed around lint and the lighter. Hmm. She flipped the coat over and investigated the other pocket.

Jackpot.

Mandy's fingers closed over a small notebook. She shouldn't open it. No way. It was a total violation of privacy. Who knew what was in there? Probably angry poetry, or maybe a list of all his hookups ranked by sexual abilities. She shook her head to clear away her stupid thoughts. What was wrong with her tonight?

Yeah, Caleb rattled her...rattle...rattler. He kind of was like a rattlesnake. If he saw any weakness he'd strike out and bite her neck and...oh wow...now that was an image that made her whole body flush.

Mandy swallowed. Her finger traced the metal coil holding the pages together. Sometimes she felt like that spiral, tightly wound and responsible for keeping everything together.

Caleb had no idea how much his "kindergartner on crack" comment hurt. Her doctor said she'd have an easier time if she took meds for the ADHD, but she didn't want to do that anymore because she'd tried it and hated the side effects. Gran had suggested the occasional puff of weed, but no way was she doing that. She didn't want to end up like her brother, whose smoking had ratcheted up from the occasional party smoking to an everyday habit that caused his grades to tank.

Most days she felt like she was white-knuckling it, especially in some of her more challenging classes, but she believed the universe gave her a squirrel brain for a reason. She just didn't know what it was yet. She closed her eyes and took another deep breath. *I am in control of my emotions. My mind is calm and clear. I am a ray of light to everyone I meet.* Even the cranky chauffeur.

She stared at the small worn notebook in her hand, wondering what secrets it held.

Caleb was a mystery, an enigma. He looked like a badass she'd cross the street to avoid, yet he was one of the smartest guys in school according to J.T., who was on the honors track with him. Even though Caleb ditched classes a lot, he still earned As and Bs. It wasn't fair, when she had to work so hard just to earn Cs and the occasional B in her non-honors classes.

She plugged the aux cable into her phone and cranked up the volume. Her music sounded awesome on his car stereo, way better than sitting in dark silence. She shoved the notebook back into his jacket pocket, unopened, proud of herself for resisting the urge to snoop. A wave of happiness at the good karma she'd just earned shot through her.

Determined to stop thinking about Caleb, and Gus and Kay sucking face, she sang along to the music. *"You're a shining star, no matter who you are. Shining bright to see what you can truly be."*

This music always cheered her up; maybe it would do the same for the broody demon chauffeur.

· · ·

Caleb took a long swig of his Red Bull before heading back to his car. He watched Mandy sing along to the annoying disco beat pounding through the closed windows. He glanced around, grateful no one he knew was around to witness his humiliation.

Sighing, he headed to his car, resigned to his fate. It wasn't like he could abandon her. For an indefinable reason, he felt a responsibility to get her home safe, especially after Gus had bailed on her.

He opened the door, slid onto the seat, and hit the power button, killing the song mid-cloying lyric.

"Hey!" she protested. "Not cool, Caleb. I love that song."

"But I don't." He held out his Red Bull. "Sure you don't want some? I hear it cures broken hearts."

She narrowed her eyes. "You're kind of a jerk, Caleb."

"Tell me something I *don't* know."

"Maybe I'm not the only one with a broken heart," she said as he pulled onto the main road.

He glanced at her, noticing her ridiculous spider eyelashes. Were those fake? Unbelievable.

"I didn't see you with Elle tonight," she pressed.

His hands tightened on the wheel. "Elle is psycho. Even more than you."

"I'm not psycho."

He snorted. "Debatable. Anyway, Elle and I split." *Even though Elle is in denial,* he thought, but he kept that to himself.

"So you shouldn't make fun of other people's love lives just because you can't keep a girlfriend."

He accelerated as much as he safely could in the swirling snow. He had to get this girl home. "I could keep a girlfriend. If I wanted to." He bit the words out, each one costing him painful life points.

She tugged his jacket tight around her neck. "I doubt it. Girls don't like jerk boyfriends, at least not on a long-term basis. But you don't do long-term, do you, Caleb?"

If only she were a guy, he'd just toss her out of his car. He glanced at her, surprised by the challenge sparking in her eyes and the stubborn tilt of her jaw. He liked what he saw.

"Maybe I haven't met anybody worth the effort."

She blinked. "Because you think you're better than everyone else."

Okay, *that* he didn't like. "I'm gonna clue you in on a secret, Disco, on behalf of all guys everywhere. We don't like crazy. We don't like stalkers. We don't like needy. We don't like—"

"Turn here."

Her voice sounded weird. He pulled into the driveway and turned toward her. Her eyes blinked rapidly, and he winced at the shock he saw reflected back at him. He was being a dick;

he knew that. But he didn't know how else to deal with her. She wore her heart on her sleeve; she always had, which was another reason he avoided her.

She'd be fine. She'd go inside and watch some cheesy romance movie and her faith in humanity would be restored.

And he wouldn't have to deal with her ever again.

• • •

"Thank you for the ride, Caleb," Mandy said formally, like he was an Uber driver, not someone she actually knew. She had to get away from him and his insults. Yeah, he'd given her a ride home, but he'd been sort of a jerk, especially at the end.

The glow of his headlights illuminated her path as she ran up the driveway, praying she wouldn't slip on the snow and embarrass herself. She opened the front door, and the headlights dipped and dimmed as Caleb reversed out of the driveway and sped away.

She texted J.T. and Cammie.

R U almost here? Horrible night. Worst birthday ever.

Their replies pinged back instantly, saying they were just a few blocks away.

She had the best friends in the world.

• • •

Caleb walked up the wide, curving staircase, carefully avoiding the cat swirling between his legs. His dad wasn't home — probably out with his latest arm candy or maybe working late at the office. Not that it mattered; he liked having the house to himself.

He cranked music while he showered, trying to drown away the night. What a complete waste of time and energy. Why the hell had he gone to that party? He hated people, especially his classmates, 99 percent of whom were morons. Especially the one he'd been stuck driving in circles with tonight, who was apparently living in some sort of 1970s time warp mashed up with some crazy New Age life-is-beautiful-if-you-just-breathe philosophy.

Never again. Even if Mandy was sort of cute, she was crazy, and he didn't do crazy.

He wrapped a towel around his waist and flopped into the overstuffed chair in the reading alcove overlooking the swimming pool. He pulled one of his favorite books from the stack on the table. Nights like this, the only thing that could make him feel better was reading about someone who got it, who got him. Not girls who couldn't even handle a Red Bull. He opened the well-worn book and read the famous opening lines.

The Catcher in the Rye. Now that was a book. He doubted someone like Mandy would get all that was going on in Holden's jacked-up life. But he did. He read for a long time, then set the book aside. Someday he wanted to write books like that, books that made people think. He wanted to be like Salinger, or maybe Kerouac or Hemingway. The type of writer people still talked about long after they were dead.

It was Mandy's fault he was in such a black mood. She'd pissed him off, saying he was a crappy boyfriend, that he couldn't keep a girlfriend long-term. He'd told her the truth when he'd said he'd never meant anyone who could keep his interest. It wasn't just girls he got bored with, it was everyone.

There was a reason he sat by himself at lunch every day with a book. Why he didn't do BS like football games and school dances. Real connection with people always led to disappointment. Or worse. Anyway, he'd rather watch people than engage with them; it was perfect training for being a writer.

Caleb grabbed his notebook from his leather jacket lying

on the floor. He opened it, flipping to one of his favorite pages. Next to *The Catcher in the Rye* and *A Farewell to Arms*, this was his favorite book, but it wasn't something he could ever write an AP essay about. No one but him would ever see this book.

Some days it was the only thing keeping him anchored to the earth.

Chapter Three
One Thing Leads to Another

Monday, September 19

Mandy's last class of the day was lit, which always made her contemplate ditching, not that she ever would, unlike Caleb. Mr. Spriggs rattled her unlike any other teacher. He was condescending and made her feel like an idiot. She liked to read, though not the books he assigned.

Freshman year, when she'd had him for comp, she'd worked up her courage to ask him for extra help on structuring an essay. He'd given her that withering stare of his and asked why she didn't know basic fifth-grade composition. She'd begged Ms. Chen, her counselor, to move her to another section of American Lit this year, but his was the only one that worked with the rest of her schedule.

Spriggs droned on about some other ancient book they had to read, and Mandy tried to take notes. Thank goodness J.T. had already read all these books in his honors classes. He could help her decipher them, make them less boring when he reenacted the most dramatic scenes.

As always, J.T. had made her laugh, cheering her up on Saturday night when he and Cammie had come over after the party from hell. They'd brought a giant tub of chocolate fudge ice cream, peanut M&M's, and a magazine with Ryan Gosling on the cover. The three of them had stayed up into the wee hours rehashing the evilness of Kay's stealing Gus from under her nose, and the drive from hell with Caleb, who they all agreed was the biggest, most self-absorbed jackass on the planet.

"Ms. Pennington," Mr. Spriggs said, right after the bell rang, "please come up here."

She glanced at Gus, momentarily struck dumb by his floppy brown curls and big blue eyes, the eyes she'd been in love with since forever. But he just shrugged sympathetically and left without looking back.

Of course he didn't bother to stick around to wait for her; he was probably in a hurry to suck face with Kay. She sighed heavily and approached the desk of doom.

"I spoke with Ms. Chen about your essay." Mr. Spriggs narrowed his eyes. "As I reminded her, I'm not in the habit of letting students have extensions for work they should've completed properly in the first place."

Mandy's heart raced and her palms sweated. Why was he so awful to her? "I-I know," she stammered. "Thank you for giving me a second chance."

The essay had been due last week, but she'd been frozen by writer's block, and she did have extra time for assignments as part of her school-approved 504 accommodation plan, so Ms. Chen had gone to bat for her. Usually Mandy handled the extra time requests on her own, but Mr. Spriggs made her brain freeze, so she'd asked Ms. Chen for help.

His face pinched and narrowed like a bird's. "I've taught for many years, Ms. Pennington. I've heard every excuse in

the book from students. This latest incarnation of excuses —
ADHD, processing disorder, dyslexia — "

"Dysgraphia," Mandy whispered. "I have dysgraphia, not
dyslexia." She couldn't believe she'd dared to interrupt him,
since he clearly didn't believe any of it was real.

"Whatever." He waved a hand as if he were tossing her
in an imaginary trash can. "I'm tired of all the excuses, the
supposed accommodations I'm to give students like you."

She couldn't believe the words coming out of his mouth.
Over the years, some teachers had been more sympathetic
than others to her learning differences, but she'd never
encountered someone so outwardly hostile. She wondered if
she should tell Ms. Chen, but worried it would backfire if she
did.

Everyone I meet on my journey is there for a reason. She
swallowed nervously and dared to meet his cold gaze. Maybe
not everyone.

"You have two weeks, which is quite generous on my
part, considering you had all summer to read the book and
prepare for this essay."

Mandy reminded herself to breathe. Two weeks to redo
the essay and to prep for Spirit Week, which she was in charge
of. And Dad was on the road for his truck-driving job, her
stoner brother Reg was skipping school, and she needed
to take care of Gran, who lived with them. Her shoulders
slumped.

And if she didn't get at least a C on the essay, she'd be
benched from the cheer dance squad, which would be awful.
She took a deep breath.

"Okay," she said, her voice tight as she kept all of the
things she wanted to say inside.

Mr. Spriggs waved a hand, dismissing her, and she escaped
the classroom only to be stopped by a familiar yet unwelcome
voice.

"Mandy! Wait up!"

Mandy spun around, her stomach tightening. Kay Ashton, stealer of Gus, president of the student council, and all-around doubter of Mandy's ability to do anything right, stalked toward her like a girl on a mission.

"Hi, Kay," Mandy said, wondering what karmic act she'd done to end up on Spriggs's bad side and now Kay's, judging from the scowl on her face.

Kay put her hands on her hips. As usual, she looked perfectly put together, not a brunette hair out of place, not a stain or wrinkle in sight. She'd been like that since kindergarten.

Mandy breathed through her nose, willing herself to stay calm.

"So this DJ you hired for homecoming, are you sure he's committed to our dance?"

Mandy frowned. "Why wouldn't he be?" Neuro Blastr was a cool guy. She'd met him at the all-ages dance club, and he was giving them a deal on his fee for the dance.

"Because I've been texting him for two days and he hasn't replied." Kay's eyes narrowed suspiciously.

"Maybe he's out of town, doing a gig or whatever," Mandy said. "The dance is still three weeks away. I wouldn't worry."

Kay snorted. "Of course *you* wouldn't worry. But some of us take our responsibilities seriously. And some of us, like Gus and me, are expecting a perfect dance. Do you even *have* a date to the dance?"

Mandy swallowed. "Y-you're going to the dance with Gus?"

Kay's perfect pouty lips curved into a smirk. "I'm sure he's going to ask me. Especially after how things went at the party Saturday."

She wasn't sure how much more she could take. First Spriggs dismissing her ADHD and dysgraphia, and now Kay getting in her face, bragging about her hookup with Gus? She closed her eyes, willing the impending tears to stop. She would *not* lose it in front of Kay. She had to keep it together until she could melt down in J.T.'s car or at least in the bathroom.

"I need you to get a hold of the DJ, Mandy," Kay barked, sounding like one of those yappy little dogs Gran wanted. "Confirm he's on for the dance. It's the least you can do."

Mandy's eyes flew open. "What do you mean, it's the least I can do?"

Kay crossed her arms over her chest. "I *mean* it was generous of the student council to let the spirit committee be in charge of music for the dance. I told everyone we should have the final say, but for some reason my other officers fell under your"—she waved her arms around— "weird spell or whatever and trusted you."

Kay had never liked her, ever since Mandy had smeared finger paint on Kay's face in kindergarten when Kay called Cammie a mean word. And that time during the fifth-grade Shakespeare festival when Mandy had shoved her wooden sword a bit too enthusiastically at Kay's stomach after Kay made fun of the costume her gran had sewn.

"You know what I mean," Kay prattled. "When you get all wound up, people listen to you, for reasons I don't understand."

Mandy recalled the eighth-grade mock congressional hearings when her team had defeated Kay's. Mandy had wowed the panel of judges. Her teacher had told her she had a future in politics because she was so good at public speaking and persuading people to her side. Kay had hated that.

It was the first time a teacher had ever complimented her. Usually they harped on what she was doing wrong, like forgetting to turn in assignments on time or how hard it was to read her penmanship because of her dysgraphia.

Kay narrowed her eyes again. "Maybe it's the freaky

clothes and the crazy hair that make people listen to you. I don't know. But you need to make sure this zero guy—"

"*Neuro* Blastr," Mandy muttered. "His DJ name is Neuro Blastr."

"What-ev-er." Kay wagged a finger in Mandy's face, punctuating each syllable, and Mandy briefly fantasized about biting it. "Just do it, Mandy. I expect a confirmation by Monday."

Kay spun on her heels and stormed off, leaving Mandy feeling like she'd had the virtual stuffing beat out of her. She was grateful the halls were empty and no one had witnessed her humiliation.

But when she turned toward the exit, she realized there had been a witness to her humiliation, after all.

• • •

Caleb leaned against the door, watching Mandy. He hadn't left yet because he was avoiding the parking lot, where his stalker ex was circling his car like a vulture, just waiting to pick his carcass clean.

He watched the whole thing with Kay go down—Kay marching down the hall like a freaky teenage CEO in her skirt and button-down blouse, lashing into Mandy, waving her finger in her face. He kind of hoped Mandy would lean over and take a bite out of her finger, but he knew that would never happen.

Even though he hadn't heard everything Kay said, he got the gist. Mandy had screwed something up, something about the dance, and now Kay wanted it fixed.

Caleb ran a hand through his hair, wondering why his body wasn't moving out the door, getting the hell away from this lunatic asylum. Mandy turned toward him, shoulders slumped, all of her usual fire snuffed out. Something twisted in his gut when her hand swiped away a tear.

Fuucckkk.

He did not have time for this. For pity. For her.

She shuffled toward him, agonizingly slowly. She met his gaze briefly, then shifted her focus to the floor.

He should go. She didn't want to deal with him any more than he wanted to deal with her.

His body didn't move.

Finally she reached the door. Automatically, he opened it for her. She brushed past him, clearly anxious to get away.

But his body, which apparently was mutinying against his brain, caught up with her.

"You okay?" he asked. So his vocal cords were in on the coup, too. *Great.*

She hesitated, then sped up, not answering him.

This time his body listened to his brain and stopped. He watched her survey the parking lot. He could guess who she was looking for, but J.T.'s car was gone. So was Gus's truck. She fumbled in a pocket of today's weird butterfly dress and texted on her phone.

And waited.

He waited, too.

She glanced over her shoulder, frowning when she locked eyes with him.

He smirked, something in him responding to the spark of fire in her eyes. He liked that a lot better than the defeated girl, the one who looked like Kay had kicked her in the stomach. Caleb could always appreciate a good old-fashioned rebel.

She turned back to her phone, texting furiously.

As he moved toward her, the breeze carried the scent of her perfume. Too sweet, just like her.

"Waiting for someone?" He stared down at her, wondering why the hell he was doing this. Why he felt some strange urge to either help her out or poke at her until she snapped at him.

He couldn't decide which he wanted more.

She shoved her phone in her pocket and raised her face, her eyes shooting sparks, that sparkly pink mouth of hers ready to argue.

"None of your business," she snapped. "You're the last person I want to deal with today."

He felt like a pinball machine, different parts of him lighting up as her words hit their targets. No one ever stood up to him, least of all the Goody Two-shoes glaring up at him. The challenge was exhilarating. "Too bad you didn't unleash some of your spitfire on Kay instead of me, Disco."

"Why don't you go pick on someone else, Caleb?"

Her eyes were bright—too bright. He knew from experience that shininess meant tears were imminent. Damn. Had he made her cry? Or had that been Kay's fault? He'd been trying for the opposite—to shake her out of her funk, to wake up her crazy side.

"I'm not picking on you," he said, meaning it.

She blinked too fast trying to make the tears go away—he knew that trick, too. He glanced away, giving her a moment to compose herself.

She cleared her throat. "So what are you doing then?"

He met her gaze again. The tears had retreated. Good. She was too tough to let a freak like Kay make her cry. He studied her. Maybe not tough, but…strong. In a weird hippie way. Spewing her karmic philosophy and running pep rallies and believing in angels and demons or whatever.

"Good question," he said, finally answering her. He ran a hand through his hair, and her cheeks turned pink, and the pinballs inside him pinged again. "I *was* going to offer you a ride home. But I'm not in the mood to be yelled at, so…"

They stared at each other for a long moment, neither of them speaking. She hugged herself like she was cold or nervous. The pink stain on her cheeks faded as the small fire he'd ignited in her sputtered out.

"So that's the perfect end to my day," she said, turning away.

He watched her walk away from him. That wasn't supposed to happen.

"Wait."

She kept walking. Frustrated, he stalked after her. She sped up. "Mandy. Wait."

She stopped and turned around, a flicker of the spark back in her eyes. "Did you just call me Mandy? Not Disco?"

He couldn't stop his lips from curling. "My bad. I'll stick to Disco since you like it."

She faced him head-on now, hands on her hips. "You know I don't like it."

"I think you do." He stepped toward her, willing her to stay put this time.

Her eyes flashed. "Are you giving me a ride home or not? Because the bus gets here in fifteen minutes and I've had an awful day."

"Yeah, I saw Kay giving you crap."

"It wasn't just her. Did you ever have a day when everything that could go wrong did? Even my breakfast was ruined, because my stupid brother left the fridge open all night so the milk was sour and..."

Her words faded away like an annoying background buzz as he watched her sparkly pink lips, her hands fluttering while she talked, her red curls blowing in the breeze...

Shit. What was *wrong* with him? And why was she still talking?

"...so then Spriggs told me he doesn't believe in ADHD. Or any learning disabilities. He's such a jerk. I don't know how you and J.T. stand him."

He stared at her, completely lost. Why was she talking about Spriggs? And learning disabilities?

"And then Kay with the 'why does anyone listen to *you*, Mandy? You're such a flake.' I can't stand her." She paused for a breath, and he opened his mouth, but she was faster. "And now she and Gus are probably going to the dance together. He hasn't asked her yet but I'm sure he will." She took another breath and plunged on. "I try to get along with everyone but, ugh. Did you ever meet someone you just can't deal with? Because they're just so…you know…annoying."

"Yeah," he said, cocking an eyebrow. "Looking at her right now."

She stopped talking. Finally. But she didn't look happy.

"You know what? Never mind about the ride, Caleb. At least the bus driver is nice to me."

She spun around, but his arm shot out, grabbing her before she could storm off again. "Nope. I'm giving you a ride."

She jerked out of his grip. "Why?" she demanded, her voice tight with anger. "Why are you doing something nice but doing it like a jerk?"

That made him laugh. "I don't know."

She frowned. "I don't understand."

"Me either," he said, steering her toward his car. "You're like a—"

"Don't you dare call me a kindergartner on crack again."

He grinned as he opened the passenger door. "I wasn't going to say that." He'd been about to call her a firecracker, but he'd keep that to himself. For now.

She swallowed and licked her lips, and the image hit him hard and fast—pinning her against the car, kissing her. Tugging on that insane red hair.

"So what insult were you about to throw at me?"

He blinked. "What?"

"Never mind. I don't want to know." She slid into the car and slammed the door shut.

This was crazy. He didn't know why he felt this weird compulsion to mess with her. To help her out.

To…kiss her.

• • •

Mandy stared out the window as Caleb drove too fast. "You're speeding."

"Thank you, Captain Obvious." But he slowed down. A little.

"Can I put on some music?"

He shot her a glare. "Not your crappy disco. Anything but that."

She leaned against the headrest and closed her eyes. She couldn't wait to get home. She still had leftover ice cream. And M&M's. And Ryan Gosling.

He cleared his throat, and her body tensed at the gravelly sound. She couldn't believe she was trapped with the demon chauffeur again, but it was better than taking the bus.

"So, you really want to go to homecoming with Gus, huh?"

Her eyes flew open. They'd stopped at a red light, and he glanced at her, his expression unreadable.

"I…well, yeah, I do, but—"

"Some guys are clueless, unless you throw it in their face."

"Throw what in their face?"

The light turned green, and the car accelerated, along with her heart rate.

"Some guys only want what other guys have."

"I don't understand." She had no idea what he was talking about, but something inside her zinged with nervous energy.

He sighed next to her, probably annoyed with her stupidity, since his brain was so big and all, and hers was skittering around like a kindergartner on crack.

"If you hook up with someone else, maybe Gus will notice you. The way you want him to."

Her body flushed with heat. What was he suggesting? "And how would I manage that?"

He sped up, shifting into third gear. "Find a fake boyfriend."

"What?!" She screeched so loudly she even scared herself. Caleb swore and swerved, then shot her a glare.

"Damn it, Disco. Calm the hell down."

She leaned forward, straining against her seat belt. "That's a horrible idea. I hate lies. And besides, even if I wanted to do it, where would I find a fake boyfriend? J.T.'s gay, and he's the only guy I'd trust enough to—"

"You're not gonna *marry* the guy. It's a business arrangement. You'd both know it's fake. You only do it until Gus asks you to the dance, then it's over."

They'd arrived at her house. He parked and turned to look at her, and she caught her breath. He was...hard to look away from, that was for sure.

"Thanks for your, uh, suggestion, Caleb, but no way is that happening."

"You'd probably only have to fake it for two weeks. Three, max, if Gus is a total loser and doesn't ask you 'til the last minute."

She sighed. Why was he so insistent? "It's not happening. Anyway, who would I ever convince to do that for me?"

He studied her, his intense gaze unnerving her, then his low voice said one simple word. "Me."

They stared at each other for so long she wondered if time had stopped, like in that *X-Men* movie when that guy froze time and ran around while that old song played, knocking bullets out of the way, and guns out of hands, and hats off heads and—

"I've got a stalker ex I need to get off my case," Caleb

said, his dark gaze locked on hers. "You've got a dork you're trying to seduce. It's a win-win."

"Gus isn't a dork," she whispered, but for a second, she couldn't see Gus's sweet face in her mind's eye. Instead all she saw was the stony-faced badass drumming his fingers impatiently on the steering wheel. She swallowed. "Gus is a sweetheart."

"Dork. Sweetheart. Semantics." His lips curved in a mocking smile that did something to her stomach.

"N-no one would ever believe it," she stammered. "That you and I would..." She blushed, unable to finish the sentence.

"That we'd what, Disco?" He unbuckled his seat belt and turned toward her. Her breath caught in her throat as he reached out and touched her hair, twirling a long strand around his finger. He leaned in so close she could see a faint shadow of stubble on his jaw. "Go to a dance together?" He shifted even closer, moving in so that his lips barely brushed her cheek as he whispered in her ear. "Or just hook up?"

This wasn't...he wasn't...but she didn't...not with him... she...Gus... Her thoughts spun out of control, just like her hormones. God, what was he—

He dropped her lock of hair and leaned back against his seat, smirking. "I think everyone would believe *that*. You did, didn't you? Just for a second?"

Her hand flew up to slap him, but he grabbed it like he'd been expecting it. "Two weeks. It won't even take that long. Lover boy Gus only needs to see you and me do that once, and he's yours. All yours."

"Y-you're such a—" He was still holding her hand, though he'd loosened his grip.

"Jackass. I know. But let me pretend to be your jackass boyfriend and we'll both get what we want."

Everything in her screamed no, but when she finally opened her mouth, the word that fell out was "Okay."

. . .

Caleb watched Mandy wobble up the cracked sidewalk. She wore ridiculous shoes, as usual. Her house was small and shabby, the opposite of the huge, sterile house he and his dad rattled around in, along with their housekeeper Helen. He probably should've walked her to the door, but he needed a minute before he drove home.

That stunt he'd just pulled hadn't gone the way he'd planned. He'd just meant to prove what a good actor he was and how easy it would be to convince everyone of the fake boyfriend act. He hadn't expected her to look at him like she actually *wanted* him to kiss her.

And he sure as hell hadn't expected a freaking tornado of lust to shoot through him when he leaned in to whisper in her ear, when he caught a scent of her perfume as his fingers played with her soft hair.

Shit.

Now he was thoroughly screwed because, for whatever reason, she'd agreed to his idiotic plan. And the last thing he needed was to fall under some freaky hippie spell.

Even though she was fun to spar with, she was still crazy. A total train wreck.

And he didn't do crazy.

Chapter Four
Stayin' Alive

Tuesday, September 20

"We need an emergency meeting," Mandy told Cammie and J.T. as soon as she spotted them in the hallway.

Cammie looked perfect as always, her dark hair and lashes highlighting her delicate olive-skinned features. J.T., on the other hand, looked like he'd just escaped a wind tunnel, his blond hair going in twenty different directions, his clothes disheveled. But his killer smile and sexy David Bowie eyes — one green, one blue — overshadowed the messiness.

Gus sauntered toward them, grinning, making her stomach flutter.

"Hey," he said, stopping next to them.

"Hi," Mandy said, wishing she'd never seen him kiss Kay. If she could just pretend it never happened...

"There you are!"

Speak of the devil. Kay bore down on them, her predatory gaze locked on Gus. She stopped next to them and looped her arm through Gus's. "We're having lunch together. Just you and me."

Gus blinked in surprise. "We are? I was thinking I'd eat with these guys today." He gestured toward them, but Kay ignored it.

"You can eat lunch with them whenever. Today, *I* need you." Kay ran a finger down his chest.

Gus's neck flushed, but he shrugged. "Okay. Sounds good."

Mandy's heart sank to her feet. She didn't have a chance, not against Kay.

"Cool with us," J.T. said. "We have stuff to do."

Mandy glanced at him, surprised. Shouldn't he be on her side? Or at least anti-Kay?

The first class bell rang, sending everyone scrambling down the hall because their principal, Dr. Harris, aka Dr. Hairy, was a stickler about tardies.

"We need to talk," Mandy said before they separated. She should've called them last night, but she'd been paralyzed by panic. She'd tossed and turned all night, stressing over Caleb's proposition.

J.T. nodded, and Cammie squeezed her shoulder. "Don't worry. Whatever it is, we've got your back."

Mandy smiled her thanks, then rushed to her first-period class. She could always change her mind. It was a crazy plan. Ridiculous. Complicated.

Doomed.

At lunch, Mandy and her friends piled into J.T.'s clunker, scarfing down fries and chocolate shakes in the fast-food parking lot. Mandy sat in the backseat while her two friends angled in the front seats to face her like she was the criminal and they were the jury.

"What do you mean, Caleb wants to be your fake boyfriend?" Cammie demanded. "This has disaster written all over it."

"Maybe," J.T. said around a french fry. "Maybe not."

"What?!" Cammie exclaimed. "Did we not establish his certified assholery after he drove Mandy home Saturday night, attacking her with insults?"

"We did," J.T. agreed. "He hates everything and everyone." He paused. "Except you, apparently." J.T. waggled his eyebrows at Mandy. "So maybe this will work."

Cammie crossed her arms over her generous cleavage, of which Mandy was not-so-secretly jealous. "I don't want Mandy getting hurt."

"Why would she?" J.T. said. "Caleb's not going to accidentally fall for her, and she's definitely not going to fall for him. And maybe this will finally make Gus see the girl who's been there for him all along."

J.T. and Cammie shot each other meaningful glances. Mandy sighed and searched for a mantra. *The universe brings me exactly who I need, when I need them.* Her friends were there for her. Always. Even when they acted like she was their little sister they had to protect. She adored them, but sometimes they made her feel incompetent, and she already had enough of that going on with her classes.

"I know it's a crazy idea. But when I see Gus with Kay…" Her words trailed away. Kay was evil. Gus didn't belong with her. He belonged with Mandy, who appreciated him. Who wouldn't suck out his soul.

"Maybe try it with Caleb for a day or two," J.T. said. "See what happens."

"Speaking of, why aren't you with him right now?" Cammie asked. "Shouldn't you be eating lunch with your fake boyfriend?"

Mandy choked on her drink, then finally managed to squeak out a reply. "I haven't seen him today." Because she'd hidden from him every time she'd caught a glimpse of the black leather jacket and rock star hair. "Maybe he'll forget," she said hopefully. "Maybe it was all a bad dream and—"

"He won't." J.T. shoved a handful of fries in his mouth.

"Why not?" Cammie demanded.

J.T. shrugged. "A guy like Caleb doesn't throw out that kind of deal and forget about it. Do you think Lucifer forgets when he makes deals for people's souls?"

"Well, I don't think you should do it," Cammie said. "Relationships built on lies never last."

"But I'm not having a *relationship* with Caleb," Mandy said, blushing as she remembered how she'd responded to him last night in his car. Jerk. She'd never get suckered in by his fake seductions again.

Cammie's face crinkled in sympathy. "Sweetie, I don't want to hurt your feelings, but I think Gus is so sucked in by the Kay spell that he's not going to notice anyone else. Not even you and Caleb trying to make him jealous."

"But he can't be," Mandy protested. "Not already. They just hooked up over the weekend. That doesn't have to mean anything, does it? If he and I could just go out, the two of us…" She thought of her favorite Chinese restaurant, the Silk Lamp. She imagined staring at Gus over candlelight, reaching across the table to hold his hand.

J.T. and Cammie gave each other *the look* again, and a jolt of anger and determination shot through her.

"I don't care what you guys say. I'm going to try it. What's the worst that can happen?"

"Famous last words," Cammie muttered under her breath.

• • •

Caleb ate by himself as usual, reading at a table in the corner of the cafeteria. He'd seen Mandy and her minions leave, and he'd felt a mixture of relief and disappointment. Mostly relief, he told himself.

She'd been avoiding him all day. She probably thought she was being sly, but it was hard to miss her darting around corners and ducking into classrooms whenever he came near her. Her shirt glittered so much it could probably be seen from outer space.

He took a swig from his soda and refocused on his book, a worn collection of short stories he'd found in his favorite used bookstore.

A freshman scurried by, tripped, and his tray flew through the air, sending an avalanche of food onto Caleb's table. The cafeteria went dead silent as everyone waited for the explosion.

Caleb wiped food off his jacket before aiming his glare at the kid, who looked like he weighed maybe sixty pounds.

"I-I'm s-sorry, sir," the kid stammered and Caleb almost laughed.

Sir? Seriously?

"Watch where you're going next time." Caleb moved his book out of the way of a spreading puddle of soda. Murmurs rose around him and he knew people were waiting for him to lose it, to go ballistic on the kid. Just because he'd lost it one time.

The story had been told and retold so many times he didn't even recognize it anymore, but the reputation had followed him for years, even though he hadn't been in a fight since ninth grade.

"Get outta here, kid," Caleb said. He stood up and the kid took off, tripping over his shoelaces.

Caleb shoved his book in his pocket and stalked out of the cafeteria, debating whether or not to stick around for the rest of the day. He had calc next, a class he wasn't doing great in. He should probably stay for that, but he could miss the rest of the afternoon since he was killing AP English and history.

Elle pounced on him as he rounded the corner. "Hey, gorgeous, where have you been hiding?"

Crap. He took in her skintight dress that barely covered her ass. He knew she'd worn it for his benefit and was surprised she hadn't been sent home for violating the dress code.

"I wasn't hiding." He kept moving, hoping she'd get the hint.

She didn't.

"So anyway…I was thinking about homecoming. It's only two and a half weeks away."

He stopped at his locker and willed her to disappear.

She didn't.

He made the mistake of glancing at her. She didn't look all misty-eyed like she was in love with him. She looked… fanatical. Scary. Like she'd be just as happy killing him as kissing him.

It sort of scared the crap out of him.

He glanced up and down the hall at the swarms of students returning from lunch.

Where the hell was his fake girlfriend when he needed her?

Chapter Five
Disco Inferno

Tuesday, September 20

When Mandy and her friends returned from lunch, she spotted Caleb at his locker, his ex-girlfriend Elle rubbing up against him like a cat. Her earlier determination faltered, but Cammie gave her a gentle push.

"Go on. If you're gonna do this, you need to go all in."

"She's right," J.T. said. "Go save him from his stalker."

Mandy swallowed and took a breath, then started down the hall, her gaze fixated on Caleb. He noticed Mandy when she was about six feet away, his expression transforming from desperation to relief, which surprised her. Then his expression changed again, from relief to…uh…Mandy slowed. He was doing it again, the fake seducer act, looking at her like she was his favorite dessert.

Elle spun around to see who he was looking at, and Mandy almost fled when she saw the angry fire in Elle's eyes. Maybe Caleb wasn't exaggerating about the stalker thing. But

Caleb was fast, closing the gap between them and draping his arm over her shoulders, his thumb rubbing soft circles on her neck and shutting down her brain functions.

"There you are, babe," he said, his voice low and sexy. "I missed you at lunch."

Elle glared daggers at her.

"Uh, yeah, I, um, was with J.T. and Cammie," she finally managed, unable to tear her gaze from Elle.

Caleb's fingers continued to massage her neck, and she wondered briefly if he could sense her panic and was trying to soothe her. Which was stupid on his part, because the last thing she felt right now was soothed, since his touch shot tingles through her whole body.

"*You* and Caleb?" Elle snapped. "Are you kidding me?" She glared at Caleb. "You dumped *me* for this freak show?"

Caleb pulled Mandy in even closer. "Shut it, Elle." His voice was a threatening growl, and out of the corner of her eye she noticed Kay and Gus watching them, with J.T. and Cammie not far behind, staring openmouthed.

Showtime. She squared her shoulders, determined to follow through on her part of the deal.

"So you're coming to the spirit committee meeting today, right babe?" she asked, turning to flutter her eyelashes at him. It gave her a secret thrill to throw *babe* back in his face.

A spark of acknowledgment and appreciation flashed in his dark eyes, and his lips curved dangerously. "Wouldn't miss it, *babe*."

She smiled at him for real because this was kind of fun, like a tennis match. And she was excellent at tennis.

"This is bullsh—" Elle began, but the class bell drowned out the rest of her protest.

Caleb steered Mandy down the hall, his grip firm around her shoulders. Everyone stared at them like they were aliens, or celebrities, or maybe a weird combination of the two. Her pulse rate ratcheted up. She hadn't considered that this fake boyfriend thing would actually become public knowledge. Like, *really* public.

He stopped at his calc classroom, releasing her from his grip.

"Thanks, Disco." He smirked. "You just saved me from being shanked by a psycho."

So he was back to jerk Caleb again. She steeled herself and decided two could play this game.

"Sure. But now you owe me, so I expect to see you at the spirit committee meeting today. Three thirty. Starbucks."

His eyes widened in surprise. "Why would I—"

She gave him the sweetest, fakest smile she could muster, adding an eyelash flutter for emphasis. "My *real* boyfriend would support me and help me out if I asked him."

J.T. appeared next to them. "Yo Torrs, Mandy. How's the new power couple?" He grinned like a kid on Christmas morning.

Caleb shot him an annoyed glance, then focused back on Mandy. "What the hell am *I* going to do on the spirit committee?"

"Lots of things," Mandy said, a bolt of mischievous excitement streaking through her. Having Caleb on the spirit committee might be entertaining, as long as he didn't mess things up. She squinted a warning look at him, grinning wickedly. "You have to promise not to ruin things, though."

He glared at her, but she wasn't deterred. They had a deal, and she intended to make him work for it.

"See you at the meeting!" She fluttered her fingers in a wave and shot him what she hoped was a smirk cocky enough to match his own. "Don't be late!"

• • •

Caleb stewed through calc, which sucked because he really needed to pay better attention in that class. But he couldn't stop thinking about Mandy and the crazy scene that had gone down.

Now the whole freaking school knew about their fake relationship. It was Elle's fault, since she wouldn't leave him the hell alone, and Mandy had only followed through on their deal by playing along with him. She'd impressed him, throwing *babe* back in his face.

Maybe now Elle *would* leave him alone, if he could convince her that his feelings for Mandy were real. Which they weren't, of course, but nobody needed to know that.

He pushed away the memory of Elle insulting Mandy, when he'd told Elle to shut up. That part had felt…very real.

J.T. slid a folded piece of paper on his desk. Caleb stared at it, then glared at J.T. What the hell? Since when did J.T. and he communicate? They hadn't really talked since the second grade, when Caleb's dad had moved him to a private school and he'd lost touch with J.T. until high school.

Before that, J.T. had been a permanent fixture at his house, the two of them sharing a little kid bromance based on a mutual love of the Power Rangers TV show and brownies. But those days were over, and Caleb liked to pretend it never happened.

J.T. tilted his head, gesturing for Caleb to open the note. Caleb expelled an annoyed breath. This fake relationship thing had gone live twenty minutes ago and already he regretted it. He made sure their teacher wasn't looking, then unfolded the note.

If you hurt her, I will kill you, Red Ranger.

Caleb's eyebrows shot up in surprise. He hadn't expected that. J.T. wasn't the type to threaten. Then again, if he didn't know J.T. was gay, he'd think J.T. and Mandy were a couple;

they were tight.

The Red Ranger part was funny, almost making him smile. Caleb had always been the Red Ranger when they'd played Power Rangers, because the Red Ranger was in charge. J.T. had always been the Blue Ranger, the geeky hacker.

He scrawled a reply.

I won't hurt her. You can't kill me because the Red Ranger always kicks the Blue Ranger's ass.

He made sure their teacher was distracted, then tossed the note onto J.T.'s desk.

He shifted in his chair. What the hell was he doing passing notes like a ten-year-old girl? He'd just discovered an unanticipated flaw in his fake girlfriend plot: Mandy came with a posse. A very annoying one. And she was the queen of school participation, so of course she'd forced him to come to a stupid spirit committee meeting. Why hadn't he taken those factors into account when he'd proposed his scheme?

The note plopped back on his desk. The blond cheerleader sitting next to him watched the whole exchange with way too much interest. He scowled at her, and she turned away. He turned his scowl on J.T., who just rolled his eyes and pointed to the note.

I've got my eye on you, Torrs. Blue Rangers are always ready for the call to action. I'll power up if I have to.

Caleb snorted a laugh, and their teacher spun around, pinning him with a warning glare. "Sorry," Caleb muttered, then he shot another glare at J.T., who was trying not to laugh.

He sighed in frustration. Maybe he'd be better off getting shanked by a psycho than dealing with Mandy's crazy friends.

• • •

Mandy sucked on a straw, relishing the cold chocolate sliding down her throat. Everyone was there for the spirit committee meeting. Correction: everyone but Caleb. So much for being a supportive fake boyfriend. Whatever. Not like she thought he'd really show up. She reached into her backpack and passed around the bright pink papers with the Spirit Week schedule.

Monday was their monthly bake sale, then the rest of the week they'd finish prepping for Spirit Week, which was the following week. Everything was geared around a seventies theme, to go along with the dance. The trivia contest, the scavenger hunt, the dress-like-a-hippie day…which wasn't a big deal for her, but would be for everyone else.

My committee is supportive and motivated, Mandy thought as she squeezed her eyes shut. *This will be the best Spirit Week ever.* She kept her eyes closed, visualizing all of the events going off without a hitch. Visualizing herself at the dance in her awesome green dress. With Gus.

"Closing your eyes isn't going to make me disappear."

She willed her eyes to remain closed as the chair next to her scraped the floor and a body settled into it, a body that smelled really good. Frickety frack. Where had J.T. gone? He'd been sitting in that chair just a minute ago.

The voice chuckled softly. "Okay, keep pretending I'm not here, Disco. I'll ask someone else what's going on."

Mandy's eyes flew open, meeting Caleb's dark gaze head-on. His self-satisfied smirk made her want to lob a hard serve in his court.

"You're late," she snapped.

He shrugged, reaching for her cup with his free hand. He took a long drink from her straw, keeping his eyes on hers. She was dimly aware that the voices around her quieted as people watched them. Well, watched *him*. It was hard not to watch those lips sucking on her straw like…like…

Mandy snatched the cup from his hand. "Apparently they

don't teach manners in hell."

He licked a few drops of chocolate from his lips, keeping his dangerous eyes on hers. "Oh, they do. Just not the kind you'd approve of." His lips curved into a wicked grin that sent her body temp into the stratosphere. "They teach us demons all kinds of bad things." He leaned in close, lowering his voice. "Very bad things, babe."

Mandy didn't know where to focus. She could barely put two thoughts together, and the thoughts she did have were totally inappropriate.

Gus, she told herself. Gus. Gus. Gus. She pictured his sweet face, grinning at her. All those years by each other's side, *that* was what she should be focusing on.

Caleb was fake. This act he was putting on was totally fake, and she needed to remember that.

He grabbed a paper from the stack of pink fliers. "A scavenger hunt?" Caleb laughed. It might sound sexy if he weren't mocking, which she knew he was. "Trivia bowl?"

"They're fun events, Caleb." She narrowed her eyes. "You just don't realize it because demons don't know how to have fun."

He turned his body toward her, his knees pressing against her thigh. "Don't we?" The gleam in his eye made her press her knees together. "I disagree." Several girls ogled him like they'd happily trade places with her.

J.T shot across the coffee shop to hover next to Caleb. "Is your *boyfriend* hassling you, Mandy? I can have security throw him out."

Caleb tilted his head back to look at J.T. "Starbucks has security. Right."

"Blue Rangers are everywhere, just waiting for the call to action," J.T. said. Caleb rolled his eyes, and Mandy wondered what the heck they were talking about.

"I believe you took my seat," J.T. said, glaring at Caleb.

Caleb turned to Mandy. "Would you like me to move?"

"Uh," Mandy said, hating her brain for freezing up. If only he'd been a jerk about it instead of asking nicely like a normal person.

"J.T.," Cammie called from the other end of the table. "Come here. I need your help with something."

J.T. shifted his glare to Cammie.

"One point to the Red Ranger," Caleb said as J.T. sighed in disgust.

"What are you talking about?" Mandy asked, looking back and forth between them.

Caleb ignored her question and reached for her drink again. He picked it up, hesitating with the tip of the straw just millimeters from his lush mouth. Since when did she think words like "lush" and "Caleb" in the same sentence?

He cocked an eyebrow. "Mind if I have another drink? Demons get thirsty."

She shrugged. "Go ahead and finish it. I don't want any."

He sucked from the straw, watching her, then paused to whisper, "My girlfriend wouldn't be afraid of my germs." He held the cup toward her and spoke loudly. "Finish it, babe."

Mandy tore her gaze away from his mouth. He was right; she needed to play along. She took the cup and put her lips on the straw. He watched her as she sucked out the last few drops. His jaw clenched, and he dropped his gaze, swallowing. She set the cup down quickly, like it had burned her hand.

"Spirit Week is going to be awesome." She picked up the flier he'd been reading. "We've put a lot of work into it."

"I'm sure you have." His voice sounded strangled. He shifted next to her, moving his legs underneath the table instead of pressing into her. She was relieved and disappointed all at once, which annoyed her. Relief was okay. Disappointment? That was bad.

Fake boyfriend, she told herself. Fake. Fake. Fake. She

stood up, determined to ignore Caleb's stare. "Okay, everyone, we all know the agenda for Spirit Week."

Everyone stopped talking to listen. "We need to put up fliers and really talk up the events, especially the trivia bowl. Encourage people to form teams and make sure they know about the prize."

"What's the prize?" Caleb asked.

"The first season of *That '70s Show* on DVD. Plus the chance to pick the first song played at the dance." Mandy answered while looking around the table at everyone but Caleb. She felt him, though, watching her, his gaze traveling up and down her body as she stood.

"Who shows up to a dance in time for the first song?" Caleb snorted, then fell silent as he looked around table.

These were *exactly* the people who showed up to a dance in time for the first song. Mandy glared at him, taking a deep breath and reminding herself that he was only around temporarily.

My committee is supportive and motivated. My fake boyfriend is not undressing me with his eyes.

• • •

Caleb wasn't sure what was happening, because for a second there, he'd had the crazy idea to pull Mandy onto his lap and kiss her until she begged for mercy. Or begged for more. Apparently his hormones were confused about whom to focus on and whom to ignore.

Very carefully, he turned his body away from her, pretending to study the pink flier listing the Spirit Week events. All of them pathetic. Hopelessly silly, not at all cool. Just like her.

Shit.

He didn't even like her, let alone want her. Not like that.

He sneaked a glance at her, his eyes exactly level with her ass as she turned slightly to answer a question from someone on the other side of the table.

Shit.

This was not supposed to happen. Not to him. His body betrayed him just because of this stupid fake relationship game they were playing. He glanced around the table. There were plenty of hot girls here; why was he reacting to Mandy instead of them? He willed his body to cool down.

"So Sunday is baking day, okay?" Mandy said, her voice annoyingly high and breathy. He rubbed the back of his neck, wishing he could mute her.

"Um, Mandy. There's kind of a problem with that." Amber, one of the cheerleaders who looked like all the others to Caleb, leaned forward in her seat. "We can't bake at my house after all. We're getting our floors refinished and my mom said no way will she let a bunch of us in there spilling icing and stuff."

Caleb rolled his eyes. If only he had his pocketknife, he could stab himself and put himself out of his misery. Save Elle the trouble.

"Uhh...wow...we, um," Mandy stammered. "I guess we could do it at my house, but it's really small—"

"Who else has a giant kitchen we can use?" J.T. interrupted.

Caleb noticed people glancing at him surreptitiously. Oh, hell no. He settled his face into a stony glare, but J.T. fixed his intense stare right on him. "Caleb, how about your house? You could fit a freaking army in your kitchen."

Mandy's head whipped toward J.T., clearly shocked.

He had to hand it to J.T.—the guy didn't seem at all intimidated by him, unlike the rest of the spirit junkies who watched him like he might suddenly zap them all with a lightning bolt.

Mandy tugged at her weird necklace—was that a *crab*?—

her gaze darting around the table, obviously desperate for someone else to volunteer their house.

What would a real boyfriend do? He sighed, then said the only thing that made sense. "We can do it at my house, babe."

She blinked in surprise. "We can?"

"Sure. It'll be fun." He almost choked on the f-word. He didn't do fun.

J.T. grinned victoriously. "Excellent. We'll show up at one o'clock."

Caleb kept a fake grin plastered on his face. "Can't wait."

"Okay then, I guess we'll meet Sunday at Caleb's house," Mandy said. "For the baking bonanza."

Across the table, J.T. locked eyes with him.

Fucking Blue Rangers. They missed nothing.

• • •

"Oh my God, J.T. I'm going to kill you!" Mandy angry-whispered as everyone else filed out of Starbucks. Caleb had been the first to leave, which was completely unboyfriend-like behavior, but whatever. She was too freaked out about the impending baking event at his house to worry about that.

"Why? I solved the problem." J.T. looked proud of himself, like he'd just conquered a warring army.

Mandy felt herself flush with anger. "I'd rather everyone try to fit in my tiny house than go to Caleb's!" She swallowed. "We're going straight into the devil's lair."

J.T. laughed. "Yeah, right. I've been in his house. No demons, I promise." He tilted his head. "And technically, it's your *boyfriend's* house so you shouldn't be freaking out." He cocked his eyebrows meaningfully toward the few committee members still hanging out.

She took a breath and spoke softly so no one would overhear. "When were you in Caleb's house?"

"Once upon a time, he and I were friends."

Mandy gaped at him. "In what alternate dimension did this happen?"

J.T. shoved his notebook in his backpack and headed for the door, waiting for Mandy to follow him. "The kindergarten T-ball dimension."

Mandy hurried to catch up to him. "Seriously? You two were actually friends?" She could hardly believe it.

J.T. snorted. "I guess. We used to be into the same stuff."

Mandy's thoughts fired like pinballs, fast and crazy. Why hadn't he told her this before?

"But you guys haven't been friends since I've known you," Mandy protested, focusing in on the pinball thought she was most curious about.

"We were up through second grade. Then he moved to a private school and we, uh, lost touch."

Mandy remembered meeting J.T. freshman year, when they'd bonded over movies and old music. "But when we started high school, why didn't you guys reconnect?"

J.T. stopped walking to stare down at her. "Seriously? Can you picture him and me hanging out?" He snorted. "I tried to talk to him a few times but he totally blew me off."

Mandy considered this new data as they crossed the parking lot. She imagined a pint-sized J.T. and Caleb, in a kid-sized leather jacket, playing with Legos and scarfing snacks. The idea made her giggle.

J.T. shot her an annoyed look. "I know what you're thinking." He paused, then sighed. "He wasn't always an asshole. I don't know when that happened." He shrugged as he unlocked his car. "Maybe after his mom bailed. She just up and left one day, when we were in the second grade…right before he moved to a private school."

Mandy settled into the passenger seat. That was awful, but it didn't give Caleb the right to be a perma-jerk. "If everyone who lost a parent to divorce or...or"—her voice hitched but she continued—"whatever...turned into a jerk, half the school would be full of people like Caleb."

J.T. reached over to squeeze her knee. "Exactly. I mean, after all you've been through you're the nicest person I know." He shot her a grin. "Crazy as they come, but your heart's in the right place."

She glanced at his stubborn profile. He'd been with her through the worst of it, when her mom died and her life fell apart. J.T. didn't give many compliments, so when he did she knew it was genuine. *The universe sends me the people I need.*

"Thanks," she said. "But none of this solves our problem. Can you picture it? All of us piling into Caleb's house?" She chewed her bottom lip nervously. "I even made a baking playlist."

J.T. laughed. "Bring it. Maybe it'll send him right over the edge."

Mandy smiled, remembering how he'd yanked his aux cable out of her phone when she'd been listening to disco in his car. "Yeah," she said. "I'd like to see that."

She couldn't let Caleb intimidate her. Besides, *she* should be the one in control of this whole situation. He had to do what she said; he was her fake boyfriend now. Plus, it was a chance to practice her compassion outreach, to see if maybe being kind to arrogant jerks really did have the potential to change them.

"I keep picturing you guys as little kids. Playing pirates or whatever." She giggled.

"Power Rangers," J.T. corrected.

"Power what?"

"It was a kids' TV show we used to watch together. Teenage superheroes battling aliens."

Mandy laughed. "Was it as good as *Sky High*?"

J.T. snorted. "Not even close."

. . .

Fine with me, Caleb's dad texted. *Glad to see you getting involved in something at school.*

Caleb didn't need to ask permission for the house invasion since his dad was never home, but he hoped it might bump his ranking in his dad's never-ending assessment of Caleb's performance as a crappy son. He'd been right.

Helen slid a plate of brownies toward him as he sat at the enormous granite-topped kitchen island. He glanced at her and smiled. She was possibly the only person in his life he liked having around. He took a bite of brownie. He should bring these to the stupid bake sale; they could charge five bucks apiece and people would pay it.

"Bad day?" she asked, wiping her hands on her apron. Helen was tall and fit, with short dark hair and sharp blue eyes that missed nothing, but she spoiled him like a sugary sweet TV grandma.

He took a drink from the glass of milk she'd poured for him. Sometimes he still felt like a little kid when he hung out with Helen. She'd been with their family since forever.

Since before. And after.

"Yeah," he said around a mouthful of chocolate. "I got, uh...drafted onto a stupid committee." He paused to drink more milk. "The kitchen is going to be trashed Sunday. The most obnoxious people in school are coming over to bake for a fu—stupid bake sale." He glowered at the plate of brownies as if they were somehow to blame, then glanced up.

Helen's hand stilled on her apron. "Really? How interesting." She picked up a cleaning rag and wiped down the spotless counter. "I'll come over to help."

Caleb almost choked. "No. You don't have to do that." It would be awful enough having to survive it; he didn't want any witnesses to the humiliation. "Besides, that's your time off. Trust me, you don't want to spend time with the psychos coming over here."

Helen raised her eyebrows. "You don't think my pastries are bake-sale-worthy?"

He grinned, knowing she wasn't serious. "Of course they are. But there's like a million people coming over. I'm sure they'll make plenty of stuff. You don't need to bake anything." He took another bite and chewed. "I'll make sure everything's cleaned up." He wouldn't leave her with the disaster zone he knew Mandy would leave in her wake.

Just the thought of Disco buzzing around his house like a psychedelic butterfly made his head hurt. He hoped Elle dialed back the crazy, and that Gus dumped Kay soon and asked Mandy to the dance, because he didn't know how much more of this fake boyfriend stuff he could tolerate.

Helen took a brownie and sat down across from him. "Caleb, I'll be here. Your dad will be out of town, and I don't want those kids ruining my KitchenAid. That mixer is like a second grandchild to me."

Caleb smiled. Helen had been the most steady person in his life for a long time. And she was at least as stubborn as he was. "Okay," he said, shrugging, "but don't say I didn't warn you. It's going to be like a Disney cartoon mashed up with a horror movie." He pretended to shudder. "Cheerleaders, pep squad, band people. Total invasion of the soul-snatchers."

Helen's laugh was deep and full. She reached across the counter to swat him on the shoulder, and it occurred to him that she was the only person on the planet who could get away with that. "You're so dramatic, Caleb. I'm sure they're great kids."

He snorted, picturing Mandy and her minions. "Yeah," he mumbled sarcastically. "The greatest."

• • •

Mandy sat in the living room of the small duplex she shared with her grandma, brother, and dad, when he wasn't on the road hauling Walmart junk across the country in a ginormous semi.

She added the final song to her baking playlist, ridiculously pleased with herself. Caleb would hate it, which made her smile, but her smile quickly morphed into a frown. It was totally bad karma to want to make someone else miserable, even if that someone was a jerk. *Everything happens for a reason,* she told herself for the hundredth time. Even the fake boyfriend thing.

Her brother Reg crashed into the kitchen, startling her out of her reverie as he banged pans on the counter and rattled through the refrigerator.

"Shh," Mandy hissed. She hurried into the kitchen. "Gran's sleeping. Keep it down."

He glanced at her, his gaze glassy and unfocused. Stoned again. Great.

"What are you doing tonight, Reg?" She hoped he'd stay home with her and Gran instead of going out with his idiot friends.

"None of your business."

"Maybe you could stick around tonight," Mandy pressed. "We could watch a movie. I'll make popcorn." *Like we used to,* she thought, *before you started smoking weed.*

"No way," he said, wincing like she'd stabbed him.

She glared at him. "I'm still mad at you for not picking me up from that party Saturday night."

"You got a ride somehow," he said, grabbing his stinky-smelling burrito from the microwave.

"From freaking Caleb Torrs!" Mandy whisper-yelled, resuscitating her four-day-old frustration with her brother.

He stopped mid-burrito bite to stare at her. "Torrs? Really?"

Mandy nodded. "It was…weird."

"Did he, uh, put the moves on you?"

Was her brother actually showing concern? That was a shocker.

"No, he didn't." Not that night, Mandy thought, trying not to think about his fake moves in the car and in the hallway today at school. And at Starbucks, with the straw sucking. She grabbed a yogurt from the fridge and ripped the lid off, then grabbed a spoon from the drawer.

Reg grunted. "Yeah, no surprise there." He took a huge bite of burrito.

"What's that supposed to mean?"

"You're not his type," Reg said around his mouthful of beans and cheese. "Too weird."

So much for brotherly concern.

"For your information, Caleb and I are…" *Crap*. What should she tell him? Her brother would know if she had a real boyfriend, right? She swallowed, then straightened her shoulders. "It so happens I *am* his type. He and I are officially a thing."

Reg's mouth dropped open, giving her a disgusting view of his snack.

"No way. No fucking way."

Her body tensed. Was it really so impossible to believe that she and Caleb could be a real couple? "Yes. Yes f-ing way." She was trying really hard not to use f-bombs, because it bugged her dad.

Reg swallowed his food, then shook his head. "Don't get knocked up, sis. There's only one reason Torrs would go out with you—"

Without pausing to think, she catapulted a spoonful of yogurt at him, proud of her direct aim. He sputtered as the pink slime slid down his face.

"You suck, Mandy!"

"No, you do! What kind of brother would assume that?"

They glared at each other, and Mandy heard her grandmother rustling in the living room. "Mandy? Is everything okay?" Her voice sounded sleepy and disoriented.

She poked Reg on the chest. "Now see what you did? Just get out of here, Reg."

He grabbed a paper towel and wiped his face, then stormed out of the kitchen, pausing only to flip her off.

Anger roiled through her like a stormy surf, but sadness was there, too, riding the same waves, drenching her with regret and guilt. She hated how things were between her and Reg now, and wondered if they would ever get along again.

Everyone's on their own path. He'll change when he's ready. She didn't know if she believed that, but she wanted to. Needed to.

Mandy cleaned up the yogurt that hadn't landed on Reg, then headed into the living room, grateful to see her gran sleeping in her chair. She sank onto the faded blue couch and shoved in her earbuds.

She opened her essay on her old laptop, muttering under her breath. She had to get a decent grade from Spriggs to avoid dance squad probation. She needed maximum extracurricular activities to make up for her borderline grades to have a shot at even a partial scholarship. It wasn't like she had Caleb's big brain or her brother's freakish math gift. All she had was… squirrel brain—spazzy enthusiasm combined with a total lack of focus. Nobody gave away college money for *that*.

The stress made her mood ring practically melt as its colors swirled from black to green to red, finally resettling on black. A heavy sigh escaped her, and she tugged at her zodiac necklace. It wasn't even her sign; it was her mom's. A crab, for Cancer. Irony in the extreme since cancer had killed her mom three years ago. She squeezed her eyes shut, willing herself to focus on the essay topic.

Holden Caulfield. What a spoiled brat. Mandy did not see what the big deal was about this book. He was a rich kid who had everything but whined constantly about how awful his life was. Not that she could put any of that in her essay. Mr. Spriggs thought *The Catcher in the Rye* was the greatest book of all time. She'd cornered him after school one day to ask if she could write about an awesome steampunk mystery instead, but he'd just given her one of those looks that made her feel like garbage on the bottom of his shoe.

She flipped through her faded and torn copy of the book, which had been highlighted and underlined by many students prior to her. The notes and yellow passages blurred as she skimmed the pages. She snorted as she read some of the highlighted dialog. Holden called everyone phonies. He should visit the twenty-first century; his head would explode if he spent even a week in her high school.

Her phone pinged with a text from Cammie.

Sorry I missed the mtg. I heard about the bake sale! R U ready for it?

Sure, Mandy replied, even though she worried Caleb might ruin the whole day.

Cammie sent back a row of shocked faces, then an eye roll.

Mandy shoved her phone aside, determined not to let Caleb get under skin. She was going to run the baking session like the committee leader she was. She'd make sure her fake boyfriend helped out, and if he didn't, she'd have to take action. She wasn't sure exactly what action, but something.

Then again…maybe Caleb needed someone to be kind to him. Maybe the reason he sulked around like he lived under a thundercloud really was because his mom had left him. That had to hurt, a lot. Her mom had died, which had been awful, but to have a mom walk out on you…she couldn't imagine that. Maybe she and her friends should be extra nice to him during his fake boyfriend tenure and see if he responded.

Kind of like a wild dog who needed to be tamed.

She giggled at that image, then squeezed her eyes shut. She couldn't think about Caleb right now; she needed to focus on her essay. For what felt like the hundredth time, she struggled to write a topic sentence. What she wanted to write, *Holden Caulfield is a spoiled brat who needs to do time flipping burgers,* was different from what she finally wrote: *Holden's experience captures the timeless angst of teenagers everywhere.*

What a line of crap.

Chapter Six
Hot Stuff

Wednesday, September 21

Mandy sat across from Ms. Chen, her special ed counselor. She played with the fringe on her purse as Ms. Chen scanned her revised essay. Ms. Chen frowned and cocked her head, her gestures increasing Mandy's anxiety. After struggling over her topic sentence and first page last night, she'd decided to write what she wanted to, not what Mr. Spriggs expected. It was supposed to be a response to the book, so how could he penalize her for not having the same response as him. Right?

She wished she could sneak in her earbuds and listen to "Blinded by the Light," this seventies song that was about ten minutes long, full of synthesizers and nonsense lyrics that always cheered her up. Unfortunately Ms. Chen had a strict no-cell rule while in her office. She sighed, resigned to sitting still. She was *not* a kindergartner on crack, no matter what Caleb said.

Ms. Chen cleared her throat and looked up from the

paper. "Well, Mandy, this is certainly an unusual take on *The Catcher in the Rye*. I don't think I've ever read anything quite like it."

"Is that good or bad?" Mandy asked, anxiety streaking through her.

Ms. Chen frowned. "I'm not sure. I suspect it's not what Mr. Spriggs is looking for."

Mandy chewed her lip. "But it's my honest response to the book."

Ms. Chen sighed and leaned back in her chair. "This grade is important for you, Mandy. You need at least a C to maintain eligibility for the dance squad."

Mandy nodded. "Yeah. But it doesn't seem right for me to have to lie on a paper just to please a teacher."

"It's not lying, Mandy. It's…meeting expectations to achieve your goals."

I call BS, Mandy thought, but she kept her mouth shut. She squeezed her eyes shut and grasped for a mantra, but she couldn't come up with anything that fit this situation. *Lies are okay if you get what you need*? No way. The universe would definitely not approve of that.

She squirmed uncomfortably as she thought of the big lie she and Caleb were attempting to pull off. Maybe the universe would give her a karmic pass on that, just this once?

"What about the, uh, mechanics? Grammar and stuff?" Mandy asked, pushing away worries about her karma. Writing papers was her biggest struggle in school. Usually J.T. helped her, but she hadn't asked him for help on this since she knew he was busy with his own AP workload.

He and Caleb were in a lot of the same classes; J.T. always complained about how Caleb sat in the back and never participated, then aced everything. Mr. Spriggs taught AP English, too, and thought Caleb was a genius. At least that's what J.T. said, usually sounding resentful. J.T. was a great writer, but according to him Spriggs only had eyes for the demon.

"You definitely need to clean up the mechanics," Ms. Chen said. "Do you have a tutor?"

No way was she going to get assigned some random person. She'd beg J.T. for help again, bribe him somehow. Not like he ever expected payment. He was awesome sauce like that.

"Yeah," Mandy said. "I do."

"Well, I recommend working with your tutor to rework the essay so it's more aligned with Mr. Spriggs's expectations. Focus on the structure and mechanics. You have interesting ideas, Mandy, but they're scattered all over the place. Try rewriting the paper so it's more…favorable toward Holden Caulfield."

Mandy sighed heavily. Holden Caulfield was a jackass. Kind of like Caleb. She sat up straight like a marionette yanked by a puppeteer. They *were* similar, now that she thought about it. Both rich, both moping around like they had terrible lives.

"What do you think, Mandy? Do you have time to rewrite this with all of the Spirit Week work you're doing?"

Not to mention my job at Build-a-Buddy, Mandy thought, and taking care of Gran while Dad's on the road. *The universe never gives us more than we can handle.* She forced a smile. She truly did believe that because she'd lived it, even when she'd thought she couldn't make it one more day.

"Sure," she said. "No problem."

She'd figure out a way; she always did.

• • •

Caleb sat at his usual lunch table, glancing up in surprise as Mandy slid onto the bench across from him, her perfume filling his nose.

"Uh, hi?" he said, making it sound like a question.

"Hi, fake boyfriend. How's your day going so far?" She flipped open her salad container and poured dressing on the wilted leaves.

"Okay," he said, watching as she stabbed her salad like she wanted to kill it. "Better than yours, I'm guessing." He tensed, telling himself he didn't really care about whatever drama she was about to unload.

She glanced up at him, her eyes flashing. "Good guess, demon," she chattered. "I met with Ms. Chen this morning and she says I have to completely rewrite my stupid *Catcher in the Rye* essay for Spriggs." She shoved a bite of salad in her mouth, then spoke around it. "I hate that stupid book."

Caleb forgot his vow to ignore her drama. "You hate Salinger?"

She nodded.

"We're about to end the shortest fake relationship at Sky Ridge High."

She stared at him, eyes widening in shock. "What? Why?"

"I can't fake-date someone who doesn't appreciate Salinger. Total deal breaker."

She set her fork down. "Of course *you* think he's a genius."

"Anyone who *appreciates* literature thinks he's a genius."

"You'd really fake break up with me over that?" She looked worried, her crazy spider eyelashes fluttering.

"Maybe." He took a drink of his soda, studying her. He wouldn't, but Mandy didn't need to know that yet. He liked messing with her.

She leaned forward and closed her hand over his, sending an expected jolt of heat through him. "Stalker sighting," she whispered, glancing over his shoulder. "Don't look. Just pretend you're telling me how awesome my outfit is."

He glanced down at their hands, noticing her nail polish

for the first time. Every nail was a different color. He tried not to laugh. "Your manicure is…interesting," he said, looking into her eyes like he was telling her he loved her, just in case Elle was getting closer. "Do you have different-colored underwear for every day of the week, too?"

Heat flooded her cheeks, and she started to pull her hand away, but he trapped her hand with his. "Is she still watching?"

Mandy swallowed and glanced over his shoulder again. "Y-yes."

"Good. Keep your eyes on mine." She refocused on him, and he gave her his sexiest grin. "Tell me about your undies. What color are they today? And when do I get to see them?"

"Caleb!" She gasped and turned an even deeper shade of pink, but he didn't let go of her hand.

This was perfect. If Elle was watching, all she'd see was him obviously saying something suggestive based on Mandy's reaction. Now he just had to reel her in so she didn't smack him and ruin the effect. He leaned across the table.

"Work with me, Disco. Now you tell me how hot I look today." He winked, hoping Elle was freaking out.

Mandy's mouth opened like a fish, then she seemed to realize she needed to perform. She leaned forward, her curls falling over her shoulders.

"Smoking," she said, her low voice matching his. "Black leather totally turns me on." Her thumb rubbed the inside of his wrist, and Caleb swallowed.

"It does?" he asked, more hopefully than he should.

She leaned back, grinning, wrenching her hand out from underneath his. "It worked! She stormed out." She sipped from her weird green juice. "And no, black leather doesn't turn me on. Not even." She wrinkled her nose in disgust.

He stared at her, keenly aware that he'd been played. By a crazy hippie. She took another bite of salad and winked at him.

Fuuckkk.

This was *not* how this was supposed to play out. *He* was running this game, not her. She was *not* supposed to impact him like—

"There you are!" Cammie slid onto the bench next to Mandy, and J.T. plopped down next to Caleb. "We looked in our regular spot, but of course you're eating with your *boyfriend*." Cammie shot him a warning glare full of implied castration threats.

J.T. reached over and stole one of his fries. "Yo, Red Ranger. How's it hangin'?"

Caleb's glare took in all three of them. "Does this look like the IHOP? Do I have a 'welcome' sign on my forehead I don't know about?"

"I'm a package deal, Caleb. Date me, date my friends." Mandy smiled again, and though her words pissed him off, there was something in her smile and the teasing lilt in her voice that made him want to laugh. And he didn't do that very often.

"Hey, Gus," J.T. said, and Mandy tensed, all the laughter disappearing from her eyes, replaced by something…swoony, misty. Completely unlike the fake sexy eyes she'd turned on him just a few minutes ago.

His gut tightened.

"Hey." Gus hesitated at their table. He shot Caleb a curious look, then glanced at Mandy, and Caleb decided it was showtime again.

Caleb stretched out his denim-clad leg, moving it against Mandy's bare leg under the table. She dropped her fork, heat flooding her cheeks again. He sent her a silent message with his eyes, reminding her they were onstage.

"So we'll meet after school in the library, babe," he said, casually reaching his hand across the table to cover hers again. "I'll help you with your essay."

"You will?" She sounded shocked.

He squeezed her hand. She needed to focus and get into her role, or else Gus was going to figure them out.

"Or you can come over to my place," he said, working his thumb on her palm like he meant it. "But we both know we won't get any studying done if you do." He gave her a simmering look that could've melted ice.

"O-okay," she stammered, her cheeks pink again.

He liked making her blush. A lot. He shot a glare at Gus. "You need something, dude?"

Gus's eyes narrowed. He opened his mouth to reply, but Kay suddenly appeared next to him, snaking her arm through his. "There you are! You keep disappearing on me." She glared at everyone, then tugged Gus away.

"Wow," J.T. said, stealing another of Caleb's fries. "That whole scene was better than *Teen Wolf*." He grinned at Caleb. "Do you howl at full moons?"

Mandy leaned forward, furious. "You weren't supposed to scare him away!"

"Your real boyfriend would." He glanced at J.T. and Cammie. "I assume you two know about our fake relationship, since the three of you share a brain or whatever."

Mandy stood up in a huff, grabbing her lunch tray. "It's called friendship, Caleb. Maybe you should try it sometime."

Before he could respond, Mandy stormed away. Cammie jumped up to chase after her, pausing only long enough to shoot a glare at Caleb.

J.T. sighed, stealing another fry. "Girls," he said, shrugging sympathetically. "Some days I'm so glad I'm gay."

Chapter Seven
Got to Get You into My Life

Wednesday, September 21

Mandy was halfway down the hallway at the end of the day, the doors to freedom in sight, when a hand rested on her shoulder, stopping her.

"Trying to ditch tutoring, Disco?"

She shrugged Caleb's hand off her shoulder and spun to face him. "You're joking, right?"

"Nope." He matched her glare with his, trying to signal something with his eyebrows. She glanced over his shoulder to see Elle leaning against the wall. Watching. Probably with an ice pick in her boot.

"I see," Mandy whispered, her voice tight with frustration. "You don't really want to help me out. You're just saving your own—"

"Let's argue motivations later." He steered her one hundred eighty degrees, pointing her away from the doors to freedom.

She glared up at him. "This better not be a waste of my time."

His eyes narrowed, but the corner of lips quirked up. "I never knew you were so feisty, Disco."

She scowled. "That makes me sound like a poodle." But she fell into step with him, because maybe he could actually help her with her essay, and she needed all the help she could get.

He grinned as they passed Elle, lifting a lock of Mandy's hair, then releasing it. "I can totally see it. You'd be a red-haired poodle with painted toenails and bows in your ears and—"

She sighed as she pushed open the library door. "If I'm a poodle, then you're a Rottweiler."

"Rotts are cool. They're actually sweet dogs, unless they're raised by assholes."

She arched an eyebrow. "So what's your excuse?" She loved the look of shock on his face as she turned away to find a table.

Who knew it would be so fun teasing the Big Bad Wolf? She was surprised she wasn't intimidated by him, but for reasons she couldn't quite explain, she had a feeling she could handle him. Well, maybe not *handle* him, but…tolerate him.

She settled at a table in the corner and spread out her notes, then dug an apple and a tub of pistachios out of her bag. She needed brain fuel if she was going to work with the big brain himself.

Caleb slid into the chair next to her, and she tried to ignore the way her pulse sped up. Her body was getting confused by this fake boyfriend thing. *Not him,* she told herself. *Gus.*

"So have you thought about reporting Elle?" Mandy asked casually, digging in her purse for a pen so he wouldn't notice her heated cheeks. "I think stalking falls under the no-bullying manifesto."

Caleb moved his chair closer to hers, and she subtly tried to inch away from him. The last thing she needed was Caleb's confusing presence muddying her already-jumbled thoughts. She was beginning to think that this tutoring session might end up hurting her grade instead of helping.

"She's not a real threat. She just needs to focus her energy somewhere else."

"So get her a poodle. She can name it after you and take it everywhere." She took a bite of apple, crunching extra loud to annoy him, and to remind herself that nothing was going to happen between them.

Caleb's eyes darkened. "You can't stall forever, Disco. Show me your paper."

. . .

Caleb didn't need to be here. He could've bailed on the fake tutoring arrangement, especially after the way she'd stormed out at lunch. But he figured just another day or two of enforced togetherness and Elle would back off and Gus would move in…though that image made his stomach clench.

"Okay." Mandy heaved a sigh. "But before we start, I just want to say that Holden Caulfield is a whiner. I can't stand him. I don't get why this book is so famous. At all." Mandy paused to take a bite of her apple.

She frowned, and the little crease over her nose distracted him when he thought about kissing it. *Focus, moron.* He reminded himself she'd just insulted one of the most important books in American literature.

"You don't mean that," he said.

Her nose crease deepened. "Yeah, I do." She rolled her eyes. "I know you and J.T. think this is an awesome book, but dude. It stinks."

His brain almost shorted out because a) since when did

he and J.T. agree on anything? and b) she wasn't kidding around. She hated Salinger.

"Have you actually read it?" he asked. "Not just the cheat notes on the internet?"

She looked ready to throw her apple. "Hilarious, Caleb. News flash: I can read. I just didn't like the book." She chewed on a thumbnail, which should've grossed him out but was oddly okay coming from her.

He closed his eyes and breathed through his nose. "Look, Spriggs must've told you about how important this book is. It basically started the whole YA genre. You wouldn't have all your...uh"—he gestured toward her weird hippie bag—"whatever books you read if it weren't for this one."

She narrowed her eyes at him and leaned forward. "Really? I wouldn't be able to read about hot aliens or teenage spies if stupid whiny Holden's story hadn't been written? There'd be no demon romance books if Holden didn't worry about how he's a sex maniac just because he likes that girl?"

Caleb's brain imploded, trying to follow her zigzagging train of thought. And what sort of books was she reading, anyway?

"Demon romance, huh? I thought you were scared of demons? Me, in particular." She scooted her chair away again, and his smirk deepened. It was a lot easier to do this with her than argue about her obvious literary ignorance. Fixing that was going to take a lot of work. Teasing her? Flirting with her and watching her panic? That was easy. And entertaining.

"I won't apologize for what I read." Her eyes flashed.

He leaned an arm on the table, watching her. "Not asking you to. But if you want a decent grade from Spriggs, you can't talk crap about Salinger."

She turned away from him, staring at her notes and nibbling on her thumbnail again. "I'm not going to lie just for a good grade." She shot him a sideways glare. "Wouldn't that be *phony* of me, just what Holden's always complaining about?"

Caleb sighed, running a hand over his chin. "When is your paper due?"

"Next week."

He studied her. This was it. If he committed to this, he'd be all in, because when it came to his favorite authors, he was passionate.

"If you really want to do this," he said, keeping his gaze locked on hers, "I'm in."

She blinked at him, her crazy spider eyelashes fluttering. "Really? Not fake tutoring to make Elle crazy? You actually want to…help me?"

He shrugged. "I can't stand to see Salinger go unappreciated."

Mandy rolled her eyes. "So you're performing a service to literature, is that it?"

He laughed. Just when he thought she was a total flake, she surprised him. "Yeah. And the clock's ticking on my offer. You have sixty seconds to make up your mind."

She stared down at her notebook covered with her messy handwriting and lots of circled question marks. He frowned, thinking of his own precise printing and organized notes. No wonder she was struggling.

"Thirty seconds," he said, grabbing a few pistachios from her Tupperware container.

"Hey!" She glared at him. "I think you have food boundary issues. First my Frappuccino, now my snacks? What are you, a freaking Chihuahua? Control yourself, dude."

"I thought I was a Rottweiler." Caleb smirked as he reached for more pistachios. Why did he like messing with her so much? "Fifteen seconds."

"Okay. I accept your offer. But there are conditions."

• • •

Mandy couldn't believe she'd just agreed to let Caleb help her. Even though her gut screamed *Danger!* her heart said, "Yes. Let him help you." Then her brain chimed in. "He's an AP English genius. You'll ace the paper if he helps you." Two out of three body parts won. This was crazy, because this whole…*whatever*…between them was based on a lie. She was probably earning vats of bad karma with this fake girlfriend act.

"Hello?" Caleb prompted. "Anybody home?" He reached for more pistachios. "What are your conditions?"

"Oh." She cleared her throat. "Well, you can't make fun of me, for one," she said, holding up a warning finger. "And you can't write it for me, or tell me what to write. We can talk about the book, and you can…um, I don't know, tutor me or whatever. But I'm still going to write the paper in my own words."

He narrowed his eyes, crunching a pistachio, then swallowing. He coughed and she slid her water bottle toward him. His eyebrows shot up. "What about my food boundary issues?" He coughed into his fist again.

"I don't want you to choke to death before my paper is done." She grinned. "Plus, tomorrow is scavenger hunt prep, so you have to be alive to help with that, too."

"Who said I'm helping with that?"

She fluttered her eyelashes. "My *boyfriend* is so awesome about helping with spirit committee."

He took a long drink of water. "Fine. Then I have conditions, too."

Mandy's hands twisted anxiously under the table, but she tried to look nonchalant. "Oh yeah? What?"

"You have to at least be open to the possibility that the book doesn't suck." He leaned forward, his dark eyes fastened on hers. "And you have to let me say more than ten words without interrupting or arguing."

They stared at each other, tension coiling around them like an invisible rope. Mandy swallowed, but she didn't break eye contact. She licked her lips, wondering where she'd lost her lip gloss today; it was the third time in as many days. Caleb's gaze shot to her lips as a muscle tightened in his jaw.

"But after ten words I get to argue?" she whispered as her own gaze feasted on his mouth. God! What was *wrong* with her? It was Gus's lips she wanted, not Caleb's.

"Make that fifteen words," he said.

A shiver slid through her at the sound of his voice.

"You can't just change the rules whenever you want, Caleb."

His lips eased into a slow, sexy grin. "Sure I can, Disco. Just watch me."

• • •

As Mandy rummaged through her bag again, Caleb told himself to focus. So he'd thought about kissing her again, so what? People were freakishly attracted to people they couldn't stand all the time. It was some weird physiological thing. Completely irrational but biologically programmed after eons of evolution. And his brain was obviously confused by this fake boyfriend thing.

She tossed her copy of *Catcher in the Rye* on the library table, and he flinched. He hated when people didn't take care of books. She probably dog-eared pages instead of using a bookmark.

"What's wrong?" she asked.

He picked up the book. It was one of the school copies, a worn paperback full of dog-eared pages and faded yellow highlights. He sighed. Someday when he was a famous author he'd have an enormous library, the kind with those ladders attached to the shelves. And nobody would get near *his* books with a damn highlighter.

"Nothing," he muttered. She wouldn't understand. Besides, he didn't tell anyone about his writing dreams.

She shrugged. "Okay, whatever. So where do we start?"

He'd never tutored anyone before, so he didn't have any idea how to start. "Do you have the rough draft?"

She opened a messy binder, crammed full of crumpled papers, and pulled out two. She glanced between them, hesitating, then set one on the table and shoved the other back in her binder. She smoothed the paper, then slid it toward him, not meeting his eyes.

"You have two drafts?" he asked.

She nodded. "Ms. Chen already didn't like the first one, so I tried again."

He noticed the slight blush on her cheeks, the way her hands fluttered nervously, picking things up and putting them down again. He remembered what she'd said about ADHD and Spriggs not buying it. He wondered how he could ask her about it without pissing her off.

"It's a very rough draft," she said, darting him a nervous glance. "I know it needs work."

He nodded and began reading. A few minutes later, he wished he could rewind time and rescind his offer. Her ideas shot all over the place, and she rambled. A lot. He ran a hand over his jaw, trying to figure out where to start.

"It doesn't completely suck," he finally said, his gaze meeting hers.

"Ah," she said, sticking out her chin. "Partial suckage. I suppose that's a compliment from you." But hurt flashed in her eyes, and he felt a twinge of guilt.

"Spriggs doesn't usually give second chances," he said. "How'd you talk him into it?"

She touched her weird crab necklace, then tucked a lock of hair behind her ears. She never stopped moving; he'd always noticed that about her. Probably why she was on twenty different committees and queen of the pep rallies he never attended.

"My counselor convinced him. Because I—" She took a breath, and something shifted in the way she looked at him. "Okay, I know we're doing this fake relationship thing, Caleb, but...can I trust you with something real?"

He swallowed, taken aback by the intensity in her gaze.

"Yeah," he said, meaning it.

She held his gaze like she was deciding whether or not he meant it, then her shoulders stiffened, like she was putting on armor. "If I don't get at least a C on this paper, I'll go on academic probation from the dance squad. And I'd miss the pep rally for Spirit Week, which I know sounds dumb to you, but..."

Heat flooded her cheeks, and he could feel the embarrassment cascading out of her in waves. He shifted in his chair as awareness hit him that she really did need help. *His* help. He nodded, weighing his next words carefully.

"Okay," he said. "But if you get a C or better, you're good, right?" He'd never been on academic probation, managing to squeak out Cs in math and acing the rest of his classes even when he skipped out.

She nodded. "But I...had some problems last year, too, so I can't start off this year with another screwup." He watched the fleeting look of panic shoot across her face and felt a twinge of sympathy for her. Writing was like breathing for him; he wondered what it was like to struggle with it.

"My fake boyfriend would want me to stay on the dance squad," she joked, but he heard the wobble in her voice. He decided to make it easy on her, to ignore the wobble and focus on the joke.

"Yeah, I guess he would. Because he'd like watching you prance around in that short skirt." He shot her an over-the-top leer, hoping to make her laugh.

Her eyes widened in shock, but she laughed. "God, my fake boyfriend is such a pig."

"Total jackass. You should dump him."

She laughed again. "I will. Once he helps me with this essay."

He liked the way this felt, sitting with her in a private corner teasing and joking. He never did this with girls. With anyone.

She reached into her bag and pulled out a packet of green Pop Rocks candy and slid it across the table.

"What's this?" He eyed it like it was poison. He hadn't eaten that junk since he was a kid.

"It's a thank-you. For agreeing to help." She grinned like a weight had been lifted off her shoulders.

He slid the candy into his jacket pocket next to his notebook. "I'll save it for later."

"Okay, just don't drink them with Coke or your stomach will explode. I'd hate for my fake boyfriend to die a gruesome death before my essay's done." She fake shuddered. "Your funeral would be crazy. Elle and I would have a fight over who missed you the most. Hair-pulling. Screaming. *Big* scene."

His gaze met hers as they laughed together. She was nuts. Completely whacked.

Not his type *at all*.

"Let's focus, Disco," he said.

So they did, even though he had to keep telling himself to stop staring at her lips.

Chapter Eight
Jive Talkin'

Thursday, September 22

"You sure you're all right, doll? You seem a little stressed." Mandy's dad shoveled a forkful of spaghetti into his mouth.

Gran had cooked Dad's favorite meal; she always did the nights he returned from road trips. Gran tsk-tsked as she reached for the Miss Piggy and Kermit salt-and-pepper shakers. "She's stressed; I can tell by her mood ring." Gran glanced pointedly at Mandy's ring.

Mandy sighed, pushing her plate away. She wasn't hungry. "I have a lot on my mind. Spirit Week, homework…"

"Your new boyfriend," Reg chimed in, leering suggestively.

Mandy considered throwing Miss Piggy at his head, but reminded herself that violence wasn't the answer, and she'd already winged him earlier with the yogurt, so instead she just glared at him.

Her dad frowned as he tore a piece of bread from the garlic loaf. "New boyfriend? Who is it? When do I get to meet him?"

Mandy squirmed on her chair. Way too many people were getting invested in this fake relationship. "Um, just a guy from school. It's nothing serious."

Reg snorted, pausing his chewing. "I still can't believe Torrs is into *you*."

Gran smacked Reg on the arm. "What the hell is wrong with you, Reginald?"

"Mother, please." Mandy's dad sighed heavily and set his fork on his plate. "No swearing at the dinner table, remember?"

Gran blinked innocently. "I can't help it; it's the pain meds talking."

Dad focused on Reg. "And next time you insult your sister like that, I'm grounding you from the car for a month."

"You can't do that!" Reg protested.

Mandy closed her eyes, willing all the voices to be quiet. There was no escaping the crazy. School was crazy; her family was crazy. Her entire life was chaos. Was it any wonder she had off-the-charts ADHD?

When *had* things gotten so crazy? She knew the answer: when Mom had died. Dad had to take on more cross-country hauls to pay off Mom's medical expenses that insurance hadn't covered. Gran had moved in with them since Dad was gone so much, as sort of a surrogate mom. But then she'd had to go on oxygen because of a lifetime of smoking. It wasn't the meds that made her swear, though; she'd always been like that.

And Reg had just…gone over to the dark side, like Anakin Skywalker. Somehow his former easygoing self had turned into someone she couldn't stand, like he'd been secretly bitten by a radioactive asshole spider.

Once upon a time they'd gotten along, and he'd even looked out for her. Now he seemed to hate her, like he was embarrassed to be her brother. It cut her to the core, but she tried to bury her hurt feelings because she didn't have time for that, on top of everything else.

Mandy stood up from the table, grabbing her plate. "I need to get to J.T.'s. We have a scavenger hunt meeting tonight, to get everything ready for next week."

"What about your homework? You staying on top of it?" her dad asked.

Mandy's stomach twisted as she thought of the stupid English paper. She'd managed to catch up in all her other classes, but this paper was killing her, though that library session with Caleb had been sort of helpful. "Yeah," she said, not meeting her dad's eyes. "I'm all caught up."

Reg snorted. "Only because J.T. does everything for you."

"That's enough," her dad growled. "To your room, Reg. You're grounded for the night."

"No way. That's bullshit!"

Dad slammed his hands on the table. "The next person who swears at my dinner table eats a bar of soap!"

"Son of a bitch, honey," Gran said. "Nobody does *that* anymore."

Mandy walked quickly, having changed from her platform wedge heels to flats before escaping her insane family. *My family is on the right path,* she told herself, increasing her walking pace. *All their choices will lead to good. Eventually.*

Cammie had offered to pick her up, but Mandy had declined. She needed to burn off her stress, and walking to J.T's house helped clear her head. She worked on her meditative breathing as she soaked in the warmth of the sun, which had quickly melted Saturday night's early snowstorm.

It was always worse the nights Dad came home from

road trips, because they all did their own thing while he was gone. When he returned and laid down the law, Reg fought back, Gran's swearing hit the stratosphere, and Mandy just wanted to hide out, even though she loved her dad. She loved her Gran, too, of course. She even loved her brother, but she didn't like him much these days.

Each day gets easier. Mandy walked faster. *One day my family will survive a dinner without an argument.*

Mandy became aware of a black car in her peripheral vision. The car slowed as it pulled to the curb. The window rolled down, and Caleb's gravelly voice floated toward her. "Wanna ride, little girl? I've got candy. And puppies."

Mandy bit back a laugh and leaned down to stare through the open window. "Perv."

"Is that an accusation? Or a proposition?"

Caleb leaned across the passenger seat and opened the car door. "Get in, Little Red Riding Hood. The Big Bad Wolf is going to the same place you are."

"I didn't think you'd really show," she said, surprised.

He smirked. "My fake girlfriend is bossy. And she's running the meeting. Don't you want be on time, Disco?"

She always lost track of time, another lousy side effect of ADHD. She tried to remember to set alarms on her phone, but sometimes she forgot. And she always underestimated how long it took to walk to J.T.'s. Sighing, she slid into his car, hardly believing she was in the hearse. Again.

"Where's your car?" Caleb asked as he pulled away from the curb.

"I don't have one," she said, irritated at his assumption. Just because his family was loaded didn't mean everyone else was. "Some of us have to share a family car." Though she could've taken it tonight since Reg was grounded.

He glanced at her, then focused back on the road. "Okay," he said. "So why didn't Cammie give you a ride?"

"Who are you, the head of the Inquisition?"

He shot her a surprised look, eyebrow raised. "You know about the Inquisition?"

A flame of anger ignited in her stomach. It wouldn't take much to transform into a raging fire, especially after all the stress from dinner tonight. "How dumb do you think I am, Caleb? Just because I'm not in the honors classes doesn't mean I'm a moron."

They stopped at a red light and he turned to face her, running a hand through his tangled hair. "I didn't mean—"

"Yeah, you did," she said. "Just because I think *Catcher in the Rye* is a stupid book doesn't mean *I'm* stupid."

She noticed his fingers grip the steering wheel tighter.

"I'm sorry. I didn't mean that. You're definitely not stupid."

She let out a long breath. "Well…that's a first. Everyone else thinks I am."

He darted a glance at her. "I doubt J.T. does. Or Cammie."

"They're my friends." She shrugged. "I meant teachers. Especially Spriggs." She mumbled something under her breath he couldn't quite make out.

"What was that?" He pulled the car to a stop in front of J.T.'s house and turned to look at her.

"Just um, a mantra. Never mind."

"A mantra?"

She nodded. "I'm sure you don't believe in them, and I'm not interested in you making fun of me right now, so—"

"What is it? *I will get an A on my essay and jump into a 1970s time warp so I can be the Queen of Disco*?"

She narrowed her eyes. "It's…bigger than that. And I'm not telling you, so give it up."

"That's one thing I don't do, Disco. Give up."

She cocked an eyebrow. "You gave up on Elle, didn't you?"

. . .

Damn. She looked innocent enough, but she had sharp kitten claws hidden underneath all that glitter and hippie perfume. "It was… I didn't *give up* on her. We just…didn't mesh."

"Hmm. *Mesh*. Interesting choice of words." She studied him intently, and he felt his neck grow hot, but he couldn't tear his gaze away from hers.

"I think I know why she's stalking you," she announced.

"Because she's crazy. We've established that."

Mandy shook her head, tapping her finger on her chin. "Nope. She needs closure."

His mouth fell open. "Closure? Who are you, freaking Oprah?"

Her lips curved into a smug smile that he really wanted to wipe off her face. With his own lips. Damn it, not again. He had to stop thinking about her like that. A car horn beeped behind him, and he realized the light had changed to green. He accelerated, telling himself to freaking focus on the road.

"It's basic relationship etiquette, Caleb. If you dump someone, you should at least try to do it respectfully."

He shot her a warning glare, no longer thinking about kissing. "I'll remember that when I dump you."

"Whoa." She put up a hand. "Maybe *I'm* going to be the one who dumps *you*."

"That's not how this is gonna go down, Disco. I'm never the one who gets dumped."

She laughed. "First time for everything. Anyway, we don't have to figure that out right now. I'm sure it will just, you know, happen organically or whatever."

As he parked in front of J.T.'s house, a surge of adrenaline shot through him. Everything in him wanted to argue with Mandy. She was not going to dump him, and he was not going to dump her.

Wait, what?

Not *yet*—that's what he meant. Nobody was dumping anyone yet. Not until they both got what they wanted. Although right now he wasn't sure *what* he wanted.

"You could try it again," she chattered, "breaking up with her. But make sure you're prepared this time. Write down a list of why you two didn't *mesh*." She glanced at him, and he thought her cheeks darkened with the hint of a blush but he wasn't sure. "Do it reasonably. Calmly. Thank her for the time you spent togeth—"

He snorted with laughter. "You're crazy, you know that, right? Tell me about the last time somebody broke up with *you* and did it reasonably. I bet all your exes ran away screaming."

"Way to treat your *girlfriend*, Caleb. Really nice." She reached to open the passenger door, but it stuck. He leaned over her to open the door, looking down into her wide eyes.

"The way I see it," he said, drinking in her definitely blushing cheeks and fluttering eyelashes, "as of right now, you're still *my girlfriend*. Nobody's dumped anybody." He had her caged in, like a butterfly trapped under glass. Her tongue darted out to lick her bottom lip, shooting lightning bolts of desire through his body. "So instead of talking about who's dumping who, maybe we ought to put our energy somewhere else."

"L-like where?" Her voice was barely a whisper, and her gaze darted to his mouth.

"Like convincing everyone we're for real, not fake." He leaned in closer, his lips just millimeters from hers. "We need to sell it. So kissing might be a good place to start."

Her eyelids fluttered like panicked butterflies. "B-but there's no one around that we need to convince."

In spite of her words, she arched toward him, and if there was one thing he was good at reading besides books, it was body language.

"Practice makes perfect, Disco." He closed his eyes and brushed his lips across hers, barely making contact, but it was enough to light him up inside. He wanted more. A lot more. Fake, real, whatever the hell this was, he wanted more.

"W-we're late," she whispered against his lips, torturing him. "We should go inside."

He opened his eyes, staring into hers, looking for answers to a question he couldn't put into words.

"Fine. Whatever." He jiggled the handle and flung the door open, then dragged his body away from hers. She blinked rapidly, then jumped out of the car and slammed the door closed.

He ran a hand through his hair, remembering how she'd arched her body toward his, and how she'd stammered. Maybe she was confused, too, about what was real and what was fake.

One thing was for sure. Before this fake gig was over, he was going to kiss her.

For real.

· · ·

Once inside J.T.'s house, Mandy made a beeline for the basement staircase. Caleb was fast, though; she could feel him following her down the stairs like a shadow she couldn't shake. Everyone looked up as they entered the chaotic room full of blaring music and laughter.

J.T.'s observant gaze swept over them. "There you are. We thought you got lost."

Mandy practically flew across the room to Cammie, whose sparkling eyes danced with speculation. Cammie leaned in and whispered, "I can't tell if you want to kill Caleb or kiss him."

"Me either," Mandy whispered back. "That's why I ran over to you."

Cammie snorted and handed her a soda. "Take a drink. Pretend he's not here."

"Right. Like that's even possible." Mandy sucked down the soda, grateful for the cool liquid because her body was on fire after that almost-kiss. She had to focus.

I can do this. I'm a leader. I'm not distracted by what was almost the hottest kiss of my life. "Okay everyone," she said loudly to be heard over the music. "Let's get to work."

• • •

Caleb sat on the floor surrounded by chattering cheerleaders, praying for the sweet release of death, or at least a coma so he didn't have to listen to them. Then again, at least they were a distraction from how much he wanted to drag Mandy out of here, back to his car, where they could finish what they'd almost started.

"Where can we hide this lava lamp?" asked a perky brunette who kept rubbing up against Caleb. She fluttered her eyelashes at him. "Maybe you'll be the one to find it during the scavenger hunt. For your bedroom." She leaned into him, and he caught the smell of grape bubble gum.

He hated grape.

"My bedroom's fine the way it is," he grumbled.

The cheerleader put her hand on his chest. "I'll bet it is. Maybe you can show it to me sometime."

Caleb sighed and glanced across the room toward Mandy, who was surrounded by a huge group of spirit freaks digging through their own box of weird seventies crap they planned to hide around the school. She'd divided everyone into teams and they all had assignments for decorating.

Mandy caught his eye, then her gaze took in the cheerleader whose hand was moving south down Caleb's chest. Mandy arched her eyebrows, looking exactly like a pissed-off *real* girlfriend. Caleb grabbed the girl's hand and moved it back to the lava lamp, but Mandy had turned away.

The cheerleader sighed next to him. "So you and Mandy are a thing, huh? For real?"

He frowned, aware that everyone in his group had stopped chattering to hear his answer. They stared at him like he was an alien species, which he figured he was since they inhabited totally different orbits at school.

"We're...yeah." He didn't even need to say a complete sentence because the cheerleaders pounced on him like kittens with a toy mouse.

"So you're taking her to homecoming?" the brunette demanded, apparently relinquishing her desire to maul him. "Right?"

"Are you doing a prom-posal?" a blonde asked, tilting her head like a little bird. "She'd love that."

A girl with coal-black dreads nodded enthusiastically. "She totally would. I mean, lots of us have already gotten ours, so you should hurry up. It's only two weeks away. Make sure you do it right."

What. The. Hell. How was he going to get out of *this*? Tell them that he wasn't really her boyfriend, that Gus was the one who needed to come through with the big prom-posal? The thought of that made his gut clench.

"I...uh...it's not really my style," he muttered, hoping they'd drop the issue. He pulled an old album out of the box his group was sorting through. The Bee Gees. Great. What a bunch of girlie guys. They even sounded like girls when they sang.

He slid the record out of the album cover and stared at the grooves on the record, then glanced up into the determined dark eyes of his prom-posal pusher. She wasn't giving up.

"We could give you some ideas," she chirped, and all the other girls perked up, scooting closer to him.

"But it's not even prom," he protested. "It's just homecoming."

They stared at him like he spoke a foreign language, then they all started talking at once.

"You still need to do it!"

"It's like a warm-up for a prom-posal! So make it big, but not something you won't be able to top when it *is* time for prom."

"You *have* to, Caleb. Mandy's so sweet, and nobody's ever done one for her before and—"

"This whole dance was her idea! The seventies theme and everything. You *have* to."

He scooted backward. They were even scarier than Elle, all of them homing in on him like hyenas on a hunt, circling and trapping their prey.

"Uh, I don't know…"

The girl with dreads sighed in frustration. "Ask some of the other guys for ideas."

Right. Like he'd just barge into the guys' locker room one day and ask for prom-posal advice.

"Anyway," the blonde said, "I'm glad she's going out with you. You guys are cute together, because you're so… unexpected."

The girl with dreads nodded. "Totally. I was afraid she'd never get over that stupid crush on Gus. He's such a tool."

Caleb frowned. "He is?"

The girls all glanced over their shoulders toward Mandy, who was engaged in animated conversation with her group, laughing and gesturing, in full butterfly mode.

They turned back to him, their beady eyes focused.

"He's got so many people fooled," the brunette said, glancing at the other girls, who all nodded their agreement. "He puts on this goofy innocent act, so girls will trust him. But after just one date, he turns into a total octopus."

The blond nodded furiously. "Hands everywhere. Down the shirt, up the skirt, and he doesn't like hearing no…"

The old record Caleb was holding cracked in half. He glanced down at his white-knuckled hands.

"Ooh," the brunette said. "Don't let Mandy see that. She loves that record."

Broken records were the least of his worries. "So, why didn't you guys warn her about Gus? When you, uh, thought she still liked him?"

"It's a new strategy for him," the blonde said. "But we know he's done it with a couple of girls already. Word's just starting to get around."

"I tried to tell her just last week," the girl with dreads said, "but she's sort of…blind about people sometimes. Sort of, uh, what's it called? When you only see the good in people, not the bad? Even when they're assholes?"

"Pollyanna," Caleb muttered. That was Mandy in a nutshell. He glanced across the room again, and this time she met his gaze. She smiled shyly, her cheeks turning pink again, and he wondered if she was thinking about their almost-kiss. He gave her his best loyal boyfriend smile.

No fucking way was Gus taking her to this dance.

Chapter Nine
Just What I Needed

Friday, September 23

Mandy dug through her closet, yawning. The scavenger meeting had gone later than she'd expected, and she'd had a hard time falling asleep last night because she couldn't stop replaying her almost-kiss with Caleb. She'd tried to replace the real memory with a fake fantasy of kissing Gus, but Caleb's face kept taking over. She kept imagining Caleb's mouth on hers, his hands in her hair.

Cammie had driven her home instead of Caleb last night. She'd bolted up the basement stairs, telling Caleb she'd see him later. Totally unrealistic girlfriend behavior, but whatever, she'd needed to get away from him.

He'd texted her after she got home, asking if she was okay, which had only contributed to the kissing replays. Because jackass Caleb was sort of turning into sometimes-nice-guy Caleb. And she hadn't expected that.

She burrowed deeper into her closet, the tangling metallic

hangers sounding like a tuneless wind chime. Her clothes were a hodgepodge of thrift-store finds and clothes her mom used to wear—really awesome stuff from the seventies, colorful and sparkly. Clothes made her happy. She tugged a psychedelic tank top off a hanger, glad the freakish early snowstorm was just a memory and warm temps had returned. She imagined standing next to black-clad Caleb and smiled at the contrast. After tugging on the top, she grabbed jeans from the floor.

Today was Friday, thank God. Tonight she was going to the movies with Cammie and J.T., and Sunday was the baking bonanza at Caleb's house. She grabbed beaded earrings from her spinning jewelry rack on her dresser, deciding not to worry about Sunday until she had to.

She put on mascara and lip gloss, gave up on taming her wild red curls, shoved her feet into platform clogs, and finally decided she was ready for another day as Caleb Torrs's fake girlfriend.

• • •

Caleb waited at her locker, along with several of her cheer team friends. He looked panicked, like a little Nemo captured by a flock of hungry seagulls. *Mine. Mine. Mine.* The image made her smile.

"Hi, Caleb," she purred, just like a real girlfriend would. Her friends giggled appreciatively. "Hi, guys." She waved to her friends. "You all officially met Caleb last night, right? This is Amber, Tonia, and Leticia. In case you forgot." She pointed to each girl as she announced her name.

He nodded, looking like he wanted to run away, but he stayed put. "Right," he said. "Last night."

"Spirit Week's going to be awesome, isn't it? I can't wait for all the events!" Mandy smiled at the girls, who nodded and chimed in their agreement as Caleb ran a hand through his hair, still looking like he wanted to escape.

She caught his eye and winked. He blinked in surprise, then his usual smirk made an appearance. Her stomach fluttered, so she focused on cramming books into her locker.

"We were just talking to Caleb about the dance," Amber said. "And how we can't wait to see whatever prom-posal he comes up with for you."

Mandy froze. What the heck? Caleb wasn't supposed to do that, Gus was. After she and Caleb broke up. Or maybe before they did…she wasn't sure exactly, but somehow…

"Oh," she managed to say, turning to face Amber. "Uh… I'm not really…expecting that from Caleb. It's not his style."

Leticia tossed her dreadlocks over her shoulder. "That's BS. Anyway"—she pinned Caleb with a meaningful look— "we'll see you guys later. We just wanted to say hi."

The girls waved, then moved away, their skirts swishing in perfect synchrony.

Slowly, Mandy turned to face Caleb. "What the heck was that about?"

He looked stricken. "Uh, it's kind of…well, last night at the meeting they sort of ganged up on me. Said I had to do a prom-posal for homecoming. That you'd be expecting one."

"Well, I *am* expecting one, but not from you."

He narrowed his eyes, suddenly morphing from nervous Caleb to pissed-off Caleb. How did he do that so fast?

"You want your prom-posal from Gus."

She nodded, staring into his dark eyes. She did want that. Didn't she?

His lips curved, and suddenly she was in his car again, those lips brushing against hers and setting her on fire.

"Maybe we didn't really think this through," he said. "If I'm supposed to be your boyfriend, then *I'd* be the one doing the prom-posal. Not Gus."

She swallowed. "But no one would expect you to, since you're...you know."

"Since I'm what?" He sounded defensive.

"Since you're Caleb Torrs. Lord of Darkness. Hater of School Activities. Scarer of Freshmen."

His lips twitched. "Two out of three, maybe. I don't scare them intentionally." He reached behind her and slammed her locker shut. "Come on. I'll walk you to class and we can keep arguing."

They fell into step together and people watched them, some smiling, some with raised eyebrows, some looking shocked to see them still together after two days.

Caleb leaned down to whisper in her ear. "Elle at ten o'clock. Get ready."

Mandy glanced over his shoulder to see his stalker glaring at them, eyes narrowed. "Ready for wh—" But she didn't finish her sentence because Caleb stopped and pulled her into his arms, squishing her binder against her chest.

"Gus at two o'clock," he leaned down to whisper into her ear, brushing her hair off her neck and making her shiver. She peeked over his other shoulder to see Gus leaning against the wall, Kay chattering in his face, but Mandy was so distracted by Caleb's hands—one on her neck and the other gripping her waist—that she couldn't focus.

"Sorry we don't have time to argue about this, Disco. Just roll with it."

Then he moved in for the kill.

• • •

This wasn't how he'd planned to do it. He'd wanted their first kiss to be private. In his car, probably, or maybe his house, if he could figure out a way to get her there alone.

But Gus and Elle were right there watching them, so he

had to make his move. Sell it, just like he'd told her. Convince everyone this fake thing between them was real. But he didn't want to be an ass and force himself on her, either.

"You up for one fake kiss, Disco?" he whispered.

Her eyelashes went into overdrive, and he felt her body tremble as a shiver ran through her. "Um, uh…maybe just one. Make it quick."

He smiled to himself as he ducked his head to her neck, inhaling her perfume as he kissed the soft skin. This was *not* going to be fast. He moved his mouth to her jawline, trailing kisses as he worked his way toward her mouth. He felt her tremble again and pulled her closer, wishing they were anywhere but the middle of a packed hallway. He needed to get rid of her stupid binder digging into his chest. Needed her closer.

Needed her to stop wanting Gus.

"Mandy," he whispered against her cheek, his mouth almost to her lips. *Let's stop pretending.* The words were almost there, just hovering in the back of his throat, waiting to escape.

"Caleb," she whispered back, just as he was about to finally taste her lips for real. "I want…"

You, he willed her to say. *Say you want me, not that tool Gus masquerading as a dork.*

"Break it up!" The barking voice startled them, and they sprang apart, coming face to face with Dr. Hairy, the anti-PDA principal. She tapped her foot on the linoleum, her mouth a thin line, while all around them people laughed and hooted and clapped.

"I'm quite sure you're both aware of the PDA policy," Dr. Hairy said. "Since I make it very clear at the first assembly every year."

Mandy swallowed, her face almost as red as her hair.

Caleb shrugged, schooling his face into a bored expression.

"I might've missed that day."

She narrowed her eyes. "Mr. Torrs, I'm quite sure you're aware of the policy, because you've violated it before."

Why'd she have to bring that up in front of Mandy? Last time he'd been busted for PDA was when Elle had jumped him in the cafeteria, trying to convince him to stick around, because at that point he was already drifting away from her.

"Detention. Both of you. After school today."

"What?" Mandy squeaked. "But it's the first time I've…" Her voice faded away, and Caleb could tell she was mortified.

"And your last," Dr. Hairy said. She glared at Caleb. "You, too, Mr. Torrs. Now get to class, both of you."

• • •

Mandy was going to die. Shrivel up and float away, like ashes swirling upward from a fire of embarrassment. She couldn't believe Caleb had done that. In front of *everyone*.

She'd rushed away from him and Dr. Harris, ignoring the catcalls as she ran down the hall. This fake boyfriend thing was done. It wasn't worth it.

No matter how amazing those kisses on her neck had been. No matter how real it had felt, especially when he'd whispered her name. Had she imagined the feelings she'd heard in that one whisper?

Probably.

Definitely.

Her phone pinged with a text from Cammie as she slid into her desk. She glanced at it, not surprised to see a row of shocked face emoticons. Her phone pinged again, with almost the identical message from J.T. As usual, gossip traveled at lightning speed. She ignored her friends' messages; there'd be time enough to deal with their joint freak-out later.

Right now she had to figure out how to get out of this

fake girlfriend deal, because it wasn't going at all the way she'd planned. She glanced to the front of the room where her teacher was distracted, talking to another student.

This sucks, she texted furiously to Caleb. *I'm going to kill you.*

Sorry babe. I'll make it up to you. Buy you lunch?

Do not babe me! I am not your BABE. I am your FAKE GF, got it?

Got it, BABE. ;)

She shot back a row of angry devil faces, then shoved her phone in her purse because she sure didn't need double detention today.

She'd kill him later. After he bought her lunch.

. . .

Caleb figured he'd better take Mandy off campus for lunch so no one would see their imminent explosion. He didn't need Elle seeing their big fight and thinking she could move back in on her imagined territory.

"Let's go," he said, cornering her at her locker.

She spun on him, hair flying, hands on her hips. "I changed my mind. I'm not going anywhere with you!"

He glanced around, aware they were already drawing an interested audience. "Dial it down, Disco. Let's get out of here and discuss this rationally."

"There's nothing to disc—"

At that moment, Gus and Kay appeared, holding hands, and Caleb wondered if maybe there really was a God, who might even be on his side.

Mandy watched them, her expression changing from

anger to wistfulness, and Caleb felt like he'd been punched in the gut. But he didn't let her see it, instead reaching for her hand. *Time to sell it.*

She stared at their clasped hands, then looked up to meet his gaze. He nodded slightly toward Gus and Kay. She blinked, then seemed to snap back to reality. He watched her expression change again, this time to one of swoony, devoted fake girlfriend.

He frowned. He didn't like that very much; he preferred authentic, pissed-off Mandy. But at least she was still holding his hand, so he'd take what he could get.

"Where are we going to lunch, *cutie*?" she asked, raising her voice on the last word. He heard a few titters from their audience.

"Wherever you want, *babe*."

He tugged her down the hall, determined to get the hell away from prying eyes and ears. As soon as they were in the parking lot, he turned on her. "Don't ever call me cutie."

She fluttered her eyelashes. "Then stop calling me *babe*."

He narrowed his eyes. "It's what I call all my girlfriends."

She blinked, and he watched her expression change from stunned to embarrassed. "T-then you better stop calling me that." She swallowed, and he could tell it took effort for her to snap at him. "I'm not like all your other girlfriends."

They locked eyes for a long moment, and he felt a weird sense of pride for her, since she'd stood up to him. "No," he finally said. "You're not. Okay then, let's go, *Disco*."

She tripped along next to him, trying to keep up with his long strides.

"Slow down, Caleb."

He glanced at her ridiculous shoes. "Why don't you wear normal shoes?"

"Why don't you wear anything besides black?"

He wrenched open the passenger door of his car. "Get in,

Disco."

She glared at him, but she slid into the car, then slammed the door in his face, making him smile.

• • •

Mandy stared out the window while Caleb drove, searching her mind for a mantra, but she couldn't find one to fit the insane situation: kidnapped by her fake boyfriend for lunch because he'd kissed her like a vampire in public and gotten them both detention. She glanced at her mood ring, which was yellow, for nervous.

"Drive-through or inside?" Caleb asked as he pulled into the parking lot.

"Drive-through. I don't want anyone seeing us together."

He grunted and pulled into the drive-through line. "Okay," he said. "I'm sorry about the detention. But you know why I did it, right? Both our targets were right there. I couldn't pass up that opportunity."

She arched her eyebrows. "Opportunity?"

He drummed his fingers on the steering wheel. "You know what I mean."

She shifted under his dark gaze, staring at his lips, remembering how they'd felt on her neck. "Um, so, okay, let's say that's true. Why didn't you just kiss me on the cheek or whatever?"

"*Cheek?* I told you we need to sell this, Mandy." He smirked. "Pretty sure I did." He accelerated as the drive-through line moved forward.

"Who were you trying to *sell*? Elle? Gus? Or me?"

His eyes widened, and she watched his Adam's apple as he swallowed. "Uh…well…"

A voice crackled through the speaker. "Welcome to Burger King. Place your order when you're ready."

"Veggie burger and fries," Mandy said. "And a Coke."

He cocked an eyebrow. "Veggie burger. Really?"

"Yes, really. Are you buying me lunch or not, *cutie*?"

He glared at her, but when he placed the order a hint of a smile curved his lips.

. . .

After they got their food, Caleb drove to a nearby park, and they sat in the car in the shade of a tree.

"So you didn't answer my question," Mandy said around a french fry. "Who were you trying to sell with all that… vampire action?"

"Vampire action?"

"Yeah. All the neck slurping."

He stopped chewing. "I don't *slurp*."

She smiled, giddy with her small victory. No way would she let him know how hot that neck action actually was, because heaven only knew what he'd do with *that* information.

"Unfortunately, you do," she said. "You might want to work on your technique." She took a long drink of soda, forcing herself to maintain eye contact as his eyes darkened. "Not for my benefit, of course, but for whoever's next in your girlfriend lineup."

He glowered at her. "I don't have a 'lineup.' And there's nothing wrong with my technique." She glanced at him, and her stomach did a devious little happy dance at the worried expression flitting across his face.

She shrugged. "If you say so." She was probably having too much fun with this, but he sort of deserved it, after earning her detention. She took another bite of fry. Mr. Dark Lord of Sexiness worrying about his technique. Now *that* was funny.

"So," he began, then hesitated. "So you're saying…that uh, me uh…"

"Selling it," she supplied helpfully, grinning at his discomfort.

He grimaced. "Right. You're saying…me trying to sell it, uh, didn't…do *anything* for you?"

"Nope." She blushed as she shook her head. This was getting more personal than she'd intended, and he could never know how much it had *done* for her. And it was bad karma to lie, even when it was sort of fun. She cleared her throat and turned away, staring out the window at a group of toddlers playing on a swing set.

• • •

Okay, this was *bullshit*. No way was she telling the truth.

Was she?

Damn it. This was crazy. What did he care, anyway? This was all for show.

But it wasn't *all* for show, because now he didn't trust Gus after what the cheerleaders had said. He didn't want to see Mandy with an octopus asshole. She was sweet. Funny. Feisty. Smart. A whole bunch of things he wouldn't have guessed after watching her flutter around the school the past couple of years.

Crap.

He chewed a bite of his non-veggie burger, thinking. He didn't want to be an asshole like Gus, forcing himself on her if she really didn't want it. Or if they weren't at least in agreement that whatever they did was for show.

That was it—they needed an agreement.

Rules.

Kissing rules.

"Okay," he said, his confidence returning. "I've got a better idea. I think the problem was you weren't expecting it. So you couldn't uh, sell it, from your side."

She whirled to face him, eyes wide. "What?"

He grinned, his confidence rising. "Next time, we'll have a plan."

"A plan? You mean…a…"

"Kissing plan. Yeah." He watched her as he chewed a french fry. Her cheeks were pink, her pupils dilated. *Didn't do anything for you, my ass.* But he wasn't going to gloat. Not yet.

"So let's work this out. Maybe each time we run into Gus, I kiss you. Your choice where." He grinned. "Cheek." He rolled his eyes. "Neck." He cocked an eyebrow and his gaze strayed to her lips. "Mouth."

"I…uh…don't think…" Her voice was breathy, nervous.

"And," he continued, feeling smug, "whenever we see Elle, I think *you* should kiss *me*." He winked at her. "Wherever you want."

She leaned forward. "Caleb! That's…you're…I can't believe you…"

"It's better this way, Disco. If we're agreed ahead of time, we can both sell it." He hesitated. "We'll both get what we want faster this way."

He didn't have much time to convince her that Gus was the wrong guy for her. But if kissing was part of the plan, he definitely had an advantage over the octopus dork.

Because kissing was something he was very, very good at.

Chapter Ten
Ain't Nobody (Loves Me Better)

Saturday, September 23

"What's *he* doing here?" Mandy whispered, catching sight of Caleb in the theater lobby. He leaned against the wall, eyes narrowed as he watched the groups of friends and families out for a fun Saturday night.

"Maybe he's on a date," Cammie said, "with a dominatrix."

J.T. snorted. "I invited him." He paused dramatically. "Technically, I'm here with Liam, and Cammie's with Jiro, so I guess that makes *you* his date, Man." He grin was evil. "It's Saturday night; you should totally be on a date with your boyfriend."

"You what?" Mandy screech-whispered. "J.T.! Why...but he...I'm hardly speaking to him right now! After what he did and detention and..." Her voice trailed away.

After lunch and Caleb's ridiculous kissing proposal, she'd avoided him, fueling rumors that their whirlwind romance was already on the rocks. She wasn't sure if that was good or bad, but she'd needed to get away from him. They hadn't spoken during detention, and he'd bolted from the room as soon as it was over, surprising her and leaving her feeling... confused.

Cammie put a hand on her shoulder, and Mandy took a breath, grasping for mantras. *Everything happens as it should. There are no accidents.*

"You're the one who told us to be nice to him. That he just needs some good people in his life," J.T. said, staring down Mandy. "But I admit, I'm surprised he showed."

"I'm not," Cammie said, squeezing Mandy's hand. "You are his *girlfriend*, after all."

"Always the drama with you," Jiro said to J.T., who grinned and pulled Liam in close.

Mandy swallowed, darting a glance at Caleb, who'd spotted them but hadn't moved. His eyes locked on hers, and her insides tumbled around like clothes in a washing machine.

"But you don't like him," Mandy whispered to J.T. as Caleb pushed off the wall, heading toward them.

J.T. shrugged. "He's not my favorite person. But...since *you* like him..." He gave her a meaningful look, reminding her that Liam and Jiro didn't know about the fake routine. He nodded as Caleb joined them. "Yo, Red Ranger. How's it going?"

Caleb nodded at J.T. "Good. You?"

J.T. grinned. "It's Friday and I'm with my favorite people in the world...mostly. I'm fantastic."

Mandy saw Caleb's face darken at J.T.'s veiled insult, so she stepped toward him, resting a hand on his leather jacket. "Just ignore him. I do."

He glanced down at her and his eyes...changed somehow. Softened maybe? She wasn't sure, but whatever it was, it sent tingles shooting through her body.

"It's, um, nice that you're here," she managed to stammer.

"We were just about to get some popcorn. Want some?"

He almost smiled. "I'll get it," he said. "Butter?"

Mandy nodded, biting her lip. His eyes shot to her mouth, then he frowned and turned to J.T. "You want anything, Blue Ranger?"

J.T. grinned. "I'm good." He patted his jacket pocket. "Smuggled in my own stuff."

Caleb arched an eyebrow. "Flask?"

"No." J.T. snorted. "Peanut M&M's. They're Liam's favorite."

Caleb rolled his eyes and turned his attention to Cammie and Jiro. "You guys want anything?"

Cammie shook her head. "You just take care of my girl here. Give her anything she wants." She pinned him with a wicked grin. "And I do mean *anything*, Torrs."

Mandy sighed in frustration. Her friends were enjoying this fake boyfriend thing way too much.

Sitting next to Caleb in a dark theater was a bad idea. Very bad. Or maybe very, very good depending on how she looked at it, but right now Mandy didn't know what to make of her predicament. Everyone else had sprinted down the aisle to sit together in a half-empty row, leaving Mandy stuck next to Caleb.

After she and Caleb sat down, a group of guys sat on the other side of her, laughing loudly and fake punching each other until one of them noticed her.

"Yo, Red, you need company? I got room on my lap." He leered at her.

A swirling vortex of anxiety and anger shot through Mandy. She hated guys like this, who just invaded her space and made rude comments like she was some toy, not a real person. She turned away from the jerk hoping to ignore him, but instead she met Caleb's stormy dark gaze. Uh-oh.

Mandy put a restraining hand on Caleb's arm, but he ignored her, leaning over her to get in the guy's face. "Shut your piehole, unless you want a taste of my fist."

Mandy closed her eyes and sighed. Great. Now she had not one but two cavemen to deal with.

The other guy tensed up. His blue eyes, which looked glazed, met hers. "You with this asshole?"

Caleb leaned in close, his spicy scent overwhelming her as his voice rumbled in her ear. "Take your pick, Disco. The devil you know or the one you don't."

Holy crap. He was practically smoldering. She grabbed her soda and took a long drink, then glanced at the blue-eyed jerk.

"Yeah," she finally said, "I'm with him."

Blue Eyes shrugged. "Your loss." He turned away, saying something foul to his friends that she chose to ignore.

Caleb leaned forward again but she pushed him back, locking eyes with him. "Caleb. If you hang out with my friends, there's basically one rule. Don't be a jerk. And no fighting." She was suddenly aware of her hands still on his chest. Muscles flexed underneath the fabric of his shirt.

"That's two rules." Caleb's hands reached up to cover hers. His eyes narrowed. "You'd rather I let that guy harass you?" His grip tightened, flattening her palms against his chest. Cammie and J.T. goggled at them, openmouthed, while Jiro smirked and Liam shook his head, smiling.

"I—I—um—" How could she possibly form a coherent sentence when Caleb was filling up her senses like this, his heartbeat racing under her hand? The theater darkened and the speakers vibrated with the soundtrack from the movie previews, but Mandy couldn't see or hear anything except Caleb.

Caleb released her hands, shifting in his seat to drape his arm over her, his fingers tangling in her hair, then drifting across her neck before setting on her shoulder. Every nerve ending in her body roared to life, and she was pretty sure that fire really was his secret superpower.

"W-what are you doing?" she managed to whisper.

In the dim light from the screen, she saw him tilt his chin toward Blue Eyes. "Being an excellent fake boyfriend. He keeps watching you. I want to make sure he gets the message to leave you alone."

Mandy glanced at Blue Eyes, who jerked away. Caleb was right. The guy was a total creeper.

How could she possibly focus on the movie now?

She stared at the screen. People did stuff, cars exploded, tornadoes destroyed an entire town, but her brain couldn't comprehend anything except Caleb. Scary hotness draped over her like a protective cloak. She took a deep breath, willing her squirrel brain to focus on the screen.

Caleb leaned in close, his voice tickling her neck and making her shiver. "Want to switch places with me? Then I won't have to hold you against your hippie will." She heard the teasing in his voice and shot him what she hoped was a withering glare. But based on his smirk, he wasn't about to wither.

Mandy glanced at Blue Eyes, who slumped in his seat, eyes closed. "I think he passed out," she whispered back.

Really, it would be disruptive to move now that the movie had started. And she always got cold in theaters. It would be a shame to lose the warmth of Caleb's arm wrapped around her. She darted another sideways glance at him.

"It's, uh, okay. I'll just…stay here."

He tossed a piece of popcorn in his mouth and winked at her. "Up to you, Disco." But his arm tightened around her shoulders, pulling her closer, and he stretched out his legs, resting his thigh against hers, marking her as effectively as a wolf in the wild.

. . .

After the movie, as the posse stood chattering in the theater lobby, Caleb debated whether to head home by himself, offer to drive Mandy home, or stick around. A real boyfriend would choose option two or three. Preferably option two.

"Anybody want ice cream?" J.T. asked.

As everyone debated where to go, Caleb caught Mandy's eye. She stood farther away from him than a real girlfriend would, but he reminded himself that she'd chosen to stay next to him during the movie, and his arm was still a little numb from being wrapped around her for two hours, because she'd been okay with that, too.

Suck on that, tool, he wanted to say to Octo-Gus.

"Ice cream?" he asked Mandy, and she nodded. She stepped closer to him, and he held out his hand. She hesitated, then glanced at her friends and tentatively put her hand in Caleb's. Her skin was warm and soft. He ran his thumb over her fingernails, smiling as he thought of the rainbow manicure.

They walked behind the posse, their clasped hands swinging between them. He wasn't an ice cream date kind of guy. Or much of a hand-holder, either, because somehow holding hands felt way more intimate than other stuff. Which was weird.

But doing this with Mandy was…good.

"So does ice cream melt instantly when you touch it?" Mandy asked, shooting him a cryptic smile.

He frowned, then shook his head when he realized what she meant. "You still think I'm a demon? I'm disappointed, Disco. I thought we'd moved past that."

"Well, I'm still trying to figure you out. Maybe you're right and I've misread the clues." She paused as they waited for everyone else to file into the ice cream shop. "Maybe you're some other type of villain."

Surprised, he glared down at her. "You think I'm a *villain*? Seriously? Just because a guy wears black…"

"And gets expelled for fighting—"

His hackles rose. Time to quash that misconception right now. "One, I only got suspended, and two, I had a good reason for fighting, but no witnesses."

Her eyebrow raised. "A good reason? What—like you were saving someone from a bad guy?"

"Yeah, I was." He'd saved two someones, in fact—two scrawny middle-schoolers who'd been jumped by an asshole on their high school parking lot after school. Caleb had only been a freshman, but he'd been in good shape even then. Unfortunately the middle-schoolers had been so worried about their own butts they hadn't stood up for him when questioned by the principal and security guards.

Mandy cleared her throat and crossed her arms over her chest. "Okay…well, I'll give you the benefit of the doubt on that one." She narrowed her eyes. "But you still sit in a corner by yourself all the time, glaring at everyone. And don't do any teams or clubs or—"

"But I *do* go out with a girl who prances around like a Rainbow Pony. And her weird friends."

Mandy's sparkling lips split into a grin. "I used to love Rainbow Ponies! You should have seen my collection. It was amazing. The best in town." She tilted her head. "How do you even know about Rainbow Ponies?"

He rolled his eyes. "Believe it or not, I was five years old once. But *I* was smart enough to collect Power Rangers, not freaky psychedelic horses."

"Oh!" She let go of his hand to put her hands on her hips. "You did not just diss the ponies."

He stepped close, catching the scent of her perfume. "I did. Rangers trump ponies every time."

She glared at him, making him laugh. He reached out to brush a stray hair off her cheek, and her skin instantly flushed. She was such a liar, saying that his *slurping* hadn't done anything for her. He could kiss her right now and prove it. The ice cream shop was full, and as usual they were attracting an audience.

"Wanna practice selling it, Disco?" He stared at her sparkly pink lips and tilted his head toward the tables full of people from school.

She glanced at the tables, then back to him, her cheeks flushed and eyes wide. "But nobody's here. I mean, you know, not Elle and Gus."

He put a hand on the small of her back, steering her back in line to place their order. He leaned down to whisper, making sure to brush his lips across the tip of her ear. "Right. But it's obviously our date night. Lots of people here who can report back to both Elle and Gus that they saw us together." And just to prove his point, he kissed her temple, inhaling her perfume as his lips imprinted the soft skin above her ear.

He heard her small gasp and smirked with satisfaction. Then he gave her a little push toward the counter where a senior citizen who clearly disapproved of PDA waited to take their order.

. . .

Mandy's skin burned where Caleb had touched her, so she had a hard time focusing on the frowning woman asking her what flavor ice cream she wanted.

"I'm guessing she wants the rainbow one, right, *babe*?" Caleb's voice was low and teasing, and way too close. She swallowed, trying to regain her composure. He had to stop doing this…this…*selling it* or whatever.

It also wasn't fair that he'd guessed her favorite flavor. She took a breath and straightened her shoulders. "Yes, one scoop of rainbow sherbet in a waffle cone, please. And he'll have a scoop of the black ice cream."

The woman frowned. "We don't have black ice cream."

"Then make it the—"

"Bubble gum."

She spun around to stare at him. "Bubble gum? Seriously?"

"Rainbow and bubble gum should *mesh* really well. In case we have to sell it later." He winked, sending her heart rate skyrocketing.

Fake. *Fake.* FAKE.

She had to remember that.

"This fake situation is sure looking real to me," Cammie whispered a few minutes later, nibbling on her ice cream cone. The guys were engaged in a heated debate about the movie and not paying attention to them, so Mandy scooted her chair closer to Cammie.

"It's not. I mean, it *is* still fake. We're just, um, working really hard to sell it."

Cammie snorted. "Uh-huh. Well, consider me sold. There's enough pent-up chemistry between you two to blow up a building." She licked her cone. "And I'm talking real chemistry, not fake." She narrowed her eyes. "Watch yourself, girl. He's trouble. Hot trouble, for sure, but still…be careful. I don't want you getting your heart accidentally broken."

Mandy frowned. "I know he's trouble. That's why I'm going to fake dump Caleb as soon as Gus makes his move…"

Cammie rolled her eyes. "Yeah, about that. We need to talk about the Octo-Gus."

"The what?"

"The Octo-Gus. It's what some girls are calling Gus.

Because apparently he fell into some vat of villain juice and has like eight different hands when he's with a girl and he doesn't like hearing no." Cammie leaned forward, her voice full of intensity. "I know you think he's all sweet and dorky, Mandy, but I've been hearing something totally different."

Mandy crunched a piece of her waffle cone and scowled as she chewed it. Why would anyone say bad things about Gus? And him being a groper? She couldn't see it. She glanced at Caleb. Now him, she could see justifying that kind of nickname. But as she thought about it, she realized his reputation was more dark and broody loner than gropey man-whore.

She heaved an exasperated sigh and brushed waffle cone crumbs off her hands. "I don't know, Cam. We've known Gus forever. I just can't see it."

Cammie tucked a strand of dark hair behind her ears and leaned forward. "Yeah, we've known him a long time, but he hasn't hung out with us much since school started. Or even last summer."

"Because of Kay," Mandy said darkly.

Cammie shook her head. "Before Kay, he was hanging out with the lacrosse guys. Not us."

Mandy nodded slowly. That was true. Over the summer, Gus had been all lacrosse, all the time, morphing from gangly nerd to superjock, sort of like Scott in *Teen Wolf* after he got the bite. But she'd liked Gus way before he turned into a sports guy, and she was sure he was that same guy he'd always been.

"Just because he's into sports now doesn't make him a jerk," Mandy said, staying loyal to her cheer dance team. Not all jocks were jerks; a lot of them weren't, in fact.

Cammie nodded. "I know. But I'm just saying maybe we don't know him as well as we used to."

Mandy considered this briefly, but pushed the thought

away as she watched Caleb debate with J.T., Liam, and Jiro. She'd never seen him hang out with other guys before; he was always brooding by himself. He leaned back in his chair, listening to Liam, then he said something that made everyone laugh, especially J.T. Mandy could picture them as little kids, laughing and fake karate fighting.

The image made her smile, and she realized she was happy he'd shown up tonight. Whatever happened with their fake dating thing, Caleb could probably use a friend.

Everyone could, even broody demons.

Chapter Eleven
Take a Chance on Me

Sunday, September 25

"Caleb," Helen called from the foyer. "Your friends are here."

Friends. *Right.*

He sighed. Hanging out with Mandy's posse last night hadn't been a complete nightmare. J.T. had made him laugh a couple of times. Liam was smart, and Jiro was pretty cool, when he wasn't putting his amateur moves on Cammie and pissing her off.

That girl was one hell of a cock-blocker when it came to Mandy. She'd even insisted on her and Jiro driving Mandy home last night, like Caleb was a threat, which had pissed him off, but in some ways he couldn't blame her because he knew Cammie was totally opposed to the fake boyfriend thing.

It was probably good that Mandy had a loyal wingwoman; she might need her around Gus. He scowled as he thought of the Octo-Gus rumors and slammed his book shut.

He clomped down the curving staircase, wondering

just how much to turn on the fake boyfriend act today. And how he'd survive an afternoon with the invasion of the spirit zombies.

Helen flung the door open, welcoming everyone with her beaming smile. *Gaggle*, Caleb thought, *a disorderly or noisy group of people.* Correction: a giggling gaggle, of pep-filled, spirit committee bouncing Tiggers.

They spilled into his house followed by their leaders: Mandy, J.T., and Cammie. The giggling stopped as Caleb reached the bottom of the stairs. He crossed his arms over his chest, skimming his gaze over the big-eyed geese. They stared back at him, some more boldly than others. He felt like he'd landed in the *Charlie and Chocolate Factory* movie, the weird one with Johnny Depp, and briefly fantasized about sending everyone down the spinning drain that sucked down Violet.

But then Mandy caught his eye, flashing him a tentative smile, and he realized he didn't want to flush *everyone* down the drain. He took in her retro unicorn T-shirt that had to be authentic seventies and smirked, shaking his head slightly. She tossed her hair over her shoulders, standing up straighter, and he saw a spark of fire flash in her eyes.

He cocked an eyebrow, silently letting her know he was up for whatever challenge she was throwing down.

"J.T., is that you?" Helen asked, her voice full of happy surprise.

Crap. She remembered. He'd sort of hoped she wouldn't. But Helen forgot nothing; he should know that by now.

J.T. grinned at Helen. "Hi, Helen. Yeah, it's me."

Caleb watched, horrified, as Helen pulled J.T. into a hug while everyone else laughed nervously. Mandy's gaze shot straight to his, and this time it was her turn to smirk.

Helen spun J.T. around like a top. "Look at you, all grown up!" She shot an accusing look at Caleb. "Why didn't you tell me J.T. was coming over?"

Caleb shrugged, relieved he didn't blush as easily as Mandy.

"Well, come on," Helen said, tugging J.T. after her. "Everyone come in the kitchen and let's get to work."

The gaggle followed Helen like she was Mother Goose. Caleb trailed behind them, wondering how a harmless fake boyfriend proposition had led to *this*.

Gleaming mixing bowls covered the granite counters, along with canisters of flour and sugar and not one, but two, enormous mixers. Helen had brought her personal one from home. The gaggle started unloading supplies from grocery bags, chattering and giggling nonstop.

"This is awesome," Mandy said, looking around with wide eyes. She turned her high beams on Helen. "Thank you so much for letting us use your kitchen."

Helen returned Mandy's smile with her own high beams.

Great. The last thing Caleb needed was those two bonding. Helen had a bad habit of telling embarrassing little-kid stories about him. He moved toward them, ignoring Cammie's glare.

"Caleb, introduce me to your friend," Helen said. He ignored the speculative twinkle in her eyes and shot Helen a warning glare. There would be no twinkling around Disco.

"This is Dis—I mean, Mandy." He nodded toward her. "And Mandy, this is Helen. She's our...my..." he stammered, shocked to find himself at a loss for words. How could he describe her accurately? "Housekeeper" sounded so formal. So demeaning. Plus she did so much more than cook and clean. He didn't dare say she was his surrogate mom, even though she basically was.

"I'm Caleb's worst nightmare," Helen said, winking at Mandy. "I'm the only thing keeping him from crossing completely over to the dark side. I feed him enough sugar to keep him on the side of angels. Barely."

Mandy's eyes widened, then she tossed back her head

and laughed, a surprisingly sexy laugh. "Thank God for that," Mandy said. She cocked an eyebrow, making direct eye contact with him. "He needs all the sweetening you can give him."

He snorted, but didn't take the bait.

Helen grinned, then dragged Mandy away to set her up in front of her personal mixer. Uh-oh. Not good. Helen didn't let anyone touch her appliances.

"Caleb," Helen said, "come over here and help Mandy."

"Yeah, Caleb," J.T. said, suddenly next to him. "Go rock that boyfriend act."

Caleb glared at him. "Dude."

J.T. shrugged. "What? That's why we're in your kitchen, isn't it? Because you're such a stellar BF." He grinned, then tore open a bag of chocolate chips and reached inside for a handful. "Want some?"

Caleb shook his head, suddenly remembering the time he and J.T. had eaten two full bags of chocolate chips when they were kids and gotten in big trouble with Helen.

"Caleb!" Helen called. "Come here."

God. He was totally eight years old again today. He stalked across the kitchen to stand next to Mandy, who was busy dumping ingredients into a giant silver mixing bowl.

"I'm going to check on the other kids," Helen said, stepping away but pausing briefly to raise her eyebrows meaningfully at Caleb. The message was clear: *behave yourself.*

"You have an Alice," Mandy said in a low singsong voice. "Just like in *The Brady Bunch.*"

He felt his eyebrows knit as he picked up the recipe card on the counter. "I do *not* have an Alice. Helen's much more than comic relief."

Mandy stopped pouring flour into the bowl and turned to him, disbelief in her eyes. "Alice wasn't just comic relief! She was Carol's sounding board. And she kept the kids in line, and she—"

"You do know it's not real life, right, Disco?" Caleb interrupted. "Those people don't live in that box with the moving pictures. It's called a sitcom. And why are you watching crappy TV shows from the seventies, anyway?"

She narrowed her eyes at him, and he wondered again if those ridiculous eyelashes were fake. If anyone belonged on a sitcom it was Mandy.

The doorbell rang, and Caleb tilted his head. "More minions?"

"They are legion. I'll get the door, since you might scare them away."

He rolled his eyes. "I can do this all day, Disco."

She grinned. "Me too, demon." Then she pranced out of the kitchen, reminding him again of a Rainbow Pony. He laughed softly and turned back to the counter, wondering what she was making. Probably something with so much sugar it would rot his teeth.

He glanced around the kitchen feeling like maybe he *had* wandered onto a sitcom set. He never would've imagined this crazy scene of noisy, laughing people from school making a mess, measuring ingredients, banging pans, and yelling and laughing over the sounds of the mixers.

"Uh-oh," J.T. said, appearing next to him again. "Time to boyfriend up, dude."

Caleb glanced up, following J.T.'s gaze to the kitchen doorway where Mandy stood looking like a deer caught in the headlights, with Kay and Gus next to her.

Caleb narrowed his eyes at Gus as bolts of suspicion and jealousy shot through him. Crap. What the hell was going on? He wasn't supposed to feel any of that, not about Mandy. But as he watched her bite her lip nervously, he felt all of those things, and more.

"Kick it into high gear," J.T. said.

"What?" Caleb glanced at him.

"Showtime," J.T. said, grinning. "Make it good, Red Ranger."

He was right. Caleb stepped away from the counter and crossed the kitchen, each step bringing him closer to the redhead who was making him crazy, making him wonder what was real and what was fake. Now was as good a time as any to figure that out.

"So you guys are on the spirit committee, too, huh?" Caleb said, resting his hand on Mandy's shoulder. He ran his hand down her back and cupped it around the curve of her waist, heat shooting up his arm and straight to his chest.

Kay's lips pursed. "Not exactly. But I told Gus we should swing by just to see how things are going, since Monday's bake sale is important for Spirit Week."

He felt Mandy tense next to him.

"Huh," Caleb said, deepening his voice. "Are you saying you don't trust the committee? Trust Mandy?" He felt Mandy turn toward him, but he kept his stare pinned on Kay, who blinked in surprise.

"Uh, n-no," Kay stammered. "I didn't mean—"

"I'm sure everything's great," Gus said, flashing a blinding smile that made Caleb think of a horror movie. Gus put his hand on Kay's waist, mirroring Caleb. "We just thought we'd swing by."

Caleb's hand tightened on Mandy's waist. "I'm sure Mandy can find a job for you guys." He turned and winked at her. "Right, babe?"

A cascade of emotions swirled in her eyes—confusion, frustration, gratitude…finally settling on feisty, which made him happy. He didn't want her intimidated by freaky Kay. Or sucked in by the Octo-Gus.

"Right," she said, turning back to Kay and Gus. "Maybe you guys can help wash bowls and stuff once we've got the first batch in the ovens."

Caleb grinned, squeezing her waist in a sign of approval.

Kay wrinkled her nose. "Wash dishes?"

"Unless you melt when water touches you," Caleb said. "Like a witch."

Gus frowned. "Dude. Not cool."

Kay tossed her hair. "Whatever." She pushed past them, Gus trailing after her, glancing over his shoulder at Mandy, a confused expression glazing his eyes.

"Caleb," Mandy scolded. "That wasn't nice." But her lips twitched.

"Demons don't play nice. Especially when someone's bagging on their *girlfriend*."

She swallowed, and a blush tinged her cheeks. "Well, I…I mean…you know I don't like Kay, but I try not to be a jerk to people—"

"That's why you've got me, Disco. Your jerk in shining armor. Or black leather. Whatever."

She shook her head, smiling. "Caleb Torrs. What am I going to do with you?"

He pulled her in before she could resist, gripping her waist with both hands, anchoring her in place. "You could kiss me. Oh wait—since Gus is here, I'm supposed to kiss you, right? That's our agreement."

Her chest rose and fell, but she didn't pull away. "We never officially finalized that agreement," she said, her voice a whisper.

He ducked his head to touch his forehead to hers.

"Caleb, I…" Her breath tickled his lips and his desire to kiss her was so far beyond fake, so real, he didn't think he could wait for her to agree. And she was giving off a million signals that she wanted it as much as he did.

"Mandy," he whispered against her lips, "let's stop pr—" But he never got the truth out because suddenly Cammie was there, cock-blocker to the rescue.

"Caleb, we can't find any more spatulas."

"Ask Helen," he growled, tightening his grip on Mandy so she didn't bolt, but it was too late—the moment shattered by her damn wingwoman. He turned to glare at Cammie, matching her challenging stare with his own.

Mandy's hands rested on his, gently prying his fingers from her waist.

Damn. They'd been so close to…to something. Something not fake. He was going to make sure to cock-block Jiro next time he went in for the kill with Cammie.

Several hours later, the kitchen counters were covered with wet, clean bowls and utensils drying on dish towels. Everyone had pitched in to clean up except Kay and Gus, who'd bolted.

Caleb carried Helen's prized mixer to her car. "Thanks for coming, Helen. I know it was kind of crazy." He set the box in the backseat and closed the door.

She beamed up at him as she started her Honda. "Wouldn't have missed that for the world. And I especially liked meeting Mandy. She's adorable. You both are." She winked at him and pulled away before he could think of a response.

He sighed and ran his hand through his hair before going back inside. All of the spirit zombies had left with their boxes and containers full of baked items, except J.T., Cammie, and Mandy. It was just like the caf, when they hung out at his table whether he wanted them to or not.

He heard the music when he opened the front door, disgusting disco crap cranked up to maximum volume. He stalked into the kitchen, ready to shut it down, but froze at the scene in front of him.

Cammie, J.T., and Mandy were dancing in the open area

of the kitchen, laughing as they did choreographed moves in time to the beat. They looked ridiculous…but they were obviously having fun. And Mandy didn't look completely ridiculous. There was a reason she was on the dance squad, he thought, watching her body move and feeling heat streak through his body.

She glanced up, meeting his gaze, and froze in place as J.T. and Cammie crashed into her during a spinning move. J.T. lunged for the speaker unit, turning down the volume.

"Sorry," J.T. said. "We were just…killing time."

"Practicing," Cammie said. "For homecoming." She glanced at Mandy. "We're going to head out."

"Yeah," J.T. said, pulling his phone off the speaker unit. "I still have homework to finish."

Mandy crossed her arms over her chest and glanced nervously at Caleb. "Speaking of homework, I was wondering if maybe you could look over my essay again? I brought my stuff, just in case you had time."

"Now?" Caleb asked, surprised. He felt the wingman and wingwoman glaring at him, like they were just as surprised as he was by the request.

Mandy glanced down at her shoes. "Never mind. I should've—"

"Yes," he interrupted. "Now is fine." He glanced at Cammie and J.T. "You guys need any help carrying stuff to your car?" As in, *leave*. Now.

J.T. narrowed his eyes. "I've got my eye on you, Red Ranger."

"Yep. Goes both ways, Blue Ranger." He quickly stacked up their boxes of cookies, then held them out to J.T. "See you tomorrow."

Cammie put her hands on her hips, clearly unhappy. "Mandy, if you need a ride home—"

"I'll take her home." This protective crap was really

pissing him off. "News flash, Cammie. I'm not the bad guy."

"Jury's still out." She glanced at Mandy. "Call me later, okay?"

Mandy nodded, looking embarrassed. He couldn't blame her; her friends treated her like a kid sometimes.

After Cammie and J.T. left, Mandy recovered her composure and pinned him with a stern expression. "We need a tutoring rule, Caleb. No shenanigans."

He cocked an eyebrow. "Shenanigans? Who talks like that, Disco? And what does it even mean?"

She blushed, but she didn't back down. "You know exactly what I mean. The tutoring part is real, Caleb, not fake. We don't…I mean, I don't need any distractions while we're working on my essay."

He nodded as he studied her worried face. It wouldn't be as much fun this way, but she was right.

"Okay. Deal."

Besides, maybe there'd be time for shenanigans later.

Chapter Twelve
Heart of Glass

Sunday, September 25

"Okay, let's start at the top. Tell me why you hate this book so much." Caleb wrapped his hands around his coffee mug. They sat in a small coffee shop Mandy had never been to before, because Caleb had insisted they needed fuel to recover from the baking session and give them energy for tutoring. Mandy sipped from her peppermint mocha. Caleb had ordered black coffee, which Mandy had called demon juice.

She was reluctant to answer because she knew how much he liked the book, but if he was going to help her she had to be honest. She took a breath. "Okay, well…I think Holden's just…so self-absorbed. He doesn't appreciate the good stuff in his life, except for his sister." She waited for him to flip out, but he said nothing, just watched her, taking another drink from his coffee.

She cleared her throat. "I mean, I know he's supposed to be the poster boy for teenage angst and all that. But he's just not likable, not to me anyway." She grabbed a napkin and started shredding it. The more anxious she got, the more she needed to fidget with stuff. Stupid ADHD.

"I don't like reading about characters I dislike." She glared at him, knowing he wouldn't agree. "I get that I'm *supposed* to read about unlikable characters, that sometimes that's the point of books, especially famous ones like this, but…I just don't like it…it's unlikable." She shredded the napkin into even smaller pieces.

Caleb set his mug on the table, watching her napkin destruction. "Okay," he said, raising his gaze from the mess, "maybe that's what you should write about—why you don't like Holden, and how it's hard as a reader to connect with an unlikable protagonist."

Mandy leaned back in her chair, surprised he wasn't arguing with what she'd said. "You think that's okay? What about Spriggs?"

Caleb shrugged. "It's a reader response question, so technically he shouldn't penalize you for not agreeing with him…or with me." He jokingly kicked her under the table. "Besides, it was obvious that you didn't believe anything you wrote in that draft I read."

Mandy felt heat flood her face. "It was?"

Caleb nodded. "I could tell you wrote what he wanted to hear. There wasn't any…passion."

Something in his eyes flickered, and Mandy's stomach flipped over. This was not supposed to happen with him, but he'd started it during the baking craziness when he'd almost kissed her, and turned on that protective act to deflect Kay.

She reached for another napkin and started to shred it, but his hands reached across the table, closing over hers and stilling her nervous movements. "Don't freak out," he said. "We can fix this."

His hands felt warm and soothing. She let her own hands

relax in his and searched his expression, hoping he was sincere
and that she could trust him.

"You promised no shenanigans," she said, glancing
pointedly at their hands.

He cocked an eyebrow. "Technically this"—he gestured
to their now-entwined hands—"is not really shenanigans. I
mean, we never did set our terms, so how am I supposed to
know what is and isn't shenanigans?" She glowered at him,
and he raised his free hand in surrender. "I am a victim of
circumstance, Disco. You can't punish me for not knowing the
rules."

"You know exactly what I'm talking about." She tried to
glare, but it was impossible, not with him looking at her like…
like he wasn't going to keep his promise. She extricated her
hand from his and grabbed another napkin to demolish. "We
need to focus."

"I'm focused." His lips curved dangerously. "Just not on
your essay."

Flustered, she grabbed her notebook. She flipped through
the pages, not sure what she was looking for, and noticed
her mood ring was turning greenish blue…for romance and
passion, which made her swallow nervously.

"Sorry," he said, raising his shoulders in the air innocently.
"Won't happen again. Swear." He drew an *X* over his heart with
his finger. "Let's get serious." He reached for her notebook,
spinning it so he could look at her notes. "Topic sentence, lay
out your argument, then wrap it up with a conclusion even
Spriggs can't argue with."

Mandy blinked at him. How could he switch gears so fast?

He frowned as he stared at her messy scrawl, and
Mandy's anxiety intensified. She had dysgraphia, which
sometimes coincided with ADHD. She'd always struggled
with penmanship; in elementary school other kids had made
fun of her, especially when she wasn't able to earn her stupid

"cursive license" in the third grade. Even worse, getting the thoughts in her head to match what she wrote on paper seemed impossible because her thoughts spun so fast and her printing was so slow.

"I know it's hard to read," she muttered. "Sorry." She hesitated, then decided if she was going to trust him and get his help, he might as well know. "I have this thing called dysgraphia." She shrugged. "It's...well, you can see what it's like. My thoughts go faster than I can write, and it's just...a mess." She reached for another napkin to destroy as heat flooded through her. She knew her face was as red as her hair.

Caleb studied her closely, glanced at her notebook again, then returned his dark gaze to hers. "Maybe you're going to end up being a doctor." His smile took her breath away, and she actually laughed.

"What? No way. I mean, I know that's the joke about doctors having awful handwriting, but doctors are scary smart. Med school, science geniuses...totally not me."

His smile disappeared. "You shouldn't talk about yourself like that. You're smart, Mandy." He hesitated, then spoke again. "You're really good at motivating people. Bossing them around, like during the baking insanity today."

Her heart fluttered dangerously. "You think so?"

He nodded. "Yeah. When Kay tries to tell people what to do, it pisses them off, but when you do it..." He shrugged. "People want to help. And you make it fun."

That was quite possibly the best compliment anyone had ever given her. And it had come from His Broodiness, of all people.

"Thanks, Caleb." She smiled at him, hoping he could see the sincerity she felt.

The universe surprises us with just what we need, sometimes when we least expect it.

• • •

Caleb leaned back in his chair, hoping his face wasn't betraying his feelings. He could handle Mandy when they were joking around and arguing…and the shenanigans…but the way she was looking at him right now?

That wasn't part of the plan, because it sure as hell didn't look fake.

He cleared his throat and pretended to study her notes, which he could barely read. Dysgraphia? He'd have to research that. He wasn't kidding when he said she was smart, because she was, in ways that continued to surprise him, in ways he was just starting to acknowledge. But she was battling more issues than he realized. He wanted to help but wondered how much he could.

He'd have to be careful, because he knew if she thought for even one second that he was condescending to her, she'd be out of there.

And that was the last thing he wanted.

He tore a fresh piece of paper from her notebook and drew a circle in the middle.

"What are you doing?" Mandy asked.

He drew lines shooting out from the circle, then glanced up at her. "Mind-mapping. It's a way to visually outline."

A heavy sigh escaped her. He stopped drawing to look at her. "What?"

"My fifth-grade teacher tried this with me."

"And?"

She frowned. "And I'm not ten years old anymore." She moved restlessly, her hands messing with the wild tangle of red curls, distracting him. *Focus*, he told himself.

"Lots of people use this method. It doesn't matter how old you are."

Her frown deepened. "I bet you don't use it."

He dropped the pencil and leaned back in his chair. "No, but I'm not you. My brain works…differently than yours."

As soon as he saw the shock on her face, he knew he'd said the wrong thing.

"Wait." He leaned across the table, putting his hand on hers again, screw the no-shenanigans rule. "That's not an insult. I'm trying to say not everybody tackles writing the same way."

She narrowed her eyes, but didn't move her hand out from underneath his. "For you it's easy."

He waited a beat, reminding himself they had a deal about the tutoring—all real, no fake. "Yeah, it is. But everybody has stuff they're good at, and stuff they suck at." He exhaled. Might as well go for broke. "I suck at calc, for instance, and my dad's an engineer so he thinks I'm an idiot."

Her eyes widened in surprise, and he could tell he'd cracked a little bit of her defensive facade.

"J.T. says you ace all your classes. Even when you ditch all the time."

He sighed. "I don't ditch *all* the time. And I'm not acing everything. Lit, history, Spanish, I'm good. Calc? Physics? Not so much." He squeezed her hand, watching her blush, then released it to grab his coffee cup. No more shenanigans. Not right now.

"So why do you? Ditch?"

He blew out a long sigh. "Let's work on your essay before we do any more *bonding,* Disco."

That spark he liked so much flickered in her eyes. "Okay. But if we make progress, you have to tell me why you cut classes." She frowned. "Unless it's something illegal or X-rated. Then I don't want to know."

He smirked. "You wish." He grabbed her pencil. "Let's get to work, Disco."

Half an hour later, they'd completed a mind map outline in a mix of Caleb's precise printing and Mandy's messy scrawl. Two hours and four cookies later, they'd finished a rough draft.

"Cheers," Caleb said, raising his coffee mug, surprised at how relieved he felt. And proud. "You did it." It had been painful for both of them, but somehow he'd helped her tease out the major points she wanted to cover. When she stuck to those and didn't wander the way her conversations did, she might have a shot at a decent grade from Spriggs.

She tucked a lock of her hair behind her ear and gave him a tentative smile that threatened to melt him.

"*We* did it." She took a deep breath. "Thank you, Caleb." Her smile deepened. She didn't look like an electrocuted disco hippie right now. Or maybe she did, but something had shifted in the way he saw her, because now she looked... amazing. Vulnerable. Sweet. Tempting.

She leaned across the table, and he caught a whiff of her perfume. It reminded him of how close they kept coming to kissing. Real kissing, not fake. He squeezed his coffee mug harder, wishing it were still hot enough to burn his hands.

"You were awesome today," she said. "I'm sorry I got so defensive earlier. It's just..." She shrugged. "I'm used to people making fun of me. But you didn't. So, thank you." Her eyes drew him in like green whirlpools.

No shenanigans.

"You're welcome." This afternoon had been good. Really good. Just the two of them. If they could just do *this*, without pretending for Elle or Gus, or fending off cock-block Cammie or the suspicious Blue Ranger, maybe they could actually... be together. For real.

But that wasn't possible. This had been a weird window

in time.

"So are you going to be a famous writer someday?" she asked, jolting him back to the present. "Since words are your superpower?"

He hesitated, then found himself telling her something he never told anyone. "Uh…I hope so. Someday."

She nodded. "That's great. I can say, 'Hey, I know that famous best-selling author! He helped me not fail American Lit!'"

She grinned at him and he grinned back, aware that he'd smiled more with her than with anyone else, ever. And then he remembered that all of this would probably end soon, because she wanted the Octo-Gus, not him.

He scraped his chair away from the table and stood up. "Come on, I'll drive you home."

She stared up at him, and he hoped it wasn't a flash of hurt he saw in her eyes. But then it was gone, and she gathered her stuff to follow him to his car.

They'd only driven a couple of blocks before she piped up. "You have to pay up on your end of the deal, Caleb. Tell me why you cut classes."

He glanced at her, debating how much to say to this girl… this weird, funny girl who might only be his fake girlfriend, but was someone he could almost see turning into a real friend. And more, if he had any say in how things went.

He sped up, accelerating through a yellow light.

"Ooh, four points off your license."

"It wasn't red." He side-eyed her, smirking. "You really need to get a life, Disco."

"So do you. Demon."

He rolled his eyes. "Can't you come up with something more creative? Demon's…so obvious. Also, it's not accurate."

"And Disco is?"

They stopped at a red light and he turned to face her. "Yes.

Accurate. Ironic. Funny. Exactly what a nickname should be."

She shrugged, brushing hair off her cheeks. "Whatever, smarty-pants."

He laughed as the light turned green. "Smarty-Pants is a crappy nickname. Try again."

She sighed next to him. "Red Ranger?"

He shot her a scowl. "That's just between J.T. and me."

She grinned. "Aw, that's so cute. You two could totally do an epic bromance. You guys have backstory and everything."

He snorted. "Now *that* was funny." He reached over and squeezed her knee through her jeans. "Keep working on it, Disco. You'll come up with something."

He was pretty sure he heard her growl in frustration before she laughed, which made something heat up inside his chest.

The sun was low in the sky, and he felt the familiar Sunday night blues he always felt, only this time it was worse because he didn't want to take her home, not yet. He turned off the main road.

"Where are you going?" She sounded anxious, reminding him of that first night he'd driven her home and stopped for a Red Bull.

"Just a park." He side-eyed her. "No shenanigans, I promise."

"You swear?"

"Demons don't swear."

"You're right. I definitely need to come up with something better."

He laughed softly as he parked the car close to a small pond surrounded by trees. "Come on." He opened his door and walked around the car to open hers.

They walked in silence toward the path surrounding the pond. He kicked at fallen leaves, wondering why he was doing this, what he was hoping for.

"Okay, I'm ready," she said as they stepped onto the gravel walking path. "Tell me your dirty ditching secret."

He wanted to hold her hand. It would make it easier, somehow, to tell her. And he just...wanted to feel her hand in his.

Damn. He closed his eyes in frustration. This was a mistake. He was falling under some freaky hippie spell, and he shouldn't. Couldn't. *Because this isn't real,* he told himself, even though it felt more real than anything he'd ever had with a girl.

"Hey." Her voice was soft as she stopped and turned to look up at him, her nose crinkled with worry. "Caleb, we can drop the whole thing. I don't mean to upset you or pry or—"

"You're not. It's just...I don't usually talk about it."

She nodded, her wide green gaze locked on his. "So, it's not a fun reason?"

He shook his head.

She did that thing he was starting to recognize, straightening her shoulders and sticking out her chin, gathering her courage to say something important. "Okay, then, I'll go first. I'll tell you the worst thing that ever happened to me. Then maybe yours won't be so hard."

"Mandy, you don't have to—"

"My mom died three years ago. Cancer."

Fuuckk.

Why hadn't J.T. warned him? But why would he? It's not like they were friends and J.T. was *his* wingman.

"I'm sorry, Mandy. I had no idea..."

She swallowed and her eyes brightened with tears, but she blinked them away.

"It's okay. Really, it is." She tilted her head toward a bench. "Let's go sit down."

He followed her to the faded wooden bench, desperately wanting to touch her...hold her hand, brush his fingers through her hair, something to let her know how sorry he was.

They settled on the bench, their legs just millimeters apart. He sighed and finally spoke. "My mom left. When I was eight." He swallowed, remembering the day Helen had come to pick him up from school instead of his mom. The worst day of his life.

Mandy's face did that crumply thing girls did when they felt sorry for you. He did his best to avoid girls like that, but he'd observed it often enough from a distance so he steeled himself.

However, Mandy surprised him. She didn't spout any mantras or move to hug him. Her eyes were full of sympathy, but for once she was quiet, which somehow felt just right.

"My brother was a senior in high school," he said, surprised at how easily the words spilled out. His hand moved to his jacket pocket, fingering his notebook, and she watched him, almost looking guilty. What was that about?

"I guess…I don't know. Maybe she figured she'd stuck with my dad long enough to raise my brother, but she couldn't stick around for me." He clutched the notebook in his pocket, his fingers brushing the Pop Rocks candy packet.

It was the question that would never be answered, the why of her leaving. When he was little, he'd begged his dad for answers, and his brother, and Helen. But nobody had answers for why she'd left to start over with a new husband. And become a mom again, this time to a daughter.

"Do you ever see her? Talk to her?" Mandy asked.

His gut tightened. She couldn't know her question cut like a knife. He shook his head. "Not since I was eleven. I've tried. Letters. Emails. She doesn't reply. Never calls. I don't even know if she gets them." He stared at the geese flying over the pond, his gaze unfocused. "It would almost be easier if she'd died." He regretted the words as soon as he'd said them. Embarrassed, he turned to face her. "I'm sorry—I didn't mean—what you went through was worse, so much worse—"

"No." Mandy's voice was soft when she interrupted him. "I think maybe you're right." She hesitated. "Not hearing from her...that's awful."

They stared at each other, and Caleb wondered how they'd ended up like this and why he'd chosen to confide in her, of all people.

"Sometimes shit just happens, Mandy," he said, his voice rough with frustration. "Not everything happens for a reason, like your mantras. Sometimes life just sucks."

She puffed up, ready to argue, then collapsed in on herself like a marshmallow roasting over a fire, shrinking under the heat of his gaze, making him feel like an asshole.

"I know about life sucking, Caleb," she muttered. "Trust me, I know. But I choose to believe...I *have* to believe there's a reason for everything."

The desperation in her voice hit him like a punch. He hoped like hell he hadn't hurt her. He reached out his hand tentatively, resting it on her knee. After a moment, she rested her hand on top of his.

"I'm sorry," he said. "For everything."

She squeezed his hand. "I know. Me, too. For you."

He pulled the small notebook out of his jacket with his free hand, his other hand still entwined with hers. "This is... all I have left of my mom. She used to write words for me. Big, complicated ones I didn't understand until she explained them." He gazed at the water, remembering. "She was a poet. Words—those were her first love. I think our family came in second place after words." He shrugged. "Maybe it's why I want to be a writer someday."

He felt her turn toward him, and he let out a breath before he faced her, unsure if he was ready for the full-on sympathetic Mandy treatment.

"I totally understand about the notebook." She fingered

her weird crab necklace. "This was my mom's." She glanced down at her T-shirt. "This was hers, too. A lot of the old seventies stuff I wear was hers." She shrugged, and he wondered if the bloom of pink on her cheeks was embarrassment.

He ran his thumb along hers as he held her gaze. Words tumbled inside him so fast he wasn't sure how to pick the right ones. "Don't ever be embarrassed about that stuff, Mandy."

She nodded, her smile brave, and he suddenly felt like hell for making fun of her clothes.

"I'm sorry I called you Disco. I'll stop."

Her eyebrows shot up. "No. Don't stop. I kind of...like it." She tugged at her dangling earrings, and he wondered if those were her mom's, too. "My mom really was the queen of disco." She laughed softly. "So it's cool." She hesitated. "Would you maybe show me what's in your notebook sometime? I promise I won't tell anyone about it. I just"—she swallowed and turned to glance at the pond—"it's...good to talk to someone else who understands about what it feels like...to miss your mom."

He didn't know how to respond. No one knew about the notebook, not even his dad or his brother. He ran his hand over the worn red cover. If he showed her, it would be like sharing his mom. Maybe that wasn't a bad thing.

Slowly, he opened his notebook to the first page. The swirling handwriting always made his chest tighten. He ran his free hand over the fading ink. His mom had started the notebook when he was five years old.

Words mean everything, Caleb, she'd told him. *I want to help you collect them, so you'll have just the right one when you need it.*

He'd listened to her, rapt with attention. *Rapt: fascinated, enthralled, spellbound.* He'd adored his mother more than anyone or anything else in the world. Where his father was like the night, scary and full of darkness, his mother was the light on a blazingly hot summer day, so bright he sometimes had to blink.

"Here's your first word," she'd said, wrapping an arm tightly around him as they snuggled on the couch. With her other hand she printed in purple ink on the first page of a fresh notebook. He liked this notebook because it was small enough to fit in his pocket, like it was made special just for a five-year-old.

He'd watched her hand as she wrote, noticing her bright red nail polish and the shiny gold bracelet that scraped across the page. M-A-G-N-I-F-I-C-E-N-T. He still remembered how the letters swam in front of his eyes. It was the biggest word he'd ever seen and he had no idea what it was.

"Magnificent," she'd whispered in his ear. "Can you say that, sweetie?"

"Mag fin is…um?" He'd glanced up anxiously, not wanting to disappoint her. She'd leaned down to kiss his forehead.

"Let's say it together, sweetheart." Her finger had traced an invisible line under the word as she spoke slowly. "Mag… ni…fi…cent. Say it with me."

So he had, over and over until he got it right. Then he'd looked into her chocolate-brown eyes and asked, "What is magnificent, Mama?"

She'd beamed her full-sun smile at him. "You are, sweetheart. You are magnificent, Caleb Torrs, and don't you forget it."

Sitting on the bench with Mandy, he wondered for the millionth time why a mother would leave a magnificent son and never come back.

Mandy traced her finger over the page. "She had beautiful penmanship. Unlike me." She smiled up at him, and he knew she was trying to make his sadness go away.

He squeezed her hand, hoping she'd know it meant *thank you…please don't go…just stay with me.*

She returned the hand squeeze and they sat in silence, watching the geese dive onto the water, then fly up again into the sky, easing into their V formation, streaking across the sky without hesitation, their honks fading in the wind.

Caleb wondered what it would be like, to be so sure of where you were going.

And to fly with someone always at your side.

• • •

As Caleb's car backed out of the driveway, Mandy wondered if he saw her wave good-bye. She watched the black car until it disappeared, wishing she could lift even a tiny bit of Caleb's darkness.

She was grateful her gran was napping and Reg was out, because she needed time to process what had happened. Safely inside her bedroom, she turned on the firefly lights draped over her bookcase and queued up her Mystical playlist, softly, so she wouldn't wake Gran.

She sat on the floor, leaning against her bed frame and staring at her bookcase.

"I can't figure him out, Mom," she said to the framed photo of her mom wearing the green dress—the same dress Mandy planned to wear to homecoming. She sighed and studied the photo more closely.

In the photo, her mom's head was tilted back and her eyes were closed. Her mouth was open, laughing at something her dad must've said, because he grinned down at her, his hair thick and long, unlike his current buzz cut. They looked so, so happy.

Her parents had been high school sweethearts—disgustingly cute even in 1981 when the photo had been taken, teetering between the disco era and the eighties New Wave and punk era. Her mom was solidly on team disco, but her dad was more of a punk guy. Their musical differences hadn't mattered, though, because it was love at first sight, at least according to her mom.

Mandy wrapped her hands around her knees. "He lost his mom, too," she said to the photo. "Only not forever, like I lost you." She tugged at the frayed carpet. "I bet he'll connect with her again someday." She hoped so. Even if it was years from now, she hoped someday his mom would reach out, or that he'd track her down.

"He's so different than I thought he was," she whispered to the bear she'd made for herself during her first week at Build-a-Buddy. "There's a decent guy hiding behind all that attitude."

She knew why he'd gone quiet on the drive home. She knew all about stuffing feelings, and she also knew it didn't work. The feelings had to come out, because if they didn't he was doomed to a miserable life.

But this whole fake girlfriend thing…she didn't know what to do about that, because now that she and Caleb had sort of bonded, it was hard to tell what was real and what was fake. And when she thought of going to the dance, she wasn't sure anymore who her dream date was.

Caleb texted her that night, just as she was drifting off to sleep.

Einstein had dysgraphia.

Mandy smiled at her screen. *Wow. Cool.*

Agatha Christie.

Awesome.

Thomas Edison. That actor who played Fonzie has dyslexia. Probably one of your favorite shows since it's ancient.

She laughed, sort of wishing they were doing this in person. *You can stop now. I appreciate the effort.*

Just saying you can be brilliant and have dysgraphia.

Got it.

Sleep tight, Disco.

You too, TDB.

WTF is that??

She sent him a row of smiley faces, but no way was she ever telling him the secret name she used for him with Cammie.

C U tomorrow Caleb.

Chapter Thirteen
Everybody Wants to Rule the World

Monday, September 26

Who knew so many people were sugar junkies? The line for the bake sale was crazy. Caleb sat at the table making change, trying to ignore the surprised faces when people saw him working the cash box. Mandy stood next to him, wearing something sparkly and fluorescent as usual. She laughed and joked, calling everyone by name. It was like she had a school photo directory in her head.

"Three dollars, Pete," she said to the hulking football player holding a bag of cookies with sprinkles. The guy handed Caleb a five and Caleb handed him back two dollar bills.

"Dude," the hulk said, "I gave you a ten."

"No, you didn't," Caleb said, raising his eyes to glare at the caveman. The guy glanced at Mandy, who looked at Caleb, a question in her eyes. He cocked an eyebrow. "I think I can tell the difference between a five and a ten."

"You trying to rip me off, Torrs?" the hulk said, his bulky

frame looming over the table, causing everyone else to stare.

"No," Caleb said, standing up. "I'm trying to teach you to count. Pretend I'm the Count on *Sesame Street.*" Caleb held up his hands, both middle fingers extended and spoke in an exaggerated Dracula accent. "Five minus three is two…"

The hulk flushed and stepped back from the table. "Whatever." He turned and stormed away.

"That wasn't nice, Caleb," Mandy said softly, leaning in so only he could hear her.

His body tensed as her hair brushed against his biceps. He knew it hadn't been *nice*, but whatever. He was still churned up after helping her with her paper yesterday, and then talking at the park. He wasn't sure what the hell to do with all the weird feelings banging around inside him. It was like he'd been sucked in by some whirlpool and couldn't escape. Even worse, he couldn't decide if he wanted to escape.

"I don't care if it wasn't *nice*, Disco. The guy was trying to rip us off."

"Us?" Mandy gave him a small smile that made his stomach do something weird.

He frowned. "Us. You. The freaky Spirit Squad of Doom. Whatever." He sat down and returned to manning the cash box.

Mandy turned back to the boisterous line of customers, and they fell into an easy rhythm, her telling him how much was owed, him making change, then J.T. foisting Spirit Week fliers on people as they walked away from the table.

Everyone knew her. Everyone. From the scrawniest freshman to the most popular seniors, she knew them all. He'd never seen anything like it. Maybe that's what happened when you photobombed every committee photo in the yearbook, except she wasn't photobombing. She actually did stuff on all those committees.

"I'm voting for you as queen, Mandy," a pretty dark-haired girl said, shooting Caleb a nervous glance like he might bite. "Maybe Gus will be king. You guys would be so cute together."

"Oh, um, thanks," Mandy said, handing a plate of cupcakes to the girl. "Four dollars," she said. Caleb heard her voice wobble. He shot her a glance as he handed the girl change, but she wouldn't look at him.

Caleb wondered what he'd have to do make sure Gus never got elected king. But wasn't that exactly what she wanted? To go to the damn dance with Gus on her arm? He could picture the two of them on stage, wearing fake crowns and waving and smiling at everyone.

A crowd surged the table as more people arrived before the first bell. Caleb was so busy he barely had time to look up to make eye contact when he made change, but whenever he did, he saw the same expression: shocked surprise. Was it really so unbelievable that he'd participate? Apparently so.

"Do I get a discount?"

Caleb glanced up at the voice. Gus. Of course he was a cheapskate. Except he wasn't being cheap, he was flirting. With Mandy. Caleb narrowed his eyes.

"Oh, uh, I don't…um…"

Mandy tittered like a delirious bird. She didn't get that way around him. Yeah, she got flustered and pissed off with him, and yesterday they'd connected in a totally different way. But she didn't act like *this* with him.

"No discounts," Caleb announced, crossing his arms over his chest.

Gus glanced at him dismissively, turning his attention back to Mandy. "Not even for me?" He winked at her.

Caleb stood up. "Are you seriously flirting with my *girlfriend*, dude?"

J.T. skittered over to them like an excited puppy. Mandy shot Caleb an annoyed look, but then she bit her lip. He hoped that mixed signal meant something entirely different from her narrowed eyes.

"Power down, Red Ranger," J.T. muttered under his breath. "Don't make a scene."

Caleb side-eyed him. "Do I look like I need a wingman?"

J.T. nodded. "Yep. Blue Rangers always be calming Red Rangers the hell down."

Caleb rolled his eyes, then refocused his glare on the tool.

Mandy, apparently oblivious to everyone but the Octo-Gus, handed Gus a plastic bag full of Rice Krispies Treats and Gus handed her a dollar bill.

"Uh, *no*," said Caleb. "Those bags are three bucks."

"I get a *friend* discount," Gus retorted, but the slimy way he said *friend* made Caleb's skin crawl.

J.T. stepped forward. "Seriously? You're gonna cheap out on the spirit committee? On your *friends*?" J.T. made the word sound even dirtier than Gus had, adding a leer that made Gus take a step back, and made Caleb grin.

"Whatever." Gus dug into his wallet and threw a five-dollar bill on the table. He smiled at Mandy. "I'll see *you* later."

J.T. turned to Caleb. "See how that worked? Blue Ranger saved the day."

Caleb snorted. "Yeah, ri—"

"What's with you guys?" Mandy interrupted, hands on her hips, eyes blazing. "Why'd you have to—"

The first class bell rang, stopping her midsentence. All of their customers scattered and Mandy turned away to stack leftover items in cardboard boxes, making her frustration clear.

Caleb grabbed a box and began tossing in items, speaking quietly so only J.T. could hear him. "Tell me straight. You think that tool is good enough for her?" He tilted his head toward Mandy. "I don't get what she sees in him."

He stopped, wondering when he'd decided to confide in J.T. But he had to make sure that this stupid ruse was worth it, for her. Because he had serious doubts.

J.T. stacked brownies in the box. "Last year I would've said yes. But something happened to him over the summer. It's like he got bit by a man-whore spider or something, from what some of the girls are saying." He glanced at Caleb. "Mandy's blind to it, since she's crushed on him since kindergarten."

Caleb glanced at her. "Maybe it's time for her to move on from kindergarten."

J.T. smirked. "Maybe. You got someone better in mind for her?"

They stared each other down, just like when they were kids battling over whose turn it was to use the Power Rangers Blaster gun.

"Maybe," Caleb finally said, wondering why the hell he was admitting it out loud.

J.T. squinted his Bowie eyes, then nodded. "Okay. I'll do recon on the Octo-Gus, see if he's really as much of a dick as the girls are saying."

"And if he is?"

J.T. smirked. "If he is, I'll let you know, Red Ranger. So you can figure out your next move."

Caleb picked up the box and stepped away from the table. "You're not gonna shut me down?"

J.T. shrugged. "Not yet. Not 'til I figure out who the real good guy is. And the real bad guy."

Caleb snorted as they passed the principal's office. "You make it sound like we're living in a comic book with villains and superheroes." He slanted him an assessing look. "And sidekicks."

J.T. grinned. "When you think about it, that's pretty much what high school is, isn't it?"

. . .

Mandy didn't like how the bake sale had ended. That had been weird with Gus sort of flirting with her. It was what she thought she wanted, but what about Kay? Why would Gus do that if he was still with Kay? She didn't like Kay, but there was still a basic boyfriend code, and she worried he'd just violated it.

She ignored her history teacher, instead staring out the window and chewing on her pencil. Maybe Gus hadn't been flirting. Maybe he was just joking around, like he used to when they were all friends. Well, all except Caleb.

Caleb. She didn't know what to do about him. Yesterday had been amazing, like a day to keep in a snow globe, under glass, preserved forever. She pictured the two of them on the park bench, talking and holding hands—like people who'd both suffered some bad stuff, and were just sort of…bearing witness with each other.

After that connection she'd been surprised he'd acted like a jerk today, but that was the weird thing about him—he ran hot and cold, and she never knew which it would be. Maybe he was regretting how much he'd confided in her yesterday, and showing her his notebook.

"Ms. Pennington, is there an alien invasion occurring outside the window that the rest of are not able to see?"

Scattered laughter jolted her out of her musings and she blinked, staring at her crabby teacher. She bet he'd never been confused about love. He probably lived alone or with a dozen cats. *Whoa.* That was seriously mean. What was wrong with her today?

"No," she said, sighing heavily. "I'm just…distracted."

Her teacher's face pinched like a sour lemon. "As usual. Let's try focusing on the Constitution, shall we, Ms. Pennington?"

Let's try focusing on your need for a nose-hair trimmer, Mandy thought, then she clapped her hand over her mouth so she wouldn't laugh out loud. That was totally not something she'd ever say.

But Caleb might.

"You want a lift to work tomorrow night?" Cammie asked as she and Mandy sat down at Caleb's lunch table.

Before Mandy could answer, J.T. joined them, plunking down next to Caleb. Mandy didn't know how Caleb felt about her maintaining the fake GF thing today, but she figured she might as well eat lunch with him. Especially because she couldn't stop thinking of the notebook in his pocket, and all it signified.

Caleb glanced up, shook his head like he couldn't believe they were swarming him again, then took another bite of his pizza.

"Sure," Mandy said.

Cammie nodded, tearing into her bag of veggie chips. "We have a birthday party. It's gonna be crazy."

Mandy sighed as she opened her yogurt container. Build-a-Buddy birthday parties could get out of control, depending on how many kids showed up and how involved, or not, the parents were. Sometimes they were fun, though. She glanced at Caleb, wondering if he'd had any birthday parties after his mom left. Had his dad planned them? Or maybe Helen? The thought of a young Caleb with no mom at his birthday parties made her want to hug him, which she knew was a bad idea, especially in front of everyone.

"You should have a birthday party there, Red Ranger," J.T. joked.

Caleb rolled his eyes and took a drink from his water

bottle. "I don't do birthday parties."

"That's ridiculous," Mandy said, forgetting her vow not to embarrass him. "Birthdays are important and should always be celebrated."

"Yeah," Cammie said. "Which is why you shouldn't have bailed on your birthday, going to that stupid party with Gus instead of going dancing with J.T. and me."

She felt her cheeks heat, remembering that night Caleb had given her a ride home. He was remembering it, too, judging by his smirking face.

"Wish I'd known it was your birthday that night, Disco. I'd have made it…special for you." He arched an eyebrow, keeping his gaze pinned on hers.

Cammie choked on her drink, and J.T. sat up straight, glancing at Mandy with an expression she couldn't decipher. It was almost like he thought Caleb was funny. Which he most definitely was not.

"In your dreams," Mandy snapped, hoping to hide how much his words had impacted her, making her whole body flush and tingle.

His responding grin was maddening. Infuriating. Stupidly sexy. "Oh, you're definitely in my dreams. Starring role, in fact."

Cammie was choking so hard Mandy had to whack her on the back, which was at least a distraction from whatever game Caleb was playing. Because it was a game. It had to be.

That real guy she'd hung out with yesterday? He was gone. Fake jackass boyfriend was back.

Jiro and Liam approached their table holding trays of mystery meat.

"Yo," Jiro said, sliding next to Cammie. "You gonna live, Cam? I don't want my girl choking to death." Cammie held up a hand, gasping for breath, then managed to stop coughing long enough to give Jiro a quick kiss.

Liam squeezed in next to J.T., who leaned over and whispered in his ear, making Liam blush. They shared a secret smile that made Mandy insanely jealous, then ridiculously happy for them, all in the space of five seconds.

She glared at Caleb. This jealousy bad karma stuff was all his fault. She leaned across the table, grateful her friends were distracted by their boyfriends. "Well, you better enjoy those dreams, Your Broodiness," she angry-whispered, "because that's as close as you're getting to kissing me."

He leaned across the table so their faces were within inches of each other. "Your Broodiness? *That's* what you came up with?" He shook his head in mock disappointment. "And who said anything about kissing dreams, Disco?"

Mandy sat back, blushing. "I-I didn't mean—I…"

He took a long drink of water, keeping his eyes on hers, then wiped his mouth with the back of his hand. "My dreams are a lot more…involved…than just kissing."

She opened her mouth to argue, to scream, something, anything, but her vocal cords seized because now he was playing footsie with her under the table and sending her look-over-there messages with his eyebrows.

She glanced over her shoulder to see Elle at a table, watching them with that freaky look made Mandy wonder if she was an escapee from *Orange is the New Black*.

Mandy turned back to Caleb. "I could ruin this for you right now. Throw my drink in your face and storm out of here. Elle would be all over you."

"But you won't do that. Right?" For once, he looked uncertain.

She grinned, happy to have the upper hand again. "Give me one reason not to."

His eyes narrowed and he jutted out his chin. "Because of that guy," he muttered. Mandy looked over her other shoulder to see Gus sitting with the lacrosse guys. Not with Kay. That was interesting. Gus caught her eye and smiled, and her heart skipped a beat. But then she turned back to Caleb, and her stomach tumbled over in a completely different way.

No, she told herself. She glanced at Gus again. Gus was always sweet. Unlike His Broodiness.

Caleb's foot jostled hers under the table, and she turned to give him her most withering stare, but his sexy smirk heated her insides like a slow burn, making her forget all about wanting a sweet guy.

Mandy was heading to the parking lot at the end of the day, having successfully avoided Caleb, when Gus caught up to her.

"Hi gorgeous," he said, blinding her with his smile.

She stumbled on her mom's platform clogs, but managed to smile back. "Hi, uh, lacrosse star."

His grin broadened and he placed a hand on her elbow, steering her away from the cars and toward the soccer field.

"Can I talk to you, Mandy? It's important."

She nodded mutely and let him lead her to a shaded enclave of trees bordering the field. *Don't get any ideas,* she told herself.

"So, here's the deal," he said, releasing her arm and running a hand through his messy curls. "I know I can trust you, right? Because you've always been there for me."

She nodded vigorously. Of course he could trust her. And of course she'd always be there for him.

He dropped his gaze and shuffled his Converse shoes. "It's…sort of embarrassing, but I need to talk to someone who will believe my side of the story."

"What is it?" she asked, finally finding her voice. "Are you okay, Gus?"

He raised his eyes, shrugging. "I don't know what to do, Mandy. People…some people…are talking crap about me. Saying stuff that's not true."

Her pulse sped up as she thought of Cammie's warning at the ice cream shop. "What stuff?"

He glanced at her, then looked away, and she could tell he was embarrassed. Of course he was! This was terrible. She *knew* those rumors weren't true. No way was he a groper.

"Is it…" she took a breath, because she was embarrassed, too, but she had to let him know she understood, and that she was on his side. "Is it stuff about…girls and you, um, maybe pushing things further than—"

"Yeah," he interrupted, his expression panicked. "God, this sucks, Mandy. I can't believe you heard it, too." He dropped his gaze again. "You know me. You know I wouldn't…" His voice trailed away, and he glanced at her from under his eyelashes, his curls shadowing his forehead.

Poor Gus. Who would spread rumors like that? She pictured the sweet little kindergartner she's grown up with. They had been by each other's sides since day one, and the thought of someone hurting him hurt her, too.

"Kay?" She felt a spark of anger as he nodded, still not meeting her eyes. Of course it was Kay.

"We, uh, broke up and she's…not handling it very well."

They'd split? She knew she should express sympathy, but a tiny part of her was secretly giddy, which she knew was totally bad karma.

Be there for your friend, she told herself, *don't try to move in on him like a skank. He's probably heartbroken.* She took a step toward him, reaching out to touch his shoulder reassuringly. "You're a great guy, Gus. I know that. I won't believe anything Kay says about you. Whatever I can do to help…"

He straightened, smiling in a way that reminded her it

was *him* she wanted. Not Caleb. But that was wrong to be thinking, when he and Kay had just split.

"I knew I could count on you, Mandy. You've always been there for me." He ran a hand through his curls. "I know I haven't hung out with you guys much since school started. But I needed to hang with the lacrosse guys. They've been playing together forever, and I just started on the team, so I needed to—"

"I totally understand," she said, her heart full of sympathy for him. Cammie had been totally unfair, saying he was ignoring them on purpose. Everyone needed friends, true friends, and Gus definitely needed them now. "You know we're always glad to hang out with you."

He frowned. "I don't know, Mandy. Lately J.T.'s been…" He shrugged again, kicking at the grass. "And Cammie, too."

Well, she would take care of *that*. "Don't worry about them. They were just hurt that you stopped hanging out with us. I'm sure they'll be happy if you do again."

He nodded, then shot her sideways glance. "What about your…boyfriend? Caleb? I don't think he likes me much."

Time slowed and her pulse raced as she tried to figure out what to say. Was it time to give up the facade? Tell him that Caleb wasn't really her boyfriend? But she needed to talk to Caleb first. Come up with a breakup plan, and fast.

Because that was what she wanted, wasn't it? Her stomach twisted. Her feelings about Caleb were so…intense. Confused. Anyway, he'd never like someone like her, not for real. As soon as Elle left him alone, he'd probably never look at Mandy again, which made her surprisingly sad. She'd miss harassing him at lunch, and he really did *need* friends.

Just like Gus did.

She blinked, refocusing on the guy in front of her, who looked so worried, so alone. "Caleb will be *fine* with you hanging out with us. Don't worry about him."

"You sure? He kind of, well… He's not the type of guy I ever pictured *you* with." His gaze locked onto hers, his blue eyes full of…something. Was that concern? Maybe, possibly, something else? She pushed the thought away, refusing to get her hopes up.

Her heart stuttered, and she ran a shaky hand through her tangled curls. This was so unexpected. So confusing.

"He's, well, he's…" She didn't know what to say about Caleb, but the snow globe day they'd shared was enough to ensure she wouldn't talk crap about him. "He's…cool," she finally said, which was pathetic and vague, but at least it wasn't insulting. She wasn't going to be like Kay and say undeserved bad stuff.

Gus nodded, his intense blue gaze still fixed on hers. "If you say so. But just remember, I'm here for you, too, Mandy. I always have been." He took a step toward her, reaching out and lightly brushing her cheek with his knuckles. "I'd hate to see you get hurt."

Mandy suddenly regretted wearing platform shoes because her knees wobbled, and she was pretty sure she was about to lose her balance. But at the last second she pulled it together, plastering a confident grin on her face. "That won't happen. I know you've got my back, Gus, just like I've got yours."

She wouldn't get hurt, now that the nice guy was back in her life. Maybe this was a sign from the universe, telling her that it was time to break up with Caleb. Get back to normal.

Even if Gus never asked her to the dance, that was okay, right? He needed friends and she knew how to be a great friend, and so did Cammie and J.T. Plus, she was tired of all this hot-and-cold stuff with Caleb. Not to mention all the bad karma she was racking up by living a lie.

She took a deep breath. Okay. She just had to fake break up with her fake boyfriend, and everything would be fine.

• • •

Caleb debated before sending the text, but then decided to just do it. He'd been kind of a dick today because of the swirl of feelings Mandy was stirring up. He was pretty good at stuffing feelings, but it wasn't so easy with her. Maybe she'd figure out this was his version of an apology.

ADHD superheroes: Michael Phelps. Will Smith.

He waited for her reply, which didn't come as fast as he wanted.

Cool. Thx.

He frowned at his phone, then typed, *Justin Timberlake. Jim Carrey.*

Her reply came slower this time.

So sounds like my career choices are Olympian, actor, or singer. No pressure or anything.

He smiled and sent her a grinning devil face. *Maybe all three.*

She sent back a smiley face, but nothing else, clearly ending their conversation.

He sighed and set his phone aside. He'd do better tomorrow—tone down the asshole routine and act like…well, like a decent boyfriend.

Chapter Fourteen
Don't Go Breaking My Heart

Tuesday, September 27

Caleb was surprised to find Mandy waiting at his locker in the morning holding to-go coffee cups. Surprised, but happy.

"Gotta love a girl who brings her boyfriend coffee." He reached for the cup she extended, brushing her fingers with his. She didn't say anything, instead staring at the floor. "Uh-oh," he said. "What's up, Disco?"

She raised her head, and he saw apprehension in her eyes. "I, um, need to talk to you. About something important."

Caleb grabbed his textbooks and slammed his locker shut. "Problem with your essay?" He felt confident he could help with that, based on how things had gone before. And he felt a little zing shoot through him at the idea of hanging out in the library at their corner table and joking together.

She shook her head, glancing around at the growing crowd of students in the hallway. "No, it's...personal. About our, um, deal."

Uh-oh. This didn't sound good.

"Okay," he said, putting his free hand on her back and steering into a small, dark alcove that housed a dusty trophy case. "What's up?" He sipped from his coffee, pretending he wasn't worried about whatever she was about to say.

She dropped her gaze again, biting her lip. "The thing is...I...we...I think we should break up. Fake break up, I mean."

He'd steeled himself before she said the words, hoping like hell his intuition was wrong, but it still felt like she'd punched him.

"No deal, Disco. I still have a stalker." Maybe that would be enough to convince her to wait, at least until he could talk to J.T. about his recon mission.

He had to play this just right. Had to talk her the hell out of it.

She glanced up, looking guilty and wary. "Um, but I... the thing is, Gus and Kay split. And he, um, well I think he might..."

"Like you?" Caleb said, only it came out more like a growl than a question.

She shrugged. "I'm not sure...but, well, he at least needs friends right now. Like me." She swallowed.

"You don't have to break up with me to be his *friend*, Disco. I'm not possessive." It was true; he wasn't that kind of guy. But Gus was a special case, and if she was going to go all BFF on the Octo-Gus, he'd be around to...supervise.

She sighed and shot him a frustrated look. "Caleb. This whole thing...it's just kind of ridiculous. I hate living a lie. It's totally bad karma."

"So let me get this straight," he said, unable to stop the anger coloring his voice. "You're ready to dump me for a guy who just dumped his girlfriend, like, two minutes ago?"

Her eyes flashed, and he knew she was about to match

his anger with her own. "Caleb, that's ridiculous! You and I aren't…real. This isn't a real breakup."

Then why does it feel so real? His nostrils flared, and he told himself not to flip out. He couldn't drive her away, not now. Not until he could prove that Gus was the wrong guy for her. Stalling, he drank more coffee, trying to figure out his next move.

"Okay, so let's say you're right and Gus is…interested in you. Maybe even wants to take you to homecoming." *Over his dead body would that happen.* "Like I said, I still have a stalker. So we can't break up. Not yet."

"Argh!" Mandy stomped her foot in frustration, sloshing coffee out of her cup. "This is ridiculous! How do we get rid of Elle?"

He cocked an eyebrow. "We already covered that. PDA, babe. That should take care of it."

"What?!" She screeched so loudly that people turned to stare. Including Elle, now hovering in the hall, eyes locked on them.

Perfect.

He smirked, moving in close, deciding to use the one advantage he had—the sparks that flared between them.

"We have a deal, babe." He took her coffee cup, and set both cups on the windowsill behind Mandy. Then he caged her in, trapping her against the wall.

"Showtime, Disco," he whispered.

She glanced over his shoulder at Elle, then glared at him. "Right now, *cutie*?" she said loudly.

He heard a few snickers at the "cutie" nickname.

"Funny," he whispered, then he raised his voice to be heard over the swelling crowd in the hallway. "You know that turns me on, *babe*. Call me cutie again." He heard more laughter from other students as he lowered his face to hers.

"We also had a deal about no shenanigans," Mandy said

softly as his lips brushed hers.

He felt her chest rise and fall against his. "That was while we worked on your essay." He heard her sharp intake of breath as his hands cupped her waist. "I'll break up with you," he murmured against her lips, "if you can look me in the eye after this kiss and tell me it's fake."

He kissed her softly at first, waiting to see how she responded; he wasn't going to be an ass like Gus and force himself on her, but he knew she wanted this as much as he did. Every time they argued the sparks crackled between them, and the times they were actually getting along...that was a whole other level of sparking.

She made a sound in the back of her throat that made him crazy, then she melted into him. He deepened the kiss, molding his body to hers. She didn't even try to resist, responding to his touch so willingly he had to remind himself they were in school. Still, he was going to push this as far as he could, because it might be his only chance to prove that this... connection...they had definitely wasn't fake.

Her mouth opened willingly, and his tongue plunged deep as his hands moved up her body, his thumbs briefly grazing the sides of her breasts, then sliding up her neck and into that mass of red hair he'd been dying to touch for days. The soft whimpers she made as theirs tongues danced drove him crazy. *Damn.* They had to get the hell out of here. Go somewhere alone. Her hands were inside his jacket, moving up the back of his T-shirt, clutching him like he was her personal life preserver.

When the bell jangled overhead, they both jumped, but he didn't let go of her. He stared down into her glazed eyes, taking in her swollen lips and flushed cheeks. "News flash, Disco. That wasn't fake. For either of us."

She blinked, refocusing, then tilted her chin to look him in the eye. "I-I disagree." She reached up to smooth her hair.

"That didn't…do anything for me."

"What?!" He was dimly aware of Elle still watching them like a creepy voyeur.

Mandy raised her eyebrows like a judgy teacher. "Don't worry, I won't tell anyone that you need to work on your technique." She turned to grab her coffee cup from the windowsill. "It's the slurping, *cutie*. You really need to work on that."

Then she grabbed her bag from the floor and stalked off, tossing a smug look over her shoulder.

• • •

As soon as Mandy rounded the corner, she stopped to lean against the wall. She was going to be late to class but she didn't care; she needed to get a grip. She closed her eyes, letting the cold from the tile walls seep through the fabric of her blouse, hoping it would cool her down because she was on fire from that kiss.

She expected to burst into flames any second, and she had no idea how she'd managed to pull off that smart-ass remark to Caleb and walk away from him like it was no big deal. Her mood ring, turning a violet color, clearly thought she'd been into that kiss.

He'd said the kiss wasn't fake, and it sure hadn't felt fake, but Elle had been watching the whole time. How much of that steaminess had been Caleb putting on a show to get rid of his stalker?

She had to remember that he had an agenda just like she did, and that she was dealing with two Calebs: fake jackass boyfriend Caleb who liked to mess with her—and kiss her, apparently—and real Caleb who helped her with her essay and told her about his mom and held her hand like it mattered.

"Come on, girl, let's get to class."

Mandy's eyes flew open at the sound of Cammie's voice. Her friend studied her with appraising eyes, assessing the messy hair and rumpled blouse. Self-consciously Mandy smoothed her mom's lime-green shirt, then reached up to finger-comb her hair.

Cammie smirked, then gave her a little push down the hall. "Don't try to hide it. I saw the tail end of that porno you two were about to make."

"Cammie! We totally weren't making a—"

Cammie snorted as they hurried down the hall. "Yeah, right. You're lucky Dr. Hairy didn't bust you. Again." She side-eyed her. "So I take it things have moved to a new level with you two? No more pretending?"

Mandy grabbed Cammie's arm and dragged her into the girls' bathroom, then checked to make sure they were alone.

"It's not…we're still pretending."

"Right. You weren't getting into that kiss at all. It was a total act. For him, too."

Mandy glared at her best friend. "It *was* an act, all because of stupid Elle. He's trying to get rid of his stalker."

Cammie's eyes narrowed. "Is that what he said?"

Mandy stared at her shoes. Today she'd worn boring flats with her jeans, which had meant she'd had to look up at Caleb, putting her at a disadvantage, though somehow it hadn't impacted how well their bodies had molded during that kiss.

"What did he say, Mandy? Don't even try to lie to me."

Sighing, Mandy met Cammie's determined gaze. "He said he'd go ahead and fake break up with me if the kiss didn't, um, do anything for me."

"So basically he told you he likes you. A lot." Cammie smirked.

Mandy frowned. "No, I…" Was that true? Was that what he meant, in his backward, cocky Caleb way?

Cammie reached into her purse, pulled out a comb, and

handed it to Mandy. "As long as you're going to class late, you might as well pull yourself together." Cammie turned to the mirror and applied lip gloss, smacking her lips together.

"I told him the kiss didn't do anything for me," Mandy said, combing her hair. "I'll give him two more days of this fake thing, then I'm dumping him."

Cammie's gaze met Mandy's in the mirror. "Didn't do anything for you? Honey, no way is he buying that. Nobody who saw you two would believe that." She shoved her lip gloss back in her purse and held out her hand for her comb. "Please don't tell me this is because of the Octo-Gus."

Mandy slapped the comb on Cammie's upturned palm. "Yes, it's about Gus. He and Kay broke up, and Kay's spreading rumors about him." Cammie scowled. "I don't know why you believe that stuff instead of trusting Gus, Cam. He's our friend! We need to be there for him."

"Mandy, this is ridiculous. You're trusting the wrong guy. Kay's not the only one who's been on the other side of the eight-handed monster." She crossed her arms over her chest. "And I'll eat my chem book if that kiss was fake."

Mandy hated arguing, especially with her friends. Sometimes—lots of times—she kept her feelings inside rather than argue because she hated it so much. But today felt different. Maybe because that kiss had stirred up all sorts of feelings she wasn't sure about. Maybe because she kept picturing Gus's worried and embarrassed face when he'd told her about the rumors.

"I thought you hated Caleb," Mandy said through gritted teeth.

"I never hated him, but I definitely didn't like him much."

"What changed your mind?"

Cammie shrugged. "You told me how much he helped with your essay. And I see how you two are with each other, teasing and poking, but also looking like you want to tear each other's clothes off."

They didn't do that, did they? Mandy swallowed and leaned against the sink, confusion swirling through her like beads in a lava lamp. "I wish I'd never started this stupid fake relationship with him."

Cammie nodded. "It was definitely one of the dumber things you've done."

Mandy's eyebrows shot up, but before she could argue Cammie continued. "You're the one always saying things happen for a reason. Maybe there's a reason for it. Like bringing you two together. For real, not fake."

"But I don't belong with someone like Caleb," Mandy protested. "He's not the type of guy who'd normally even notice me." She thought of Elle, who oozed sexiness, like she'd just stepped out of a photo shoot for a motorcycle calendar full of scary-hot models.

"Opposites attract, right? You two are polar opposites... and you definitely *attract*."

Stubborn resistance streaked through Mandy. "But it's supposed to be Gus. It was always supposed to be Gus." She thought of his puppy dog eyes, his messy brown curls. His shy smile. Completely unlike Mr. Tall, Dark, and Broody.

Cammie rolled her eyes. "You need to look at reality, Mandy, not fantasies about crushes you've had forever."

Mandy stepped away from the sink. "*Reality* is that Caleb and I are pretending. *Reality* is Kay and other girls are spreading lies about Gus." She reached for the door, shooting a glare at Cammie. "Reality is that my best friend is giving me bad advice."

Then she yanked the door open and stormed down the hall, not even caring that she'd get stuck on the tardy detention list.

• • •

"Recon update, Blue Ranger checking in," J.T. said, sliding into the desk next to Caleb in calc class. "Two confirmed Octo-Gus reports."

Caleb shot him a glare. His day had sucked after this morning's ridiculously hot kiss with Mandy. He was still reeling after she'd given him that bullshit line about it not doing anything for her. She'd avoided him all morning, and every time he turned around Elle had been hovering like a shadow.

Maybe Mandy was right and he needed to report Elle for stalking, but somehow that seemed like an overreaction. She was just a girl who couldn't get over him. He supposed he should be flattered.

"Did you hear me, Red Ranger? Octo-Gus is confirmed as a real threat."

Caleb shrugged. "Whatever. She's determined to go to the dance with him."

J.T. tilted his head, confusion clouding his expression. "Still? Even after this morning's epic face-sucking?"

Caleb flinched. Was everybody talking about him and Mandy? Probably. They were the school's least likely couple to hook up, so therefore the whole school was curious. He sighed, staring blankly at the whiteboard full of equations. Maybe there was a reason opposites didn't usually work out.

Their calc teacher burst into the room, papers falling out of his armload of binders.

"*She* didn't think it was epic," Caleb muttered. He had no idea why he was telling J.T. this.

J.T.'s eyebrows shot up in surprise. "But Cammie said it was like watching a porno."

Caleb almost smiled. It sure had *felt* like that to him, but not to her, apparently, even though he would've sworn she was as into it as he was.

"You can't give up," J.T. said. "You can't let Octo-Gus win."

Caleb shrugged again. Maybe he was better off with a stalker than a fake girlfriend, especially if he was the only one who wanted to move things from fake to real. He fingered the notebook in his jacket pocket, his thumb brushing the Pop Rocks candy Mandy had given him.

He knew this would happen if he was dumb enough to let someone in. He'd confided in Mandy, and what had she done? Thrown it back in his face, saying their connection wasn't real.

"Dude," J.T. whispered. "I have more recon data."

Caleb ignored J.T. and focused on his droning calc teacher, because he didn't want to bomb this class and get on his dad's radar again. And he didn't want to hear more recon data.

People sucked and couldn't be trusted. He needed to remember that the next time he was tempted by a crazy redhead who made him laugh and pushed his buttons and smelled amazing and…

Shit.

He couldn't give up. Red Rangers never walked away from a battle. He tore a page out of his notebook and scribbled on it, then passed it to J.T.

You sure about the recon?

J.T. unfolded the paper, wrote quickly, then handed it back.

Positive. Tim on lax team said G made a bet he can hook up with 3 girls by winter break. Starting with homecoming. Told Tim he's got an easy target.

Caleb glared at the paper, wishing he could set it on fire with his fingers. Since he didn't have that superpower, he crumpled it into a ball. He'd set it on fire later, in the parking lot.

Right before he beat the crap out of Gus.

Chapter Fifteen
Save It for Later

Tuesday, September 27

Caleb avoided Mandy the rest of the day because he wasn't sure what he'd say if he saw her. His gut churned, thinking about J.T.'s intel about Gus, and about the way Mandy had sashayed away from him after their kiss like he hadn't just rocked her world.

Whatever. So maybe she'd been faking the kissing. He still didn't want her ending up with Gus on homecoming. Mandy was the perfect "easy target" for Gus because of her stupid crush, and her Pollyanna worldview that blinded her to big-time douchiness masquerading as dorkiness.

He stalked down the hall, debating whether or not to confront Gus, when Elle emerged from the shadows, blocking his path.

"Caleb, we need to talk." Her voice sounded anxious as her gaze darted nervously up and down the hall.

He didn't have time for this. "Uh, sorry. Can't right now."

She put a hand on his jacket, and he flinched. "Please Caleb. It's important. It won't take long."

He huffed out a sigh, but tilted his head toward the parking lot. "Talk fast," he said, jerking his arm out of her grip and pushing through the door.

"Fine, make it difficult," she muttered, stalking next to him in her thigh-high boots that were, yeah, smoking hot, but he didn't care about that. Not anymore.

He surveyed the parking lot, hoping like hell Mandy wasn't around to see this.

"So, it's like this," Elle said, keeping pace with him as he moved toward his car. "I wanted to apologize. For, um, stalking you."

He stopped, turning sharply to face her. "What?"

She lowered her eyes, and he was shocked to see she was embarrassed. "Stalking you," she muttered. "I was being a total freak." She glanced up. "But I'm, um, seeing someone. Working on getting closure."

Holy shit. Wait 'til he told Mandy…but damn, he couldn't tell Mandy! This couldn't happen.

"That's…good. I mean, really good. But, uh…" He ran a hand through his hair, not believing what he was about to say. "Do you think you could, uh, keep doing it? Just for a couple more days?"

Her mouth dropped open, and she took a step back. "Are you *kidding* me, Caleb? Do you have any idea how hard I've had to work at getting over you?"

He frowned. They'd dated for like, three weeks. She clearly needed help if she wasn't over him already. And it was good she was getting help, but damn it, he wished she'd waited another week.

Okay, that was a selfish wish. But damn…if she stopped stalking them, and Gus kept moving in on Mandy…

"It's not just you," she snapped. "I'm having trouble with

a lot of…closure stuff." She sniffed and he panicked, because now she was about to cry. "My therapist says it's because my parents are divorcing. My sister's away at college. And my dog ran away. I mean, he came back after a day, but still, why would he leave in the first place?" She sighed dramatically. "So I guess I have, like…abandonment issues or whatever."

What he should really do is put Mandy and Elle in a room together. They'd be BFFs once they bonded over all this stuff. Plus Mandy would have a closure mantra for her. And they'd probably both decide he was a jerk and vow never to speak to him again.

"So for you to…to"—she was ramping up to a full-on meltdown now—"even suggest that I *pretend* to stalk you? Force myself to watch you and that weird hippie girl have eye sex in the caf every day and…" Her voice trailed away as tears spilled out of her eyes.

Eye sex? Were he and Mandy doing that? Hmm…maybe she hadn't been faking that kiss, after all. He sighed and looked around the parking lot. He needed a wingman to save the day, but since he basically had no friends he was stuck with dealing with this on his own.

He stared into her mascara-smeared eyes. "I'm really sorry, Elle. I didn't mean for our breakup to be so, uh, hard on you." He was baffled. They'd only gone out maybe three or four times. No sex. Not even eye sex.

She wiped her eyes and hiccupped. "I know. It's just that, I really give *so much* of myself, you know? To everyone." She sighed heavily. "I'm a total giver, but no one cares." She fluttered her smeared eyelashes at him. "I made a scrapbook about us, did you know that?"

Okay—*that* was creepy. He took a step back.

"I kept the movie tickets and even the candy wrappers you threw in the trash."

He swallowed, desperately regretting that he'd suggested

she fake stalk him.

"I was going to get your name tattooed on my thigh. In a heart, with a thorn stake for the *l* in Caleb."

He took another step back, looking around frantically for help. "I...uh...wow. Look, I've gotta go—"

"Torrs!"

They both turned to see J.T. heading toward them, a weird smirk on his face. "Where'd you go, man?" J.T. said. "We were supposed to meet at your car." He glanced at Elle. "Hi."

Relief zoomed through him. Maybe he did have a wingman, after all.

Elle nodded dismissively and wiped her nose. "Anyway. As for your *request*? No. I refuse."

J.T. shot him a suspicious glare.

"It's not what you think," Caleb said to J.T.

"Caleb wants me to keep stalking him," Elle announced. "Even though my therapist tells me I need to move on."

J.T. cocked an eyebrow.

"All because of that redhead he's trying to hook up with."

"You mean Mandy," J.T. said. "She has a name."

Elle tossed her raggedly cut black hair over her shoulder. "Whatever."

"Not whatever," Caleb said. "Her name is Mandy."

Elle bit her lip, looking ready to cry again.

"Look, I'm sorry, Elle, but uh, I've...moved on. You should, too."

"He sucks at this," J.T. said. "I can see why you broke up with him."

Elle nodded furiously. "He totally sucks."

"Train wreck," J.T. mouthed to Caleb, wide-eyed, then he turned back to Elle, who was staring at her black boots. "You're better off without him," J.T. said. "Really. Plus I hear he's a lousy kisser." J.T. shot Caleb a smirk, and Caleb couldn't decide if he wanted to laugh or slug him.

Elle raised her head. "Oh, that's not true," she protested. "His kisses are so hot." She glared at him. "Or they were. Until he lost interest."

Guilty as charged. Once he'd figured out Elle was crazy, Caleb had lost interest in the physical stuff. Though he hadn't realized just how crazy she was until today.

J.T. took a step back, and Caleb shot him a questioning look.

"We've gotta go," J.T. said, staring hard at him. "Caleb's giving me a ride…and I can't be late."

"Yeah," Caleb agreed, stepping backward with J.T. "Forget about what I asked. It was crappy of me. You just… keep on doing that closure thing. And the therapy—definitely keep doing that."

He spun around and headed for his car, J.T. keeping pace. As soon as they got in his car, they collapsed into laughter.

"Keep on doing that closure thing?" J.T. said between gasps of laugher. "Dude, that was cold."

"I know, I know. But damn. You saw how crazy she is!"

"Yeah. Wow. She makes Mandy look boring."

Caleb stopped laughing. "You did not just slam your friend and my girlfriend."

J.T. grinned. "You mean fake girlfriend."

Caleb turned away and scowled out the windshield.

"Kidding," J.T. said. "I know you like her. For real."

Caleb glanced at him. "You do?"

J.T. rolled his eyes. "Benefits of a gay friend. I don't miss much when it comes to that stuff."

Friend? Caleb turned to stare out the windshield again.

"Anyway, you don't need a stalker. That was just getting in the way."

Caleb turned back to him. "But it was my excuse for the whole idea. How I got Mandy to agree to be my fake girlfriend."

J.T. leaned back to study him. "Excuse? So you're saying you were into Mandy from the start? This didn't just happen because you guys started the fake thing and you accidentally fell for her?"

"I don't know. Maybe. Yes. Damn it. I'm so confused." Caleb blew out a long breath.

"Well, then. It's a good thing the Blue Ranger is here to save your ass and help you get the girl."

Caleb locked eyes with him, and then he grinned, daring to hope that maybe it was true. "Yeah. Maybe it is."

Chapter Sixteen
Lies

Thursday, September 27

Mandy hovered at the edge of the parking lot watching Elle and Caleb. That was some serious drama going down. Her stomach twisted in knots as she wondered if maybe they were getting back together. Just thinking about it made her want to…to…

"Hey, Mandy. You working tonight?"

She whirled around to see Gus approaching, his crooked grin making her forget about Caleb for a second.

She nodded, tugging at her hair. "From five until closing."

"Cool. Mind if I come by?"

Her heart rate picked up considerably. She glanced toward Caleb and Elle, who were still in high drama mode, Elle's hands flying around and Caleb stepping away from her.

"Sure. Oh, but there's a birthday party from six until seven thirty. Don't come then—it'll be crazy." She smiled.

Gus nodded. "Awesome. Maybe you can take a break

with me?" He kicked his feet on the ground. "I just...sort of need to talk to someone. Someone nice, like you."

Her pulse fluttered. This was what she needed. Sweet, adorable, perfect little Gus. Not smart-ass, broody, hot-kissing Caleb. She nodded. "Sounds great."

He shot her another grin. "Hey, do you need a ride home?"

Wow. Totally unexpected. "Uh...Cammie's giving me a ride." She glanced around, for once wishing her best friend didn't have a car.

"Okay, cool. I'll see you later." He lifted his chin and strolled away, whistling. Which was so dorky and cute...just like him.

She stared after him, wondering how her day had turned so crazy. Kissing Caleb this morning and now...this. She took a deep breath. Things were getting out of control. She had to fake break up with Caleb, especially now.

She glanced across the parking lot and saw J.T. and Caleb practically sprinting to Caleb's car. Huh. That was weird.

"Mandy? Can I talk to you for a minute?"

She flinched at the sound of Kay's voice, then turned to face her.

"I heard from Neuro Blastr. He's confirmed for the dance."

"That's great." Kay looked almost nervous. "I know..." She cleared her throat and started again. "Look, you and I aren't really friends, but I wanted to warn you. About Gus. He's not..."

Mandy felt her hackles rise defensively, but she waited.

"He...uh...let's just say, he's not such a good guy when you're on a date with him." She frowned. "Do you get what I'm saying?"

Righteous anger boiled inside Mandy. How could Kay do this? Kay had major gossip reach, which was probably why her lies were spreading. Mandy glared at her. "I can't believe this, Kay. Why are you spreading lies about Gus? Is it because he broke up with you? You don't want to see him with someone else?"

Kay stepped back, looking as if Mandy had slapped her. "No! That's not it at all." She stuck her hands on her hips, glaring. "Look, Mandy, the truth is Gus is only interested in one thing from you. He doesn't actually *like* you."

Mandy felt like she'd been sucker punched, almost crumpling from Kay's words. Then she reminded herself that Kay was just jealous. That Kay had always hated her. She stood up straight, inhaling and exhaling like she did when she meditated. She would *not* go ballistic on her, because that was totally bad karma.

Anger only leads to more anger. Deflect and redirect it, and peace will take its place.

"I'm sorry you're so hurt from the breakup, Kay. But it's not okay for you to spread lies just because you're not over him. I *know* Gus. I've known him since kindergarten. He's a great guy. You may have convinced other people in this school, but you're never going to get his oldest friend to turn on him. Give it a rest."

Kay's mouth dropped open. "It must be nice to live in that dreamy little hippie bubble of reality, Mandy. He's *not* a great—"

Mandy put up a hand. "We're done here, okay? And please stop spreading lies. It's totally bad karma, in case you didn't know." Then she spun around, making a beeline across the lot toward Cammie's car. Out of the corner of her eye she noticed Caleb's car tear out of the lot. It almost looked like he and J.T. were laughing together. But that didn't make sense...

She shook her head and shrugged her shoulders. This had been the craziest day ever. The thing was, she'd given Kay a hard time for lying, but she needed to stop lying, too. Stop pretending to be Caleb's girlfriend. She had to break up with him, no matter what he said about Elle stalking him.

No matter how special their snow globe day had been.

No matter how much that kiss had almost convinced her to stick around for another taste…or made her wonder if he might actually have feelings for her.

The whole thing was a total fiasco and had to stop. She'd call him tonight after she got off work and convince him that they had to fake break up, before things got any crazier.

Chapter Seventeen
Through Being Cool

Tuesday, September 27

Caleb and his dad sat across from each other at their long dining table, eating a casserole Helen had made and wilted salad from a bag. His dad drank scotch on the rocks and Caleb drank water, wishing he could have a scotch, too, because dinners with his dad were always painful.

"So how was the baking on Sunday?" His dad sipped from his glass, eyeing Caleb over the rim.

This was the first dinner they'd eaten together in over a week, which in a normal house might mean they'd have a lot to talk about it. But their house wasn't normal.

Caleb shrugged. "Okay."

"Just okay? Helen told me the kids were nice, that it was a lot of fun."

Helen. Always trying to find a way to force a connection between him and his dad. He loved her, but he wished she'd stop trying to force something that wasn't ever going to happen.

"Yeah," Caleb said, deciding to give an inch, but no more. "It wasn't as awful as I thought it would be."

His dad set his glass on the table with a *thunk*. "Caleb. Why is it so hard for you to get along with people?"

And they were off to the races.

"It's not hard. I just prefer being by myself."

"Just like your mother," his dad muttered under his breath, and Caleb's fists clenched under the table.

They sat in silence, chewing and swallowing, staring at the table instead of each other, until his dad spoke again.

"How's calc going?"

Another crappy conversation topic. "It's going. Not great, but I'll pass it."

His dad frowned. "I've told you I can help—"

"I don't want your help. I'm not going to be an engineer. Writers don't need calc."

His father drained the last of the scotch from his glass and sighed. "Caleb. You still want to get into a decent college and—"

"*If* I go to college. Maybe I'll just hit the road and—"

"You're going to college, Caleb. You can do whatever crazy road trips you want during the summers, but you're—"

"I think you forgot this is my life we're talking about, not yours."

"And you're not going to ruin it before it's even started."

They glared at each other across the table, and Caleb wondered if he'd look like his dad when he was fifty—wrinkles around his eyes, strands of silver in his dark hair, and a face as determined and pissed off as he knew his own was.

Caleb pushed back from the table, grabbing his empty plate and glass. "I've gotta be somewhere." He turned to leave the dining room, but his father called after him.

"This conversation isn't finished, Caleb."

"Yeah," Caleb muttered. "It is."

The mall was surprisingly busy for a weeknight. Caleb took in the groups of giggling girls carrying tiny shopping bags with tissue paper peeking out of the tops, moms pushing strollers, senior citizens power walking, and tourists wandering wide-eyed, hand in hand, like they'd never seen an Urban Outfitters or a pretzel shop before.

Maybe he'd write a story about this later, the way people congregated in these shrines built to spending money, instead of doing something real.

Yeah, he was in a lousy mood, judging hundreds of people all at once. Whatever. He wasn't even sure why the hell he'd come here after he'd stormed out of the house, pissed off at his dad. But when he stopped to study the mall directory, he knew exactly why he'd come here. Because he was stupid.

Stupid in love.

Build-a-Buddy was smack in the middle of the mall, by the indoor play area full of screaming kids and exhausted parents lounging on benches, ignoring their offspring. If the government needed to get secrets out of foreign spies, this would be the perfect place to take them, because this place was a freaking nightmare.

His gaze zeroed in on the brightly lit store packed full of kids and parents smiling indulgently as their evil spawn tore through the aisles clutching tiny clothes and creepy unstuffed animal carcasses.

How the hell did Mandy stand working there?

He spotted her right away; as usual she was hard to miss with that fiery red hair. She wore a blue polo shirt and khaki pants, which he knew she must hate. He smiled, imagining how much it must gall her to trade in her disco clothes for that awful uniform.

Cammie was there, too, her hair piled on top of her head, a pencil sticking out of it. She looked frazzled as swarms of little kids danced around her, shoving limp animals in her face.

Caleb moved closer, hovering in the entrance. This must be the crowd from the birthday party. Some of the little kids wore party hats and one girl whose hair was as red as Mandy's had a giant "I am 6!" button on her T-shirt and chocolate icing smeared on her cheek.

"I want the raccoon *and* the bear!" the little girl demanded, stomping her foot. Mandy smiled at her, not losing patience the way he would.

"Hey, Gilly, take a chill pill."

Caleb glanced toward the guy who'd just reprimanded the little kid. He lounged against the wall, his arm draped around a girl with short spiky dark hair. He recognized them from school. Lifeguard dude. Weird name—Suede? Slade? The girl was one of those overachiever types; he was surprised she hadn't been at his house baking on Sunday.

Maybe the little redhead was related to one of them. He didn't have any cousins, but he imagined that chaperoning a birthday party might be something people with actual families did for each other. The tiny redhead looked up at Slade and grinned, looking sort of misty-eyed like Mandy did when Gus was around. Okay, so definitely not Slade's little sister.

"Gillian," said Slade's girlfriend. "What did we talk about? Best behavior, remember?" She glanced up at Slade and they shared one of those disgusting couple smiles, the kind that usually made him roll his eyes.

Annoyed, Caleb refocused on Mandy, who hadn't noticed him yet. She knelt down to talk to the birthday girl. "You're having a great birthday, aren't you?" Mandy asked, sounding like she was the excited six-year-old.

The girl nodded. "But I want *two* animals, not just one."

A dark-haired little boy wandered over, holding out an unstuffed bear to the girl. "You can have mine if you want," he said.

No *way*, little dude, Caleb thought. Do *not* let that chick walk all over you.

Mandy glanced up at Slade and his girlfriend, who were frowning like they wanted to open a can of whoop-ass on the little redhead. Caleb glanced around, wondering where the birthday girl's parents were.

He remembered the last birthday party his mom had arranged for him. Chuck E. Cheese's. Totally unoriginal, but it was what he'd wanted when he turned seven. J.T. had been there, along with a handful of other kids from the second grade. He squeezed his eyes shut, shoving away the memory of his mom carrying out a chocolate cake covered with candles, singing off-key and making him laugh.

"What are you doing here?"

He opened his eyes, startled to find Cammie staring him down, arms folded over her blue polo shirt, which couldn't hide her impressive rack. Which he totally shouldn't be noticing since he was here to see his fake-need-to-make-it-real girlfriend.

"Just came by to say hi to my girlfriend. Didn't know I needed your permission."

He glanced at Mandy, who'd just now noticed him, her eyes wide with surprise. She frowned, then refocused on the birthday girl, who was launching into a nuclear meltdown. Slade and his girlfriend rushed over to help, and Caleb decided there wasn't enough money in the world to make him work at a place like this.

"Don't mess with my girl, dude," Cammie said, her voice full of I-will-kick-your-ass warning. "Maybe it's time for this stupid fake thing to end and for you to back off. I don't want to see her get hurt."

He closed his eyes, frustration snaking through him and making him want to lash out, but instead he faced Cammie head-on, deciding he didn't care if she could read him like a book. "I would *never* hurt her," he said through gritted teeth.

Her eyes widened and she stepped closer. "Holy crap. You really do like her." She darted an annoyed glance at Mandy. "That girl's an idiot sometimes."

"Don't call her that," he snapped. He glowered at her, and she grinned.

"Maybe there's hope for you yet, Torrs."

A scowling older woman appeared from the back of the store motioning Cammie to get back to work.

"Come back around eight forty-five," Cammie whispered. "Our manager will be gone and you can hang out while we close up."

Surprised by the invitation, Caleb watched Cammie rush back into the fray of hysterical kids. Mandy sat at the giant stuffing machine now, her foot working the pedal as she stuffed the wild birthday girl's raccoon.

Slade and his girlfriend watched, laughing together, their arms wrapped around each other, and Caleb's gut clenched.

He turned and left the store, glancing at his phone. He had a lot of time to kill before closing time. He decided to get something to eat, even though he wasn't really hungry.

There was a line at the pretzel shop, so Caleb opened the Kindle app on his phone and resumed reading a depressing novel about a guy whose family had abandoned him as a child, leaving him to make it on his own. Perfect for his mood.

As he moved closer to the counter, he glanced up and saw Gus paying for his purchase. Shit. He shoved his phone in his pocket and glared at Gus's back until he turned around, carrying two drinks and a bag.

Gus hesitated when he saw Caleb, then a smug smirk spread across his stupid face.

"You don't seem like a mall guy," Gus said, pausing next to him.

Caleb narrowed his eyes, imagining doing all sorts of un-Mandy-approved things with the lemonade.

Gus shifted his feet, and Caleb hoped that meant he was feeling intimidated. "So...you taking Mandy to homecoming?" Gus asked, and something about the look in his eyes really made Caleb wish they were alone in a parking lot.

"Yeah," Caleb said, hoping to convey all sorts of back-off messages with one word.

"Huh. Haven't seen you do a prom-posal." Gus's eyes narrowed.

Shit. Back to that stupid stuff. Not to mention the fact that he'd just told the guy Mandy wanted to go the dance with that she already *had* a date. With him.

"Not my thing," Caleb growled.

"That's too bad, since it's definitely *her* thing. You'd think her boyfriend would know that."

Caleb stepped out of the line, getting in Gus's face. "You don't know anything about Mandy and me, dude. So back the hell off."

Gus swallowed and blinked, but then that stupid smug look was back. He shrugged and stepped back. "Whatever. Just looking out for my friend." Then he turned and walked away, whistling.

Caleb contemplated what he'd just done.

Crap. Mandy was going to kill him.

. . .

Mandy wiped a hand across her damp forehead. Tonight had been exhausting. That birthday party had been crazy, especially the birthday girl, who'd been hell on wheels. Trina, the birthday girl's babysitter, had warned her but she'd still been surprised.

At least everyone was gone now, including their cranky manager. She couldn't wait to get out of here and maybe stop by Starbucks with Cammie on their way home. And talk about why Caleb had shown up, and what he and Cammie had been whispering about before he left.

Mandy went to lower the metal gate closing the store off from the mall and almost screamed when Caleb appeared, ducking under the gate.

"What are you doing here?" she gasped.

He shrugged. "Teddy bear emergency. I hear you can hook me up."

She narrowed her eyes, trying not to reward him with a smile. "Sorry, but we're closed. Try Walmart."

He took a step toward her, his smile sly and sexy. "But I want one that *you* make for me, to sleep with when I'm scared."

She turned away to hide her heated cheeks and closed the gate. "Whatever, Caleb. Look, we need to close up. You have to leave."

Cammie came out from the storage room and surprised Mandy by grinning at Caleb. "Perfect timing! Come back here and help we with some boxes." She glanced at Mandy. "You can close out the register. I'll help you clean up the disaster zone in a few."

Baffled, Mandy stared at her friend. Since when did Cammie like Caleb enough to ask him for a favor? And she didn't seem surprised to see him, either. Suspicion licked at her nerve endings. Had Cammie told Caleb to come back tonight? And if so, why?

She watched Caleb disappear into the storeroom and picked up her nearly empty lemonade cup from the counter, sucking down the last of it through the straw.

Gus had come by tonight, too, after the birthday party madness, bringing her lemonade and a pretzel "just because." It had totally rattled her. And pissed off Cammie, which in turn pissed off Mandy. Cammie needed to remember that Gus was their *friend*.

Sighing, she turned to the register, reminding herself to focus. *Everything happens for a reason.*

. . .

"Okay, dude," Cammie said, whirling on Caleb as soon as they entered the storage room. "Your competition was here earlier. Sucking up to her with lemonade and a pretzel."

Caleb gaped at her. "Gus?" Than son of a bitch. He should've dumped the lemonade on his head when he had the chance.

Cammie yanked the pencil out of her hair, clearly frustrated. She peeked around him to make sure Mandy was still at the register. "He came by looking all sad and mopey, totally working it."

Caleb's gut twisted, picturing the scene, and how easily Mandy would fall for his act. "I saw him earlier. He gave me hell about not doing a prom-posal."

Cammie's face lit up. "That's a great idea! You totally should."

Caleb shook his head. "I screwed up—I told him that I was taking Mandy to homecoming, but she wants to go with him." He ran a hand through his hair.

Cammie narrowed her eyes. "Dude. You are not giving up on this. You could kick Gus's ass from here to the moon."

Caleb cocked an eyebrow. "Yeah, I'd like to. But that would just piss her off more. 'Violence is never the answer.'" He mimicked her breathy voice, surprised at how easily he was able to call it to mind.

Cammie smirked. "I didn't mean fighting, though I know you'd win. I meant you can kick his ass by winning Mandy. Get her to fall for you for real." She poked him in the chest. "I think she's already halfway in love with you. You just have to close the deal, dude."

What. The. Hell. Caleb felt like he'd wandered into one of those weird old carnival fun houses with the bizarre mirrors that distorted reality. Because in what reality was Cammie on Team Caleb instead of cock-blocking him?

And in what world was Mandy halfway in love with him, after she'd walked away from their kiss telling him it hadn't done anything for her?

"I don't get it, Cammie. A few days ago you wanted to kill me. Now you don't? What's going on?"

Cammie peeked out the storeroom door again, then refocused on him, whispering fast. "Okay, I'll make it easy so your guy brain can understand. Gus is a tool. I've talked to three girls now, including Kay, who just dumped him. There's a reason everyone's calling him the Octo-Gus." She pinned him with a fierce glare. "Mandy's totally vulnerable to his 'dumb jock, sweet guy' act."

Caleb's skin crawled with heat as she spoke, and his muscles coiled like he needed to be ready for an attack. "That's what J.T. said, too."

"Yeah, he's got his sources and I've got mine." Cammie tugged at the collar of her polo shirt. "Honestly, Gus has never been my favorite person. I used to think he was just boring and I never understood Mandy's infatuation, but J.T. and I let him hang out with us because he was harmless, and because Mandy thought he walked on water."

"But he's *not* harmless," Caleb said, his brain firing on all cylinders again. He sighed. "She's never gonna believe it. Not unless..." He tensed, not even wanting to picture it.

Cammie nodded furiously. "I know. Not unless he pulls

the same crap on her." She poked him in the chest again. "And I know you don't want that any more than I do. I've tried to warn her, but she won't listen to me."

This time Caleb was the one who checked to make sure Mandy was still occupied. She stepped away from the cash register, talking on her cell, one hand gesturing frantically as the other held the phone.

He refocused on Cammie. "This sucks," he muttered. "The whole reason we started this stupid fake thing is because she wants that asshole to ask her to homecoming. And it sounds like he's moving in on her, just like she wants."

Cammie sighed. "But that's the problem, Caleb. You're *not* faking with Mandy. I can tell." She shrugged and smiled. "It's why I'm telling you all this. Because I can tell you *do* like her."

His eyes widened as his hand closed around the notebook in his pocket. "Maybe I'm just good at selling it." But as soon as he said it, he felt the lie and hated himself for it.

Cammie snorted. "Bullshit. You're totally into her. Don't even try to deny it." She tossed her hair. "And she likes you, too, but the problem is, in her mind she's not *supposed* to like you. She's supposed to end up with a dork like Gus. Except he's *not* dorky innocent Gus."

"He's asshole Gus," Caleb growled.

Cammie nodded. "I was kind of testing you earlier tonight, when I told you to back off. I wanted to see how you'd respond." She glanced at the stack of boxes he'd moved for her. "Sometimes the scariest villains look the most innocent. And heroes don't always wear white."

"You into comics, Ramirez?"

Her shoulders straightened. "What if I am?"

"Then you're cooler than I thought you were."

They grinned at each other, and Caleb decided if he *was* going up against a villain, Cammie'd be a hell of a sidekick.

Assuming he was the hero, which he wasn't sure of. He wasn't really sure of anything right now.

Suddenly Mandy flew into the storeroom, her face wild with panic. "I have to go. Gran's sick. I can't reach Reg and dad's on the road and—"

Cammie moved toward her, putting a hand on her shoulder. "Take a breath, sweetie. What happened?"

Mandy squeezed her eyes shut, breathing deeply, and Caleb knew she was saying a mantra.

"She's having a hard time breathing. I told her to call 911 but—"

"Let's go," Caleb said, taking a step toward the door, wanting to grab her hand but not sure if he should.

Cammie nodded, pushing her gently toward Caleb. "I'll finish up here. You go with Caleb and call me as soon as you can." Cammie smiled reassuringly. "She'll be okay, sweetie. She's tough."

Mandy turned toward him, fear shooting out of her like sparks, and his chest tightened. He grabbed her hand, squeezing it. "Come on." The words came out rough, urgent.

They ran to the front of the store, and Cammie raised the metal gate so they could leave.

"Call me!" Cammie yelled after them as they ran hand in hand through the empty mall, their shoes echoing on the tile floor.

"Did she call 911?" Caleb asked as they reached the doors to parking lot. He pushed on a glass door, but it was locked.

"This way." Mandy pulled him to a metal door marked EMPLOYEES ONLY. They shoved through the door and ran toward Caleb's car. "No," Mandy gasped between breaths. "She hates doctors. I called our neighbor who's a nurse."

Caleb yanked open the passenger door and Mandy slid in. He slammed the door and ran around to the driver's side. Adrenaline surged through him as he sped out of the parking lot, calculating the fastest way to Mandy's house.

"Not too fast," she said. "The last thing we need is to get into an accident."

She was right, so he slowed down.

"Damn it, Reg," she muttered, phone to her ear. "Pick up your damn phone."

Caleb sped up as he merged onto the highway, but not too much. Damn, she had a ton of crap going on in her life. Her dad gone, her idiot brother not being around, her gran… all the stuff at school with the spirit committee and Spriggs crawling up her ass. He glanced at her as he shifted into fifth gear. She was kind of amazing, juggling all of it.

Her phone rang once and she answered, sounding breathless. "Mrs. Cleary? Thank God you're there. I'm on my way home. I'll be there in…" She glanced at Caleb.

"Five minutes," he said, and she raised her eyebrows, clearly indicating he shouldn't drive so fast.

"Ten minutes," she said, shooting him a look that made him want to laugh…and kiss her…and just…

He refocused on the road, telling himself he'd think about everything Cammie had said later.

Right now he just needed to get her home.

Chapter Eighteen
Love Rollercoaster

Tuesday, September 27

Mandy's pulse pounded in her ears as Caleb turned down her street, tires squealing. He really needed to chill out, but she didn't have time to argue with him. He pulled into the driveway and she jumped out of the car, not bothering to close her door.

She burst into the house, scanning the living room for her gran. When she saw her sitting in her rocking chair, blanket draped over her lap, holding a cup of tea, she expelled a huge sigh of relief.

"Gran, are you okay?" She crossed the room to kneel next to her.

Gran nodded. "Everyone needs to calm down. Just because I'm old doesn't mean I'm fragile."

Mandy sighed, glancing at Mrs. Cleary, sitting on the small love seat. "She's okay, sweetie. I adjusted her oxygen. But she really ought to see her doctor to have her levels reevaluated.

She tells me it's been a while."

Mandy sighed. Her gran was so stubborn about that stuff. The front screen door squeaked open, and she glanced up to see Caleb hesitate as he entered, glancing around the house. She was surprised to see him, since she'd assumed he'd left.

"And who is this fine specimen of manhood?" Gran asked, perking up.

Mrs. Cleary laughed, and Mandy felt a blush spread across her face and neck. "Gran," she whispered. "Stop it."

Gran glanced at her, blue eyes sparkling with mischief behind her glasses. "But honey, you have to admit I'm right." She glanced at Caleb. "A very fine specimen indeed. Even with the hippie hair."

Mandy laughed out loud at that, knowing Caleb would hate being called a hippie just because he had longer hair.

"Um." He cleared his throat, and she knew he was pretending he hadn't heard her Gran. "I just wanted to make sure everything was okay."

"Come in here, young man," Gran said. "Don't be shy."

Caleb approached them slowly, his gaze darting between Mandy and her gran. She sort of felt sorry for him, especially because it had been sweet of him to come inside to check on her gran.

"So you must be the new boyfriend Reginald told us about. What's your name?"

Mandy wanted to die a thousand deaths. Her gran certainly seemed fine now, and she was relieved, but she really wished Gran would take a nap instead of humiliating her. She shot Gran a warning glare but Gran was focused on Caleb, who looked as embarrassed as she felt.

"I, um…Caleb. Caleb Torrs."

"Torrs? Your father owns T&R Engineering, doesn't he?" Mrs. Cleary asked.

Caleb nodded.

"Engineering?" Gran said. "Are you planning to follow in his footsteps? Take over his business some day?"

"Gran!" Mandy gasped, embarrassed for Caleb. "Don't be so nosy."

Gran peered at her over the rims of her eyeglasses. "Any boy who dates my granddaughter can answer a few questions. Your dad's not here so I have to be the hard-ass." She winked at Caleb. "Lucky for you, I'm a sucker for bad boys in leather."

Mandy closed her eyes, praying the floor would swallow her. Reluctantly, she half opened her eyes to see Caleb smiling at her gran. Now he looked more amused than embarrassed. *Great.*

"I don't plan on going into engineering," Caleb said, glancing at Mandy. "And, um, I should go. I just wanted to check on things."

"Oh no you don't," Gran said. "Mandy was just about to get me some ice cream. You have to join us."

Caleb shot Mandy a smirk. "Rainbow sherbet?"

Gran sighed happily. "It's about time," she said cryptically, and Mandy jumped to her feet, desperate to get Caleb out of earshot before Gran declared him the perfect boyfriend.

"Come on," she muttered, heading into the kitchen.

Gran was okay; that was what mattered most. Yeah, Mandy was dying of embarrassment, but it was a small price to pay in the scheme of things.

Caleb leaned against the doorframe, surveying their small kitchen, which was nothing like his gleaming granite showplace. She wondered if he felt sorry for her. She hoped not, because there was nothing for him to pity. Yeah, their place was small, but it was home. And it was full of people who loved her—except maybe Reg, but she hadn't given up on him yet.

She yanked open the freezer, grateful for the blast of cold air that refocused her brain. Ice cream. Bowls.

"Who's this?" Caleb asked, studying the collage of photos on the wall. Mandy set the tub of ice cream on the kitchen table and moved next to him, swallowing as she caught a whiff of his spicy Caleb scent.

Focus. *Focus.* "It's my family." She pointed to the photo of her parents, a smaller version of the one she had in her bedroom. "That's my parents." She pointed to a faded photo of Reg and her dressed in matching red jammies in front of a Christmas tree. "Reg and me, before we hated each other." He shot her a curious look, so she pointed to another photo of her mom and a group of girls dressed up for a night of disco, glittering and laughing at the camera. "Mom and her friends." She glanced at him, an embarrassed smile tugging at her lips. "Disco night."

He met her gaze, his own lips quirking in response. "You definitely inherited the disco gene." He glanced at the collage again, then back at her. "You look like your mom, but your dad's the redhead."

She nodded, suddenly feeling vulnerable and exposed, wondering if he was making fun of her in his thoughts. She sneaked another glance at his profile as he studied the collage.

"I don't have many pictures of my mom," he said softly. "I wish I did."

She swallowed, overwhelmed by guilt. Of course he wasn't making fun of her family photos. This felt like the day at the park, and part of her didn't want to move because she didn't want to break the snow globe spell.

He turned toward her. "Grab the bowls. I'll scoop."

"You...don't have to stay."

He frowned. "You want me to go?"

"It's up to you. Go or stay. I don't care." Total lie, but suddenly she was thinking of their hallway kiss, and then Gus bringing her lemonade, and her mind spun in confusion.

She turned to the cupboard and grabbed four bowls. His

lips quirked when he saw how many bowls she'd grabbed, and she knew she'd revealed more than she wanted to. She handed him the ice cream scoop, giving up on pretending she didn't want him to stay. He took it without a word and began filling bowls.

And even though she was confused by the way Gus was acting, somehow when she was with Caleb—*this* Caleb, the real one—she definitely wanted him to stay.

After Mrs. Cleary reassured Mandy that her gran would be fine, Mandy called her dad and promised to take Gran to the doctor as soon as possible.

"I hate to put his burden on you, doll," her dad said. "I'll be home by next weekend, but she should get in ASAP."

"It's okay. I'll take care of it." God, she wished she could rely on her brother to help out. But she couldn't.

"Homecoming's next Saturday, right?" her dad asked. "I'll definitely be home for that, so I can meet your new boyfriend."

Mandy's heart thrummed as she glanced at Caleb. Too bad he hadn't asked her. Wait, that wasn't what she wanted, was it? And he wasn't her boyfriend. Frowning, she said good-bye to her dad and sat down next to Caleb on the love seat, careful to sit as far away as possible.

He stayed to eat ice cream and watch an episode of *Arrow*, Gran's favorite show. Gran furthered her humiliation by commenting that Caleb looked he might do a workout routine as intense as Oliver Queen's.

"You're hiding a lot of muscle under that leather, aren't you, young man?"

Caleb rubbed his neck and stared at the floor. "Uh," he mumbled.

Mandy giggled because it was sort of hilarious that the one person who seemed to discombobulate Mr. Tall, Dark, and Broody was her gran. He glanced at her, and his embarrassed smile made her insides twirl around like a disco ball.

He set his empty bowl on the coffee table and stood up abruptly, shoving his hands in his jeans pockets. "I should go."

She stared up at him, flashing back on that hallway kiss again. "Okay. I'll walk you out."

He said good-bye to her gran, who winked at him but fortunately didn't say anything else embarrassing…until they reached the front door, when her gran called out, "You can show him your room, sweetie, but keep the door open!"

Mandy buried her face in her hands. "This is the worst day of my life," she muttered, and Caleb laughed softly.

"Want to show me your room, Disco?" he murmured, reaching out to gently pull her hands off her burning face. "So I know exactly what to picture late at night?"

She yanked her hands out of his. "Caleb! You're— you're—"

He grinned. "I think it's the least you can do, after your gran flirted with me all night." She groaned, squeezing her eyes shut, but that didn't stop him from stepping in close. "Come on, Disco. Just one little peek."

Her body was on fire standing this close to him. The sudden desire to kiss him overwhelmed her. She swallowed and stepped back.

"One peek. Then you have to leave." This was crazy, but the idea of him thinking about her in her bedroom late at night…well, apparently she had no willpower about some things.

He followed her down the short hallway and into her bedroom, lit only by the string of amber lights draped over her bookcase and the orange glow of the lava lamp next to her bed.

"Wow," he whispered. "It's like a shrine to the seventies." He stood next to her, his arm brushing hers, setting every nerve ending on fire.

She followed his gaze as he lazily surveyed the posters on the wall—posters that had been her mom's—of Earth, Wind & Fire and Blondie and the Bee Gees. Posters of the old *Soul Train* TV show and *American Bandstand*. He took in the packed bookshelf and shot her an approving smile, then his gaze moved to her bed, which was a tangled mess of blankets and pillows, and she thought she might melt into a pool of mortification.

At least she hadn't left any underwear lying on the floor.

"So you've seen it. You can go now." She moved away, but his hand reached out to grab hers.

"Wait," he said, his voice low, making every hormone in her body do cartwheels and backflips. He reached out and tipped up her chin with his other hand, his fingers grazing her throat.

The room wasn't so dark that she couldn't tell his eyes were burning up. Just like she felt.

"We need to talk," he said, his fingers brushing down her neck and sending shivers shooting straight to her girl parts.

For once, talking was the last thing she wanted. But that was crazy…mixed up…not right.

Or was it exactly right?

"W-we do?" she whispered, licking her lips. He swallowed, then grasped her waist, pulling her in close, his other hand cupped around the back of her neck.

"It can wait," he said roughly, then his lips were on hers, and just like the last time she was gone…drowning in a sea of Caleb, in surging waves of hot, urgent kissing, his tongue dancing with hers, his body molded to hers, her throat making sounds that were embarrassing, but only made him kiss her harder, deeper.

Her hands moved of their own accord, trailing up his chest, his neck, and into his glorious rebel hair. She tugged her fingers through it, reveling in the silky, tangled strands, and now he was the one making embarrassing sounds and moving against her body in a way that made her understand why Gran insisted on leaving the door open.

Fake? Real? She had no idea what this was…which meant she should stop, even though she didn't want to. She untangled her fingers from his hair and pushed gently on his chest, wrenching her lips away from his.

"Stop. We have to stop." It sounded like she was talking more to herself than to him.

He didn't let her go, staring down at her with stormy dark eyes. "Why?"

She swallowed, staring up at him. A girl could totally forget her own name staring into those eyes. "Uh, we…well, because this isn't…we aren't…"

"Aren't what, Disco?" He kept one hand wrapped around her waist and brushed loose curls off her burning cheeks with the other.

"Y-you said we have to talk. What about?"

His hand stilled on her cheek, then dropped to his side. He sighed heavily. "Yeah. So…don't freak out, but I sort of told Gus that we're going to homecoming together."

She stepped back, and this time he let go of her. She crossed her arms over her chest as warring emotions streaked through her—confusion, excitement, apprehension, suspicion. She couldn't decide which feeling to focus on, but she knew the question she had to ask. "Why?"

His face hardened, and he was back to His Broodiness. "Because I don't want you to go with him. I don't like him."

One emotion rose to the top from the messy pool swirling within her.

"What the hell, Caleb? Who put you in charge of my life?"

The dreamy haze of their kiss dissolved as she lashed out, thinking of Kay's lies about Gus, and how rude Cammie had been to Gus earlier tonight. What was wrong with people?

He crossed his arms over his chest. "You shouldn't go with him."

"But…but you didn't even *ask* me to go the dance! You just made the decision for me because you don't like him! And it's totally the opposite of our plan, Caleb."

His eyes narrowed. "So you still want to go with him? Even after…" He grimaced, and she knew he was referring to the kissing.

She flushed, embarrassed. He was right—how could she kiss him like that and still want Gus? Because of this stupid fake thing, that's why. Because she'd lost sight of what was real and what wasn't.

She made herself look into his eyes. "I'm not going to the dance with someone who didn't even *ask* me."

He stared at her long and hard. "Fine. I think we should give up our stupid plan."

That felt like a slap. So apparently all the kissing *was* fake for him. Just something he did when he had a girl alone in her bedroom, a girl who lost all functioning brain cells once his lips touched hers.

"I think you're right. It was always a dumb idea." She tossed her hair over her shoulders, determined not to show how hurt she was. "Guess you're stuck with your stalker."

He shrugged. "Nope. She got *closure*, just like you said. She's not gonna be an issue anymore."

"Perfect," she said, baring her teeth in what she hoped was an I'm-done-with-you smile. "Then we're done."

They glared at each other, and Mandy's mind reeled, wondering how they'd gone from another snow globe night to that toe-curling kissing to *this*.

Because it's not meant to be. Because the universe doesn't support fake relationships.

"I'll let myself out." He turned and stalked out of her room.

When she heard the front door close, she sank onto her bed and curled up in a ball, trying to make sense of what had just happened, because the hole in her heart definitely felt real, not fake.

Chapter Nineteen
Please, Please, Please Let Me Get What I Want

Wednesday, September 28

Caleb watched the cheerleaders swarm Mandy's locker the next day, shooting him dagger eyes. Word of their fake breakup had spread like wildfire. Today might be a good day to ditch, because he sure as hell didn't want to be here dealing with this crap.

"Dude," J.T. said, sidling up to him. "What the hell? I thought you were moving in for the kill, not trashing everything."

Caleb slammed his locker shut and glared at J.T. "You can leave me alone now, Blue Ranger. The fake gig is over."

J.T. ignored him, keeping pace as they moved down the hall, past Mandy's locker and the escalating whispers as they passed.

"Just tell me this," J.T. said. "Who dumped who?"

Caleb hesitated, trying to recall the argument. "Uh...I

think it was mutual." Wasn't it? They'd both been pissed off. It had been crazy, after that hot-as-hell kiss. He still couldn't believe things had derailed so fast.

"Was it because you didn't do a prom-posal for homecoming? Dude, that's like *mandatory*."

They'd reached their Spanish classroom. It was weird how many classes they shared. He hadn't really noticed before.

"No," Caleb growled. That wasn't it, was it? She'd been angry that he hadn't asked her, that he'd just told Gus they were going. "I was trying to protect her. Gus asked me if we were going to homecoming together, so I said we were. So that he wouldn't ask her."

They found seats in the back of class, and J.T. shook his head in disgust. "You should've asked her *first*, Red Ranger. Done the prom-posal thing and swept her off her feet. She totally would have said yes and Gus would've backed the hell off."

Caleb shot him a glare. "I panicked, okay?"

J.T. smirked at him, then glanced at their teacher, who was focusing on the girl in the front row who didn't know the difference between *saltar* and *soltar*. Caleb definitely knew the difference, because *soltar* meant to let go, something he was apparently struggling with.

J.T. leaned sideways out of his chair and whispered, "Was there more kissing? Between the panicking and the breakup?"

Caleb stared into his crazy green and blue eyes. Freaking wingman. "Yeah," he muttered. "But it didn't matter."

J.T. sat up straight in his chair when their teacher darted a suspicious glance in their direction. "Kissing always matters," he said out of the corner of his mouth. "Trust me."

A few minutes later, a piece of paper landed on Caleb's desk. He sighed and rolled his eyes, then unfolded the note.

Prom-posal Making 101. My house. Saturday. 2:00.

You still have time to save your ass. And hers.

No way. He and Mandy were done. He drew a huge *X* through J.T.'s words and tossed it back. He heard J.T.'s disgusted snort but refused to make eye contact with the Blue Ranger.

He wasn't just done with Mandy, he was done with her posse, too. It was time to work on his *soltar* moves, and let go.

• • •

Mandy felt like she was sleepwalking through her day. She heard the whispered remarks and felt the stares as everyone speculated as to why she and Caleb had broken up. *Fake* broken up, she reminded herself.

At lunch, she ate by herself under a tree by the soccer field, ignoring Cammie's and J.T.'s worried text messages. She needed to regroup, to center herself. She ate her sandwich and apple, not even tasting the food.

"Hey. You okay?"

She turned, shocked to find her brother staring down at her.

"Yeah," she finally said, staring at him as if he was a mirage.

Reg sat on the grass next to her and grabbed her bag of chips, briefly reminding her of Caleb's food-stealing. But she didn't want to think about Caleb right now.

"I heard about you and Torres. Sorry. Want me to beat him up?" Reg tore open the bag of chips and dumped half the bag into his mouth.

She smiled, almost cheered up by his ridiculous offer. "Violence is never—"

"...the answer. I know." He chewed and swallowed, then frowned at her. "For real, Mandy. You sure you're okay?"

She was so touched by his concern that she wanted to hug

him, but she knew it would totally shatter the moment. "I'm fine. Actually, *I* broke up with him." She had, hadn't she? It was hard to remember exactly who had done the dumping. They'd both been upset.

Reg tilted his head, looking like a confused puppy. "Really? Wow. Didn't expect that." His expression morphed to a glare. "Did he try to, you know... Because I will totally kick his ass if—"

"No!" Mandy didn't want Reg getting the wrong idea, not like everyone had about Gus. That was totally unfair. "We just...I don't know..." No way could she tell him about the fake deal.

She thought about the kiss in her bedroom again, that kiss that had practically merged her soul with his...until he'd confessed his idiot move with Gus. She sighed. She'd definitely miss the kissing. And the bickering. The teasing. And that sweet side of him that nobody else saw.

"Shit," Reg said. "You're about to cry, aren't you?"

She blinked, surprised to realize he was right. She swiped at the tears. Damn it, this was ridiculous. None of it had been real. *None* of it. Except maybe the tutoring. And that day in the park when they talked about their moms. And maybe the kissing?

"I don't want to talk about it anymore."

"Okay, whatever you want." Reg grabbed her water bottle and took a swig. "Hey, Dad texted me that Gran needs to get into the doc. Want me to set up the appointment and take her? I know you'll be slammed with Spirit Week crap."

Her mouth dropped open. Had somebody switched out Reg with a pod person overnight?

He scowled. "Don't look at me like that. I'm not a total loser."

"That'd be...fantastic, Reg. Really. Thank you."

"Sure." He shrugged and stood up. "Let me know if

you change your mind about Torrs. He's bigger than me but I could probably land one punch before he destroyed me." He grinned, reminding her of the brother she used to know, and warm fuzziness unfurled inside her, chasing away her confusion and sadness about Caleb.

"You're not a loser, Reg," she said, meaning every word.

"Not all the time," he said, then he flipped her a salute and sauntered away, leaving her to ponder a lot of things... like what was real, what was fake, and how people could change in surprising ways.

The universe is full of surprises.

• • •

Caleb decided to ditch calc, even though he was falling behind in that class. Whatever. He needed to be by himself and write, what he always did when he ditched. He remembered how he'd laughed when Mandy had asked if he did something illegal when he ditched. He shook his head to chase away the memory. He stalked across the parking lot, anxious to get the hell away from the same place Mandy was.

He was almost to his car when he saw them—Gus and some girl wound around each other so tightly they looked like one person. His fists clenched as he stared at them. He should take a picture with his phone, so Mandy would believe that Gus was a player. He thought of J.T.'s and Cammie's recon and wondered if the girl was as on board with the escalating dry humping as Gus obviously was.

Shit. He didn't want to get in the middle of this, but if Gus was—

The girl's laughter skittered through the air as she tilted her head back, giving Gus access to the shirt he'd tugged out from her short skirt, his hands moving deftly underneath the fabric.

Okay, whatever was happening over there was *definitely* mutual. He huffed out a relieved sigh as he opened his car and slid inside. He started the engine, watching Gus and the girl through the windshield.

The realization hit him like a punch—maybe this meant that Gus wasn't into Mandy, after all. He was shocked at the bolt of relief that shot through him, at the upsurge of…of… crap, was he actually feeling…hopeful?

He closed his eyes, and a kaleidoscope of images swirled through his mind—Mandy teasing him, arguing with him about her essay, holding his hand on the bench when he told her about his mom.

Kissing him like her life depended on it.

What he felt for her…it wasn't fake. Not even close. He pulled out his phone and sent the text before he could wimp out.

2:00 Saturday. Your house.

J.T.'s reply flew back.

You're on, Red Ranger. Bring peanut M&M's cuz Blue Rangers don't work for free.

Caleb tossed his phone into the passenger seat, smiling. As he reversed out of the parking space, he told himself that he didn't care what the hell Gus was up to as long as he stayed the hell away from Mandy.

Chapter Twenty
I Want You Back

Saturday, October 1

Caleb sat at J.T.'s kitchen table drinking soda and eating popcorn while J.T.'s little sister danced around them, holding a poster covered with glitter and rainbows, and surprisingly decent printing that spelled out, GO TO PROM WITH ME!

Mandy would love it.

"Nice, Mira," J.T. said, "but Caleb needs to go big or go home, so we're working on some other ideas here. Maybe you could go watch a movie or something."

Caleb smirked as he watched J.T. try to rein in his irritation with his little sister. Mira was a cute kid, and she was freaking giddy about the whole prom-posal thing.

"But I helped you with one of Liam's posters," she protested. "I did the glitter and it was my idea to say 'Liam, L I AM Yours.'"

Caleb cocked an eyebrow. "That was you? Give me some skin, Mira." He held up a hand to high-five her. "Excellent wordplay." She high-fived him, giggling and blushing, and J.T. shot a rubber band at him.

"Dude. Not with my sister. Save your flirting for Mandy."

"I'm not *flirting* with your little sister. I'm acknowledging a fellow wordsmith."

Mira giggled again, twirled in a circle, and ran out of the kitchen, still carrying her poster.

J.T. sighed, running a hand through his crazy blond hair. "We need to focus, Red Ranger." He tore a page from his notebook and started writing. "Top three prom-posal criteria: one—it has to be personal, ideally something only you two would get. Like a secret joke or some special memory only you two know about." J.T. cocked an eyebrow. "And keep it PG-13 since you're doing this at school."

Caleb scrubbed a hand down his face, wondering if this whole thing was a big mistake. He didn't do big gestures or make scenes. It went against everything he believed in. He sighed and met J.T.'s steady gaze. "Whose criteria are these, anyway? Some girlie prom magazine?"

J.T. snorted and shook his head. "My criteria. And I know what the hell I'm doing, so pay attention." J.T. grabbed a handful of M&M's from the bag Caleb had brought. "So do you have any special memories? Secret jokes only you two would get?"

Caleb stared at the cluttered kitchen table, focusing on the salt and pepper shakers. Special memories? Secret jokes? The time at the park wasn't something he could use in a prom-posal, and besides it was something he wanted to keep between them. He met J.T.'s narrowed stare.

"Other than the big secret of our entire relationship being fake, you mean?"

J.T. rolled his eyes. "But it wasn't fake. Irony, man—you could write a paper on it." J.T. doodled on the notebook page. "Maybe you could work something in, like 'I was never faking with you, babe.'" His eyebrows danced suggestively.

"No," Caleb growled. "That's pathetic."

"Okay." J.T. shrugged. "We'll think about that one later and move on to the next criterion: it has to be unique. You see all those guys showing up with cupcakes or flowers and a stupid sign asking girls to go with them? Total amateurs." J.T. leaned back in his chair, looking smug. "Let's use my outstanding prom-posal for Liam as our example."

Caleb snorted. "Ego much, Blue Ranger?"

"Just working what I've got, Red Ranger, and I've got mad prom-posal skills." He rubbed his chin. "Actually, my overall boyfriend skills are outstanding. You could learn a few things."

"I don't think so." Caleb reached for a handful of M&M's. "I haven't had many complaints."

J.T.'s eyebrows shot up. "Uh, except that your most recent ex is in *therapy*, dude."

Caleb squirmed on his chair. "That's an aberration."

"Maybe. She did seem to have an excessive amount of baggage, based on that parking lot meltdown. And a penchant for drama."

"I hate drama," Caleb said. "Which is why it's gonna kill me to do this stupid—"

"Prom-posals are not stupid, okay? Just get that through your thick skull. They're a tangible way to express all the feelings that guys don't usually know how to express."

Caleb shook his head. "No. They're a competition to show up other guys. And pretentious. Totally unnecessary."

They glared at each other as Caleb thought of all the stupid and over-the-top "asks" he'd seen over the past couple of weeks: the guy who'd brought a pizza to his girlfriend with a note in the lid that said, "I know it's cheesy but my heart will be sliced in two if you don't come to homecoming with me."

The golf team asshole who'd filled a girl's locker with golf balls and left a sign that said, "It took all my balls to ask — will you go to homecoming with me?"

There'd even been a few literary ones: the guy who'd made a sign asking, "Will you be the Daisy to my Gatsby?" and another poster with the *Fault in Our Stars* quote about falling in love slowly then all at once. The poster said, "Come to homecoming with me? Okay? Okay."

And the worst one: a guy who'd lain on the parking lot with a chalk outline drawn around himself and a chalk message that said, "I'll die if you don't come with me to homecoming." Probably the perfect match for Elle.

Caleb squeezed his pencil, wondering how he'd gotten *here* — sitting with his childhood best friend and arguing about the worthiness of prom-posals.

God, he hated high school.

"Back to my example," J.T. said. "If you recall, in addition to the Liam wordplay on the first poster, I also did a nerd box of love on the big ask day. Sort of a nerd-o-gram, if you will."

Caleb groaned, wondering if maybe they should settle this debate with an old-fashioned Power Rangers beatdown. "You still have that Power Rangers Blaster gun? Because I sort of want to shoot you right now."

J.T. grinned. "It's in the special memories box my mom keeps. She's got all kinds of weird stuff in there, like my Tickle Me Elmo doll, Power Rangers toys, Thomas the Tank Engine stuff…"

Caleb's shoulders tensed, and it took him a minute to realize why. He had no idea if his mom had ever started a memory box for him. And he'd probably never know, since she'd apparently forgotten he existed.

"Hey…sorry," J.T. said, the humor gone from his voice. "I wasn't thinking…"

"Whatever. It doesn't matter." He exhaled, forcing the tension out of his muscles. "So, the nerd-o-gram. That was the personal part? Not generic?"

J.T. nodded, looking relieved to be off the topic of moms. "Yeah. I made a box that looked like the Death Star. Not easy making a round container, but I did it. Then I stuffed it full of comic books and Lego Star Wars guys. And then of course, the pièce de résistance: moi."

Caleb stared at him, torn between confusion and the desire to laugh. "You?"

"Yeah. Me. Dressed as Darth Vader. With a sign that said, 'I can't Force you to say yes, but I'll stay on the Dark Side if you don't come with me to homecoming.'"

Caleb couldn't hold back his laughter anymore. "How the hell did I miss *that*?"

J.T. shrugged. "I did it at lunch, outside, when you were hiding out in your corner of darkness in the caf." He grabbed another handful of M&M's. "Before we started hanging out."

Caleb nodded, thinking of all the stuff he'd missed hiding out in his corner. "So Liam's a nerd."

"You'd better not be insulting my boyfriend."

"Just stating prom-posal facts. Nothing wrong with nerds." Caleb took a drink from his soda. "What's the third criterion?"

J.T. rubbed his hands together. "It has to be un-rejectable."

"That's not even a word."

"But you get what I mean. She, or he, has to be so wowed that they'll say yes. No possibility of rejection."

Caleb sighed. "This whole thing is bullshit." He glanced at J.T., who was puffed up and ready to go all Blue Ranger on his ass. "Not bullshit for everyone. For you, it's great. For a lot of people it works. But not me."

J.T. narrowed his eyes. "So after your big screwup, you think you can just walk up to Mandy and ask her to homecoming and she'll say yes? No prom-posal at all? Like it's the 1970s or something?"

And suddenly it clicked in his head. If he had to do this stupid thing, and apparently he did, that was exactly what to do: a 1970s theme. He glanced at J.T., whose eyes widened like he'd just read Caleb's thoughts.

"*Dude*," J.T. gasped, looking like an excited little kid.

"*Dude*," Caleb growled. "Chill. We're not going crazy with this. Maybe just a few things from the seventies but—"

J.T. jumped up from the table, sending M&M's scattering across the table and onto the floor. "Come on, Red Ranger. Time to power up."

The Party It Up store was Caleb's worst nightmare, next to the Build-a-Buddy store. He froze in the lobby, overwhelmed by the riot of colors and the obnoxious eighties music floating through the store. He sighed as J.T. tugged on his jacket sleeve. Mandy probably loved this place.

"Disco aisle, here we come," J.T. chirped. He grabbed a cart, got a running start, and hopped on the back, riding it like a scooter and pissing off the moms who yanked their toddlers out of his way. Caleb followed him, shrugging apologetically to the scowling moms. If he survived this day without killing the Blue Ranger it would be a miracle.

The disco aisle reminded Caleb of Mandy's bedroom, which made him think of that kiss and the subsequent argument that had led to this insanity. He surveyed the fluorescent and shimmering party supplies hanging in the aisle and decided that if this stupid prom-posal meant he got to kiss Mandy again, for *real*, it would all be worth it.

"Look at this!" J.T. exclaimed, holding up a portable, spinning disco ball. "You should get it."

"She already has one in her bedroom."

J.T.'s eyes narrowed. "You've been in her *bedroom*? When

the hell did that happen?"

Caleb contemplated saying something dirty, but decided he couldn't risk pissing off his wingman by yanking his chain. "I gave her a ride home that night her gran was sick."

"Yeah." J.T. nodded. "But I still don't see how that ends up with you two in her room."

"She wanted to show it to me." Caleb smirked. Maybe a little chain-pulling was okay among friends. "Nothing happened. Well, okay, *something* did but not what you're thinking."

J.T. put the disco ball back on the shelf. "That was the night you blew it, right?"

Caleb sighed. "Yeah. Don't rub it in."

"I'm not. Just assembling prom-posal facts." J.T. studied him closely. "First you sloppy-kissed her, then you told her about how you screwed up with Gus."

"I am *not* a sloppy kisser."

"That's not what she says."

An older lady who'd started down their aisle shot Caleb an amused glance, then hurried past them, laughing softly to herself. Caleb wished he could light the whole store on fire.

J.T. grinned and tossed him a package of "disco fever" buttons that said stuff like *Boogie Down, Disco Diva, Can You Dig It*, and *Funky Town*.

Caleb tossed the buttons back to J.T. "No way."

"Go big or go home, Red Ranger. Picture yourself covered in these buttons." J.T. glanced back at the spindles of party supplies and yanked off a rainbow Afro wig with muttonchop sideburns. "And this." He chucked it at Caleb, laughing, then turned back to the shelf and gasped, yanking a package off the shelf.

"This!" He spun toward Caleb, gesturing like a game show host to the package displaying a guy wearing white disco suit, one hand pointed in the air in a stupid dance pose.

"You. Have. To."

"Never." Caleb lunged for the package, but J.T. was faster, backing up and holding it over his head.

"This is it, Red Ranger. If I can dress like Darth Vader, you can do Travolta." J.T. grinned maniacally. "I'll even teach you the Hustle. You know she loves to dance."

Everything in Caleb wanted to yell or hit something and get the hell out of this crazy store. But instead he took a long breath and stared down J.T. "You think I'm going to wear that fucking suit? And do a disco dance in front of everyone?"

J.T nodded enthusiastically. "Un-re-*jectable*. Trust me."

"I'd rather…rather…" He couldn't think of anything worse than what J.T. was suggesting.

J.T. grabbed two pairs of fake rhinestone-studded glasses like Elton John used to wear and tossed them in the cart. "Those are for Liam and me." He crossed his arms over his chest, looking smug. "Dude. You pull this off and it will go down in history as the best prom-posal Sky Ridge High has ever seen."

"If I do this…and that's a big *if*…I'm doing it where no one else can see it."

J.T.'s mouth opened in surprise. "But the public display is half the fun! Then she gets bragging rights with everyone telling her how awesome it was and how lucky she is that you did such a kick-ass prom-posal."

Caleb squinted. "Seriously?"

"Dude, have you been paying at attention *at all* the past three years? Or do you just sit in that dark corner and tune out everything?"

Instead of pissing him off, that almost made him laugh. "Pretty much tuning it out."

J.T. shook his head. "Well, maybe it's time you tune in, Red Ranger."

Caleb's sigh was long and loud, but he grabbed a disco

ball necklace off a rack, thinking how much Mandy would like it. Maybe his wingman was right, and it was time to tune in.

"I don't like dancing," Caleb growled, but he took the stupid white suit from J.T. and tossed it into the cart, along with the necklace.

J.T. did a victory fist pump. "Don't worry. I'll teach you the steps and you only have to do it once. Well…maybe twice, because once she sees you can do the Hustle she'll want to do it at homecoming, too."

Caleb squeezed his eyes shut, hoping to make everything fade to black, but instead all he saw was a rainbow of colors: Mandy's laughing face framed by her red hair, her sparking green eyes when they argued, those same eyes wide with sadness when he told her about his mom, and the glow bouncing off her that day in the coffee shop when they'd finished the rough draft.

He opened his eyes. "One dance, Blue Ranger. That's it."

"Deal."

Chapter Twenty-One
No More Mr. Nice Guy

Monday, October 3

Mandy surveyed the spirit committee members as they scattered down the hall with their boxes and bags of items to hide for the scavenger hunt. She'd assigned people different areas of the school, and they had exactly thirty minutes before the bell rang and the madness began.

She brushed hair out of her eyes and sighed with relief. Everyone had shown up ready to work, even…Caleb. She'd been shocked when he walked into the caf with J.T., where the committee had huddled before dispersing to hide the items. He'd barely glanced at her, instead focusing on J.T., who'd shot her his most obnoxious smile.

"*Interesting*," Cammie had whispered in her ear, making the word sound dirty as she stared pointedly at Caleb.

"Not interesting," Mandy had snapped in reply.

Cammie had rolled her eyes. "I don't think he's here because he's suddenly turned into a spirit freak."

Mandy had ignored Cammie and focused on her instructions, dividing people into groups and telling them what areas of the school to cover. J.T. and Caleb were in a group with Amber, Leticia, and Tonia. Mandy's stomach clenched as Amber cozied up to Caleb and he didn't exactly push her way. He smiled down at Amber as she chattered at him, hands fluttering, and Mandy felt like a steamroller had crushed her flat.

It doesn't matter, she told herself. She and Caleb were over. They hadn't really even been a couple in the first place, not really.

She took a long drink of the giant mocha she'd bought on the way to school. She was exhausted because she'd stayed up late finishing her stupid *Catcher in the Rye* essay that was due today. It had been a struggle to focus on the essay and not think about Caleb and all the time he'd spent helping her with it.

Part of her wanted to let him know she'd finished and was turning it in to Spriggs today, but another part of her—the part who'd watched him smile at Amber—wanted to dump her mocha on his head.

"Violence is never the answer," she whispered aloud, then stood up straight. She needed to focus. Today was the kickoff to Spirit Week, and she had to be in top form, not distracted by broody demons.

Besides, Gus had texted her last night asking her to lunch today. That was something positive to focus on. She wasn't sure if it was a "just friends" invite or something more, but either way she'd rather spend time with a nice guy than His Broodiness.

Just keep telling yourself that…

Oh, shut up, universe.

• • •

Caleb and J.T. stashed all kinds of junk around their assigned area of the school: clackers, mood rings, a retro Six Million Dollar Man doll, troll dolls with orange hair, and psychedelic unicorn stickers. Mandy had outdone herself pulling all the items together, just like she'd wrangled the committee this morning, getting people to actually shut up and listen to her, and making them laugh.

She was a kick-ass leader. He wanted to tell her that maybe being ADHD had good side effects—stuff she wasn't even aware of, like being able to multitask and keep the big picture in mind, too.

Maybe he'd have the chance, if this stupid prom-posal thing actually worked. Amber, the blond cheerleader, was pressuring him to do it today at lunch, since his lousy sidekick had outed him and told the cheerleaders that Caleb's prom-posal was going to be epic.

"Finally!" Amber had chattered at him while they waited for Mandy's assignments in the caf. "I knew you two would get back together. You're like, destined for each other. A prom-posal is the perfect way to do it."

He'd smiled instead of blowing her off because even though she was kind of ditzy, she liked Mandy and she didn't treat *him* like he was…unworthy or whatever.

After stashing the Six Million Dollar Man in the tampon dispenser in the girls' bathroom, Caleb and J.T. emerged into the hall, laughing together and high-fiving.

"Mr. Torrs. Mr. McIntire." Dr. Harris said, eyebrows raised. "I see you've been busy."

They froze, and Caleb hoped she didn't decide to inspect the girls' bathroom, because in addition to the Tampon Man, they'd taped troll dolls on all of the toilet paper dispensers.

"Yeah," J.T. said. "Very busy. Should be a great scavenger hunt."

She patted her helmet hair and glanced at Caleb. "It's

good seeing you participate, Mr. Torrs. Keep up the good work."

Dr. Harris nodded and started to walk away, then turned back, gesturing to her ears. "I found these disco ball earrings in my office. Did you put them there?"

How had he missed the spinning silver orbs dangling from her ears? He tried to hide his smirk.

"Not me." He glanced at J.T., who was grinning.

"Suck-up," Caleb muttered under his breath.

"You know it," J.T. mumbled, keeping that stupid grin plastered on his face.

As soon as she was out of sight, J.T. spun toward him. "Lunch. Prom-posal. You ready?"

Caleb sighed and stared at his boots. He'd left the poster and costume in his car. If he went through with this—still a big if—he'd grab the stuff right before lunch and change in the bathroom. And beat the crap out of anyone who dared to mock his outfit.

"We'll make sure that Mandy's in the caf at your table."

"She's not gonna want to sit there."

"Whatever," J.T. scoffed. "I'll make it happen."

"I'm never gonna live this down," Caleb said with a scowl.

"Probably not," J.T. agreed. "But it'll be worth it."

• • •

Gus met Mandy at her locker right before lunch, smiling his dopey sweet smile and brushing his hand through his curls. "Hi," he said. "Where do you want to go?"

She shrugged, shoving her books in the locker and slamming it shut. "I don't care. Somewhere not here."

He grinned. "I can do that."

They walked down the hall together, and Mandy caught Kay glaring at them, or at Gus anyway, and Elle giving her a curious look.

Whatever. She pulled her crocheted sweater tight, like she could block out other people's judgments.

"So the scavenger hunt was great," Gus said. "I found a Pet Rock in the guys' bathroom. Those things are so weird. I can't believe people actually paid money for them."

Mandy smiled as they headed toward the doors to the parking lot. Her mom had a Pet Rock, still in its original box, complete with care instructions. Totally weird, but it seemed to fit with all the other funny stuff from the seventies her mom had told her about.

"Mandy! Stop!" She froze at the sound of J.T.'s panicked voice, then turned to find him running down the hall looking frantic. "Where are you going?" He glared at Gus. "She's already got lunch plans."

"No, I don't," she said, annoyed. "Gus and I are going to lunch."

J.T. looked wild-eyed. "But you can't. We have a…a thing to do! You need to come with me to the caf right now."

This had gone from annoying to pissing her off. She wasn't in the mood for J.T.'s bossiness today. "J.T., what are you talking about? We don't have any plans. I'll see you after lunch, but right now I'm going with Gus."

Gus stepped closer, putting an arm around her shoulders. "She's right, J.T. Take a chill pill and we'll see you later."

J.T. looked furious, which made no sense, but she was so distracted by Gus's arm around her shoulders she was having a hard time focusing on J.T. So maybe this wasn't a just-friends lunch? She wasn't sure how she felt about that, but it was weird, almost like she was being disloyal to Caleb, which was stupid. Her phone buzzed in her jeans pocket, and she pulled it out.

Caf. ASAP.

Cammie. What was going on? Why was everyone acting so weird?

Gus pulled her toward the exit, his grip tightening around her shoulders. "Later, J.T." He pushed through the door, tugging Mandy along next to him.

"Wait." She blinked in the bright sunshine as they stood on the steps. "Maybe I should check to make sure everything's okay."

Gus dropped his arm from her shoulders and rolled his eyes. "It's fine. J.T.'s just being possessive. I told you he doesn't like me much anymore." His face crumpled, looking like a little boy who'd just lost his favorite toy. "Come on, Mandy. I really need a friend today."

She hesitated briefly, then put her hand on the railing and took a step down. She'd turned her paper in to Spriggs first thing, darting into his classroom before going to her homeroom, eager to get the essay out of her binder. She should celebrate turning the paper in, and she could do that with Gus.

Not Caleb, even though it was because of him she thought she had a shot at getting a decent grade, for once.

• • •

Caleb stood in the guys' bathroom, staring at the costume still in the package. J.T. had told him to take it out and iron it last night, but he'd refused. He had to maintain *some* dignity.

The door burst open and J.T. flew inside, eyes wide and hair sticking up. "Mayday, Red Ranger!"

Caleb frowned at him. "What the hell, dude? I don't need a hair and makeup guy."

J.T. blinked and almost smiled. "Actually, not a bad idea. But we have more important things to worry about. Do not put on that costume."

"Best idea you've ever had," Caleb said, then his gut clenched. "Why not?"

J.T. swallowed and started peeking in the stalls.

"I already checked. No one's here."

"Okay." J.T. nodded like he needed to bolster himself. "So the thing is…"

"She refuses to sit at my table, right? That's okay. I can do it…wherever, I guess."

J.T. bit his lip, looking agonized. "It's…worse than that. She just left campus for lunch."

Caleb frowned. "By herself?"

J.T. shook his head, and Caleb saw the answer in his eyes. "With *Gus*?"

Shit. He threw the costume on the floor. "I told you this was a stupid idea. I'm out of here." He pushed past J.T., out the door, and down the hallway.

Mandy was right. He belonged in his world, and she belonged in hers. He was done with this crap, all of it.

If she wanted the Octo-Gus, she could have him.

• • •

Gus and Mandy sat at a corner table in the fast-food restaurant, which was packed with other kids from school. She noticed one girl glaring daggers at them, a girl she didn't know. Maybe a sophomore? She glanced at Gus, who seemed oblivious as he dipped fries in ketchup.

"So," he said, "you and Torrs split, huh?"

Her hand holding a forkful of salad paused halfway to her mouth. "Yeah," she finally said, wondering when people would tire of the gossip and stop asking her about it. She'd fended off a lot of questions this morning, mostly from her cheer friends, who'd been sort of weird and giggly when they asked about it, asking if there wasn't a chance they'd get back together.

Gus shoved the fries in his mouth, reminding her of Reg and how gross he was sometimes. She frowned and refocused on her wilted salad.

"What's up with homecoming then?"

She felt her cheeks flame. He wasn't asking her, was he? Because if so, this was kind of a weird way to do it. She glanced up, meeting his blue-eyed gaze. He blinked, smiling innocently.

"I, uh, I don't know. Maybe I'll just…stay home."

He frowned. "You don't want to do that. You planned the dance, didn't you?"

She shrugged. "The seventies theme was my idea, but a whole lot of people planned it together." She hesitated. Maybe…maybe…it was a crazy idea, but what if she asked Gus? They were friends, and yeah she maybe sort of still had a crush on him, or…maybe not, but it would be better than going as a fifth wheel with J.T. and Cammie and their boyfriends.

"Are you…" she began, and cleared her throat, feeling shy. "Do you, um…"

He smiled in a way that made her heart speed up a tiny bit. Not nearly as much as with Caleb, but she couldn't think about him right now.

"I don't have a date either, not since Kay dumped me." His expression shifted, like he was remembering something really sad, and Mandy wanted to tell him it would be okay, that Kay was a jerk, but she didn't want to make him feel worse, so instead she just nodded.

"There should be a reject homecoming," Gus said, swirling his fry in his ketchup but not looking at her. "For losers like me." He glanced up. "Not you, I didn't mean that. Torrs was an idiot to break up with you."

Mandy blinked, feeling her cheeks heat. "He didn't, I

mean, it was…mutual, I guess."

Gus tilted his head, studying her. "Well, I always thought you were too good for him. He's kind of an asshole."

Mandy felt her whole body tense up. It was one thing for her to call Caleb an asshole, but hearing someone else say it, someone she thought of as a friend…it was weird. Even Cammie and J.T. hadn't done that thing where they totally took her side and rejected Caleb. Instead they were still hanging out with him, which confused her. And sort of pissed her off. And, oddly, made her a tiny bit happy, because he needed friends.

But what was she supposed to do with that? How could they all be friends together, if she and Caleb weren't dating? Fake dating. Whatever. And why weren't they being nice to Gus? They'd been friends with him long before Caleb. She frowned and stabbed her salad, wondering if they would turn on her one day, too.

"What would you do if someone asked you?" Gus asked, twirling his cup between his hands.

She glanced at him, trying to recall what they'd been talking about before her mind wandered down the rabbit hole of Caleb.

"To homecoming," he clarified. "What would you do if someone asked you? It's sort of last minute and everything, since it's Saturday. But what would you say?"

They stared at each other, and she wondered if he was saying what she thought he was. "I…don't know," she finally said, because it was true. "I guess it would depend on who it was."

Gus nodded and took a bite of his burger, chewing slowly, seeming to have lost interest in the conversation. Okay, maybe he wasn't sending her coded messages after all. She turned to stare out the window.

Staying home on Saturday was sounding better and better.

Chapter Twenty-Two
We Will Rock You

Tuesday, October 4

Caleb stood at his locker ready to bolt for the day when Spriggs approached him, eyes narrowed behind his wire-rimmed glasses.

"Mr. Torrs. I understand you helped Ms. Pennington with her *Catcher in the Rye* essay, is that correct?"

A flash of apprehension shot up Caleb's spine as he faced his teacher. "Yeah." He shrugged, wondering what this was about, then he realized the paper was due yesterday. His stomach knotted with worry for Mandy.

"I'd like you to come with me. I have a few questions for both of you."

"Now?" Caleb asked as the warning flames increased along his spine.

"Yes, now. Ms. Pennington is waiting in my classroom." He spun on his heel and stalked away, clearly expecting Caleb to follow.

Crap. This wasn't good. Maybe he'd been wrong to encourage Mandy to go ahead with her honest reader response. But that was bullshit, because Spriggs shouldn't penalize her for that. Caleb slammed his locker shut and followed Spriggs to his classroom, wondering what the hell he was supposed to do.

Mandy perched on a desk, her purple dress reminding him of a spring tulip. She tugged nervously at her mom's necklace, and Caleb wanted to cross the room to her. But he couldn't. Instead, he stared at her until she met his gaze, defiant and nervous, that crazy combination that did something to his gut. And his heart.

Spriggs moved behind the desk and grabbed the paper, holding it out like it was poisonous. Caleb saw a giant red "B–" circled on the top. Exactly what she needed. He shot her a questioning look, but now she was staring at the floor, biting her lip.

"All right, *children*," Spriggs said. "Tell me who really wrote this essay."

Anger shot through Caleb fast and hot, lighting him up like a missile needing a target.

"I did," Mandy said, her voice high and quivery.

Damn it. Caleb ground his teeth. She needed to sound tough, confident. She couldn't give this asshole any more room for doubt.

Spriggs turned his attention to Caleb. "Is this true, Caleb? I know you were…*tutoring* Ms. Pennington." He cocked an eyebrow. "You didn't write this for her? Granted it's not your usual style, but it's suspiciously coherent." He studied Mandy through narrowed eyes. "Quite unlike your usual work, Miss Pennington."

The missile of anger inside of Caleb threatened to ignite. It took every ounce of his self-control not to leap across the desk, but instead he breathed through his nose, fists clenched at his sides. He needed one of Mandy's stupid mantras but all he came up with was *Don't hurt your teacher.*

"I wrote it, Mr. Spriggs," Mandy said.

She sounded less wobbly now. In fact, she sounded almost as pissed as he felt. He shot her a sideways glance, and she met his gaze. For a long moment their eyes locked in unspoken conversation, and it was almost like their breakup never happened.

Don't go ballistic, demon.

I won't if you won't, Disco.

But I wrote the paper!

I know, babe. But we've gotta stay calm.

Mr. Spriggs snapped his fingers in Mandy's face and Caleb was seconds away from breaking his silent promise to Mandy.

"Prove it," Spriggs said.

Mandy blinked, refocusing on Spriggs while Caleb reminded himself Spriggs was *not* a punching bag.

"What?" she asked. "What do you mean, prove it?"

"I'm going to quiz you about the book." He shot Caleb a warning glare. "And you keep quiet, Mr. Torrs."

Shit. Caleb wished he could brain dump everything he knew about this book into Mandy's beautiful, spazzy squirrel brain, because Spriggs would do his damnedest to trip her up.

Mandy tugged at her crab necklace. "Um, okay. I—uh—go ahead. Ask me anything."

Caleb closed his eyes. He wasn't sure what deity he believed in, but for the first time in a long time he sent up a plea to whoever might be on duty.

. . .

Mandy's pulse pounded in her ears. She knew she hadn't cheated, but with Spriggs challenging her she felt guilty anyway. She glanced at Caleb, shocked to see how worried he looked.

She turned away, because she needed to focus on Spriggs, not Caleb. *I can do this. The universe supports truth, justice, and the American way.* Wait, what? She shook her head slightly to force herself to focus.

Spriggs leaned against his desk. "In your essay, you took issue with Holden Caulfield's treatment of women. But how do you justify that statement when he loves his sister so much?"

Relief washed over Mandy. This was the main reason she hated the book, and she could rant about it forever if she had to. She and Caleb had debated it hotly that day in the coffee shop.

"Phoebe was the only female he treated decently!" she exclaimed. "He's horrible to everyone else. He lies to that mom on the subway, telling her that her son is so popular at school when really everyone hates him. And when he goes to that nightclub and dances with those women from out of town? All he talks about is how ugly and stupid they are!"

Mr. Spriggs's face pinched with a frown. "One could argue that—" he began, but Mandy cut him off, her confidence quickly overtaking her anxiety.

"And he takes Sally on a date but complains about her the whole time! How her voice sounds, how phony she is, how stupid. He only asks her out because she's pretty and he wants to, uh, kiss her or whatever. He doesn't respect her at all."

"What about the little girl in the park?" Mr. Spriggs snapped.

Mandy frowned, trying to recall the scene. "Oh, when he's looking for his sister? And he helps the girl with her skates? What, like he deserves a medal for being nice one time?"

She glanced at Caleb, who gave her a thumbs-up, his lips curving into the smirk she loved. God, she wanted to…to… she couldn't think about what she wanted because now wasn't the time.

Mr. Spriggs didn't look happy. "Did you notice any other times he was nice to children?"

Mandy sighed. "Like when he showed those boys the mummies in the museum? Or when he tried to erase the graffiti at Phoebe's school so the kids wouldn't be scarred for life by an f-bomb?"

Caleb snorted, and Spriggs shot him a glare.

"And the little boy singing the song, the one the title's based on." Mandy was so fired up she wasn't nervous at all anymore. "I know what you want me to say. That Holden was good to little kids, that they were innocent and he thought he was their protector. That he was still devastated by his brother's death."

Spriggs sighed. "So why didn't you put any of that in your essay?" He shook his head. "So unfocused. An undisciplined mind," he muttered.

"Because those parts weren't enough for me to love this stupid book!" She glanced at Caleb again, but this time he frowned, giving her a subtle thumbs-down. "He's still awful to girls, and he calls gay guys perverts and flits, and he's so condescending! He thinks everyone who goes to the movies is an idiot! He makes fun of his brother because he's a screenwriter instead of writing books nobody wants to read, nobody but Holden."

Spriggs scowled, and Mandy guessed he had his own unfinished great American novel stashed in a drawer somewhere.

"I think you've missed most of the point of this novel, Ms. Pennington."

Mandy felt like her head was about to explode. "Then why did you give me a B minus?"

"Because your response to the book, while wrong, was typical for today's modern reader, and you did manage to back up your…opinion…with examples from the book." He brushed imaginary lint from his shirt.

Caleb made a noise that didn't sound human.

"How can my response be wrong?" Mandy demanded. "How can anything a reader feels when reading a book be *wrong*? You can't force people to love a book just because you do!" She whirled on Caleb. "You tried to make me love the book, too, but it didn't work."

His head snapped back like she'd slapped him, and she was hit with a stab of guilt. That wasn't fair, not after all the time he'd spent helping her with her essay. She tugged at her hair and closed her eyes. Breathe. *All things work together for good.* Even bad things? she wanted to ask the universe, because suddenly things felt really bad—Spriggs questioning her intelligence, and her lashing out at Caleb when he'd shown up to back her up, even though they weren't…whatever… anymore.

Caleb cleared his throat. "Mandy wrote this paper herself. I just helped her with the structure. But all of the ideas—and they're solid ideas, by the way—those are hers." His lips curved in a crooked smile. "Just because she doesn't like the book doesn't mean she didn't *get* it."

She stared across the room, her gaze locking with his. She wanted to run to him, jump in his arms, have him twirl around while he kissed her, just like in a movie. But instead she took another breath and mouthed him a silent "thank you" instead. He tilted his head in acknowledgment, but his smile faded as he looked at Spriggs, who was scowling.

Mandy squared her shoulders and faced Spriggs head-on. She'd organized Spirit Week. She'd had a big role in planning the homecoming dance. She'd taken care of gran. She'd done a great job with the little kids at Build-a-Buddy. She could handle a crabby old teacher.

"Okay, so I'm *not* an honor student, Mr. Spriggs. But I

could be, if teachers like you gave me a chance. I read all the time, did you know that? Not the type of books you'd approve of, but still." *Some of them have big words and everything*, she thought, but she kept that part inside. She glanced at Caleb, whose eyes sparked—with admiration, she hoped—but she wasn't sure.

"A lot of people have ADHD—really successful people like Justin Timberlake and Michael Phelps. Will Smith." She paused, wondering if he was too old to get her references. "Einstein had dysgraphia, just like me." She shot Caleb a conspiratorial smile and held his gaze, remembering their late night text convos.

The fire of determination built inside her, banked and fueled by Spriggs's outraged expression. She wasn't scared. Not anymore, because none of it mattered when you did your best but people still didn't believe in you. She took a breath, deciding to go for broke.

"Mr. Spriggs—you have to give people a chance. Not just your star students like Caleb." She glanced at him and was momentarily stunned by the way he looked at her. She cleared her throat. "Give students like me a chance, too. Please. You act like it's our fault if we can't process the way *you* think we should. But our brains don't all work the same way. And that doesn't make us wrong. Or…or…lesser than."

Spriggs blinked, looking momentarily off balance. "I never—"

Caleb stepped away from the wall where he'd been leaning. "I think…" He hesitated, and Mandy watched him run his hand through his hair, his glorious rock star hair that she really, *really* wanted to touch again. "Look," he said, "it's obvious that Mandy wrote this paper, right? She just told you all about the book. She obviously read it, and her opinions are totally valid."

Mr. Spriggs narrowed his eyes behind his glasses. "Yes."

He pushed his glasses up his nose. "I'm convinced that she read the book." He glanced at her. "As for the rest of our discussion, I will take it under advisement."

Mandy glanced at Caleb, who shrugged, then winked, making her heart beat wildly against her rib cage.

"So...I still get a B minus?" she asked.

Mr. Spriggs sniffed. "Yes, Ms. Pennington. You're cleared for dance team participation. I'm sure the whole school will be delighted to see you at the helm of the pep rally this Friday."

Caleb shot across the room, grabbing her hand before she realized what was happening. "Thanks, Mr. Spriggs," he called over his shoulder, tugging Mandy out of the classroom.

She stumbled after him, thrilled at the sparks shooting up her arm from his warm touch. He tugged her down the hallway and into the dusty alcove, the same one where he'd kissed her senseless.

"You did it," he whispered, wrapping his arms around her waist. "You got a B minus, but even better you stood up to him." He pulled her in close. "And you didn't go all shit-storm on him like I would've."

"Firestorm," she corrected. "You would've lit him on fire."

He grinned down at her, and she held her breath, waiting, her eyes locked on his, her heart beating so fast he must be able to hear it. She watched his expression change, from happy to anxious to...something else. He released her and stepped back.

"Do you need a ride home?" he asked, but he kept glancing at the guys' restroom, like he had some sort of emergency she didn't want to know about.

She frowned. "Uh...no. Reg drove today so I can catch a ride with him." Reg had taken Gran to the doctor this morning, and reported back with a list of to-dos Gran wasn't happy about. Mandy had been so thrilled that Reg had followed through on his word, she'd ignored Gran's grumbling voicemail about idiot doctors.

He glanced at her, surprised. "Yeah? Okay, cool." He took a step back. "I'll, uh, see you tomorrow, Disco." Then he turned and rushed across the hall into the restroom.

Okay, that was weird. Totally weird.

Her mind still reeling from the meeting with Spriggs, and the hot and cold way Caleb was acting, Mandy texted her brother.

Be right there. She hesitated, then typed, *Got a B– from Spriggs. Off probation.*

Awesome. Fraps on me.

The universe continued to surprise her.

• • •

Where's the Travolta suit? It's not in the bathroom.

Simmer down, Red Ranger. I've got it.

Good. I need it for tomorrow.

You're gonna do it? Pull off the most epic prom-posal in history?

Yeah. But you'd better be there, Blue Ranger.

Never fear, Red Ranger. I live to serve. But I will need more M&M's.

Chapter Twenty-Three
You're the One that I Want

Wednesday, October 5

"You need to do it before school, in the parking lot," Cammie insisted.

"No," J.T. argued. "Lunch in the caf. Bigger audience because of the trivia contest today. Better acoustics for the music."

"We can do our cheer anywhere," Leticia said as Tonia and Amber bobbed their heads in agreement.

Caleb groaned, tilting his head back against his seat. The six of them were crammed in his car in the Starbucks parking lot. J.T. had rallied the troops last night, organizing everyone to meet before school and plan the prom-posal execution.

Not for the first time, Caleb wondered how the hell he'd gone from avoiding everyone to being the center of attention in this crazy posse. And why a freaking *cheer* was now part of the ridiculous plan.

"Did you text her last night?" J.T. asked, and Caleb

shrank against his seat as the girls laser-focused their heavily mascaraed eyes on him.

"Uh, no."

All of the eyes widened in shock, then narrowed suspiciously.

"Why the hell not?" Cammie demanded.

"Well...I..." Because there was so much he wanted to say, but he was waiting until today, until after she said yes. *If* she said yes...

"It's okay," J.T. said. "You showed up for her yesterday with Spriggs. I'm sure she's still feeling all gooey about that, so you should be good to go."

The cheerleaders side-eyed each other.

"What?" Caleb demanded, wondering what stupid rule he'd accidentally broken now.

Amber shrugged. "I strongly recommend daily communication with your girlfriend. In person, calls, texts, Snapchat, whatever." She narrowed her eyes again. "Don't ever skip a day."

Tonia and Leticia nodded. "Going dark is the same as breaking up," Tonia admonished.

Caleb glanced at J.T., who shrugged. "You know me. I've never skipped a day with Liam. Not even an hour."

"She's not my..." His words trailed away. She *had* been his girlfriend. Whether either of them acknowledged it or not, she had been. And this time he wanted to make it official. Real, not fake.

"Not at the moment," J.T. said, glancing at his phone. "But if all goes as planned, in exactly four hours she will be."

"I still say he should do it this morning," Cammie said. "Seal the deal and make it real."

"Aren't you the little poet?" J.T. smirked, and Cammie knocked him on the back of his head.

J.T. angled himself in the passenger seat to face Caleb,

then he grinned and shot his hands out, making a weird crossing and swirling motion with his arms that looked vaguely familiar, and yelled, "Dino Thunder! Power up! Ha!"

The girls collapsed into hysterical giggles while Caleb glared at him, trying not to smile. "You did not just—"

"Yeah, I did. Let's go, Red Ranger. Time to do this."

· · ·

Mandy yawned as she approached her locker. She'd tossed and turned last night, replaying her confrontation with Spriggs and her interaction with Caleb. When he'd dragged her to the trophy case, she'd thought maybe he was going to kiss her. That maybe they were going to pick up where they'd left off… only this time, it wouldn't be fake. But that hadn't happened.

As she approached her locker, she noticed people smiling and watching her curiously. Something was on her locker. Was that a poster? Her heart skipped a beat as she stepped closer and took in the block printing and the single red rose taped on the white cardboard.

"Will you go? Yes or No?"

Her pulse rate zoomed. Maybe Caleb had…she squinted her eyes, looking for a signature, something to indicate who this was from.

"Well, will you, Mandy? Yes or no?"

She spun around and came face-to-face with Gus.

"I…wow." She bit her lip and glanced at the poster again, her brain reluctantly processing that the poster was from Gus, not Caleb. It looked like he'd spent maybe five seconds making it. She thought of J.T.'s over-the-top nerdy prom-posal for Liam, and Jiro's super-romantic one for Cammie, where he'd made a trail of rose petals from his car to hers in the parking lot.

But that was different; they were in love, and she and

Gus definitely weren't. Not yet, anyway. Then again, what was wrong with going together as friends? They were both recovering from breakups so there wouldn't be any weird sexpectations, especially not from a nice guy like Gus, no matter what Kay said. They could have dinner together, maybe even at the Silk Lamp, then have fun at the dance. And who knew what might happen under the shimmering light of the disco balls?

"Okay," she said, straightening her spine. It was time to forget about Tall, Dark, and Broody, especially when a nice guy she'd crushed on forever had just asked her to homecoming. "Yes." She smiled tentatively, and Gus grinned in return, like he was genuinely happy she'd said yes. A few people standing around clapped and cheered, and she glanced down the hallway…and her heart stuttered.

Caleb and J.T. stood just a few feet away, staring at her, looking shell-shocked, along with Cammie and a group of her cheer friends, all of them looking like they wanted to kill Gus.

And maybe her, too.

She glanced at Gus and blinked, because for a second there he looked like a different person, his face briefly twisting in a smug, self-satisfied expression she didn't recognize. She blinked again and his normal smile was back; she must have imagined the other face.

"Cool. We'll finalize the deets later." He tilted his chin and swaggered away, leaving her feeling sort of…empty.

Not at all like a girl should feel after a prom-posal.

• • •

"Son of a bitch!" J.T. exclaimed as the girls burst into animated chatter. Caleb just stared. He couldn't take his eyes off Mandy, who stood looking at that pathetic poster, not moving.

"I will kill him," Cammie said. "Before the day's over, I'll wrap his—"

"No," J.T interrupted. "We need a plan B."

Caleb finally snapped out of his daze. "There is no plan B. She said yes. She got...what she wanted, I guess." Even though it all felt wrong and ugly and black inside him, he had to let this go. In a crazy way, they'd both ended up with what they wanted: Elle had stopped stalking him, and Mandy was going to the dance with Gus.

"You can't give up," J.T. protested. "She just said yes because of karma, and she's still got this ridiculous idea that poor Gus is being judged unfairly."

"No," Caleb growled. He glared at the posse. "Drop it. All of you."

Then he turned and stalked down the hall, wishing he'd never, ever given the redhead a ride home from that stupid party.

• • •

J.T. and Cammie cornered Mandy outside her first period classroom.

"What the hell were you thinking?" Cammie demanded while J.T. tugged fingers through his crazy hair.

"Worst prom-posal I've ever seen," J.T. crabbed. "Generic. Totally rejectable." He glared at her. "I'm disappointed in you, Mandy."

Frustration shot through her. "Easy for you guys to say! You're going with your boyfriends and you'll have an awesome time. I was either stuck going by myself, or fifth-wheeling with you or—"

"Or holding out for an awesome prom-posal," J.T. said, crossing his arms over his chest.

Mandy snorted. "Yeah, right. It's *Wednesday*, guys. The dance is in three days. I'm lucky to have a date at all. Lucky I even got a prom-posal."

Cammie cocked an eyebrow. "Better to go dateless with friends than on a date with an asshole."

Mandy put a hand up. "Stop. I don't want to hear any more about Gus or about us going to the dance together." She sighed. "Just give me a break, okay? I need to focus my energy on the trivia contest at lunch. We're ready to go, right?" She pinned J.T. with a stare, since he was in charge of the AV setup.

He glared at her, then blinked, his eyes widening, suddenly looking like he was hiding a smile. "Yep. We are *ready*." He nudged Cammie with his elbow. "I think it's going to be the best trivia contest ever. Full of surprises."

Cammie frowned at him, then mirrored his smirk. "Yeah. Possibly epic."

"See you at lunch, Mandy," J.T. said, dragging Cammie with him.

She watched them go, wondering what the heck they were up to. She sighed and walked into her classroom.

What a weird day, and it had hardly even begun.

• • •

"I'm not."

"You are."

"No."

"Yes."

"We'll all be there, dude. Don't panic."

Caleb clenched his pencil and stared straight ahead. Breaking up with an entire posse was gonna be tough, even tougher than getting rid of a stalker. It would be weird to sit by himself again at lunch, but it had to be that way. He didn't belong with them.

He turned toward J.T. and scowled. "Just forget the whole

thing. I don't need backup anymore, dude. You're released from Ranger duty."

J.T. frowned, looking five years old again. "You're breaking *up* with me?"

Caleb rolled his eyes as a couple of girls glanced at them, tittering.

"Don't be dramatic. I'm just… I need a break. From everyone." He tried to listen to Spriggs, who kept darting him suspicious looks, but honestly he didn't care about whatever book Spriggs was rambling out.

He didn't care about anything. Or anyone.

He was full of crap.

· · ·

Mandy ran through the trivia contest plan in her head instead of listening to her history lecture. She and J.T. were going to take turns calling out questions. Some of the spirit committee members were in charge of patrolling the caf and making sure no one was cheating by looking up answers on cells.

She'd hoped Caleb would be the main enforcer, but after they'd split, she hadn't asked him. Maybe she should've, since he'd helped with the scavenger hunt. He'd be a kick-ass enforcer, since he'd just have to glare at people and they'd drop their phones. She smiled at the image, then told herself she needed to stop imagining anything with Caleb.

She *should* focus on her homecoming date, now that she had one. She'd have to find out what Gus planned to wear. Hopefully he could still find something seventies-related. She'd take him to the thrift store tonight or tomorrow; they'd have to work fast.

Flipping to a blank page in her notebook, she drew a disco ball shooting out sparkling light in a darkened room. Her drawing wasn't great because of her dysgraphia, but she didn't care. She tried drawing herself in her mom's awesome green dress, but she ended up looking like a Q-tip with red flames for hair.

Trivia contest. *Focus.* She jotted notes on the page: Five questions each, from her and J.T. Tally the votes. Grand prize of *That '70s Show* on DVD for the winner. Small prizes of seventies candy like Pop Rocks and Laffy Taffy for the second- and third-place winners. Cammie was supposed to take photos since she was documenting Spirit Week for photojournalism class. She'd already taken a million pics of different prom-posals.

Mandy frowned, thinking of Gus's plain white poster that was so generic it could've been for anyone. Then she shook her head, telling herself that it actually had been sweet. When Gus had taken her to Burger King, he'd been sort of feeling her out to see if she was open to an invitation. Then he'd followed through.

Her phone buzzed with a text, and she sneaked it out of her pocket to read it.

Can I talk to U B4 lunch?

Gus. She really didn't have time since she had to get ready for the trivia contest, but he was her date, after all.

Sure.

Meet me at the north doors.

That was weird. Why couldn't he just meet her in the caf?

Okay.

• • •

If ever there was a day to ditch, today was it. Caleb headed to his car, not giving a crap who saw him leave. He'd drive up the highway, straight to the mountains. Hike some trail and maybe get lost. Get eaten by coyotes and leave his skeleton behind.

Okay, he needed to get a grip. Just because Mandy was going to homecoming with Gus, he didn't need to go all James Franco like in that movie where the guy had to cut his arm off to survive. It was just a stupid dance. Three weeks ago, he couldn't have cared less, but now after all the work they'd put in, it felt like a big deal. Caleb hated that. He was *not* supposed to be the type of guy who cared about a freaking school dance.

He was almost to his car when Elle appeared like a creepy ghost, swishing out from behind a stand of trees. The universe pretty much hated him today. He wondered what Mandy would have to say about his karma.

"Caleb, hold up."

He couldn't deal with this right now. "I'm in a hurry," he said through gritted teeth.

Elle hurried up to him, brushing her dark hair off her face. She didn't look as emo today. She almost looked…normal. "I bet you've had a shitty day. I heard about Mandy and Gus."

He glared at her. "Look, I know you're still mad at me, but you don't have to—"

"Stop right there." She put up her hand and met his glare with her own determined gaze. "I told you I'm working on closure, right? And I'm mostly there. One of my assignments is to do something that proves I'm over you. So that's what I'm doing."

He had no clue what she was talking about. He just knew he had to get away. He moved toward his car, but she blocked his way as he tried to open his door.

"You need to know something. Gus has a…a plan. He's

renting a hotel room. For homecoming night."

What the hell? Why was she telling him this? Octo-Gus. The word echoed in his mind like an echoing villain name from the *Power Rangers* show.

His fingers clenched around his key chain. "So?"

She blinked in surprise. "So I thought you'd want to know that he plans on spending the night with Mandy. Whether she wants to or not."

Fire ignited inside him, pulsing through his veins like hot lava. "What do you mean?"

Elle glanced around nervously, but they were the only ones in the parking lot. "He was bragging to some of the guys on the lacrosse team that he's going to get her drunk. Really drunk. So he can…you know…"

Caleb's fist slammed into the hood of his car, making a perfect fist-sized crater. The angry lava still scorched through his veins. He needed somewhere to erupt, and he knew exactly where. He turned back to the school, stalking across the parking lot. He didn't care if he got detention. Expelled. Whatever. The Octo-Gus was going down.

He cut around to the north doors, so he could sneak in without attracting attention from the security guards. He was almost running, fueled by his rage, and something else… something underneath the anger.

He'd think about that later.

• • •

Mandy hurried to the north doors, pushing her way through the lunch crowd. She'd texted J.T. and Cammie that she'd be there ASAP, and they'd given her major text grief but whatever.

She pushed through the door, the warm fall sunshine making her smile.

"Hey, gorgeous." Gus pushed off the railing where he'd been leaning.

"Oh. Hi." She shuffled nervously. This felt weird, meeting him here and him calling her "gorgeous."

He stepped close and twirled a strand of her hair around his finger. "We need to talk about homecoming."

"Okay. But can we do it later? I really need to get to the trivia contest." *And get your finger out of my hair*, she wanted to say, because somehow it didn't feel right.

"Yeah, yeah, I know." He stared down at her, his gaze intense. "I wanted to talk in person, not text. Tell your dad you're spending the night at Cammie's on Saturday, okay?"

She frowned. She probably *would* spend the night at Cammie's after the dance, but why did he care?

He stepped closer, his finger still twirling her hair. She reached up and grasped his wrist. "Please don't."

He looked surprised and irritated. "Come on, Mandy, it's not like we're strangers. And we're going to the dance now." He backed her against the brick wall. "I've got us a hotel room for Saturday night. So we can, you know...hang out. Just the two of us."

Her mouth opened in surprise, and goose bumps rose on her arms. Her mind swirled with faces: Cammie, Kay, her cheer friends, all of them saying the same thing: Octo-Gus... Octo-Gus...echoing in her mind like an echo from a cheesy movie.

"N-no," she finally managed. "That's not happening."

"Oh, it's happening. You. Me." He gripped her shoulders so tightly she winced, and all the innocent sweetness she'd associated with him vanished, replaced by something definitely not sweet. "Come on, Mandy. I know how you feel about me. Just think—we'll have a bed all to ourselves, babe—"

It was the *babe* that did it.

"Nobody calls me *babe* but my boyfriend," she growled,

pushing off the wall so hard he let go of her shoulders. And then she cocked her arm, pulled back, and hit him on the nose as hard as she could.

"Shit!"

Gus doubled over, clutching his nose, but he wasn't the one who'd sworn. She whirled around to see Caleb racing up the stairs, his face furious and panicked all at once.

"Are you okay?" He scanned her up and down, but before she could answer, he spun to Gus. "You're lucky she hit you first, asshole. I would've put you in a coma." He took a deep breath. "Maybe I still should."

Gus looked up at Mandy, his body still bent over, blood pouring between the fingers clasped over his nose. "I'm gonna turn you in, you stupid—"

"For what?" Mandy demanded, crossing her arms over her chest so he couldn't tell she was shaking. "Defending myself?" She glanced at Caleb. "I have a witness." Her breaths came fast and short, and nervous adrenaline rocketed through her, but so did a surging sense of empowerment.

Caleb scowled at Gus. "A witness *and* a whole pack of girls who'd back up her story."

Gus backed down the steps, glaring up at them. "Whatever. You two deserve each other. Fucking losers." Then he turned and scurried away, like a rat scuttling to a sewer.

Mandy faced Caleb, who stared at her like he'd never seen her before.

"You sure you're okay, Mandy?" He ran a hand through his hair. "I thought I'd be the one to clock him. Not you." He stared at her in awe.

She nodded, her pulse pounding in her ears and her body trembling slightly with adrenaline. "Yeah, I'm fine. And I think I just learned something."

He frowned, still scanning her like he wanted to make sure she was okay. "What?"

"Sometimes—in *extremely* rare cases—a little bit of violence might be the answer."

He blinked, then his beautiful smile appeared, just like sunshine breaking through storm clouds, but she didn't have time to stick around and enjoy it.

"I've gotta go! The trivia contest already started!" She opened the door and ran down the hall, her boots echoing on the linoleum, suddenly feeling free...and happy...and stupidly in love with that guy she'd left standing on the steps, who might or might not go to homecoming with her, if she asked him.

And she *was* going to ask him, as soon as she finished with the contest.

Chapter Twenty-Four
Fooled Around and Fell in Love

Wednesday, October 5

J.T. and Cammie went apoplectic when she ran into the caf.

"Where have you—"

"Why did you—"

She shushed them with a finger to her lips. "Later. I'll tell you everything later.

"Okay everyone!" Mandy's voice bounced back through the speakers, making her wince as the microphone whined with feedback. "Oops, sorry." She held the mic away from her face while people laughed.

"Let's get this show on the road!" Mandy's voice pulsed with energy. Who knew that punching a bad guy could give a person such a rush? Not that she was going to make a habit of it, because that would definitely mess up her karmic scale.

"You all should have score sheets at your table. Make sure to put your team's name on your paper."

J.T. leaned in and whispered in her ear. "You sure you're

okay? You look sort of weird." She rolled her eyes at him and turned back to the crowd.

"And no cheating, okay? It's more fun this way, if you don't use your cells to look up the answer." She waved the DVD case over her head. "And check out the grand prize for the winner!"

Scattered boos sounded around the room and a few crumpled lunch bags sailed toward the front of the room, landing at her feet. She leaned into the mic. "Knock it off. If you don't want to play, you can leave. But if you're staying, you're playing. By my rules, people." She shot Cammie a grin, and Cammie stared at her like she didn't recognize her.

"I like this new Mandy," J.T. whispered in her ear, then he gave her a low five.

Maybe he was right. After standing up to Spriggs and then defending herself with Gus, she did feel like a new person. She thought of Caleb telling her how strong she was, and felt a glow light her up from her toes up to her head.

"We're starting with an easy question," Mandy said, grinning. "What famous TV show featured three beautiful women detectives and a boss who gave orders over the phone?"

J.T. leaned over and spoke into the mic. "Here's a hint." He held a foil halo over Mandy's head. She glanced up, laughing, folding her hands in prayer like an angel.

She finished the next four questions, ready to turn over the mic to J.T., but he'd stepped back, texting furiously on his phone and gesturing wildly to Cammie, Leticia, Tonia, and Amber, who'd lined up behind her, and for some reason couldn't stop collapsing into giggles every time she glanced at them.

"Okay," she said, darting a glare at J.T. "Time to switch it up. I'm passing the mic to my partner, J.T. Get ready for the really tough questions now." She handed the mic to J.T., who didn't even look at her. His gaze scanned the caf wildly, like he was looking for someone. Liam was sitting right up front, so she didn't know why he looked so stressed.

She grabbed a water bottle and took a long drink, wondering if Gus really would report her. Whatever. For once in her life, she wasn't worried. Maybe it was the adrenaline buzz and she'd crash later, but right now, she was in her element, running an awesome trivia event, keeping people laughing, and getting everyone excited for tomorrow's dress-like-a-hippie day.

She poked J.T. in the back, since he hadn't asked a question. "We need to keep up the momentum," she whispered, and he arched an eyebrow.

"Momentum is not gonna be a problem." His mouth curved into a secretive smile, as he glanced at his phone one last time, then put the mic to his mouth. "We interrupt this trivia contest to bring you an important message from one of our sponsors."

"What?" Mandy whispered, stepping next to him. "What are you—"

But the lights in the caf suddenly shut off, and since there were only a few windows in the mostly cinder-block room, Mandy's eyes had a hard time adjusting.

"Do not panic," J.T. boomed into the mic, quieting the crowd. "This is all part of the show. Stay seated, and prepare to be amazed."

He turned back to Cammie and nodded. Mandy saw Cammie's teeth gleaming in the dim light like a Cheshire cat as she raised her camera and started snapping. Tonia, Leticia, and Amber shot past her and cartwheeled into the middle of the caf, then executed a perfect cheer.

"We've got spirit, yes we do! We've got spirit, how 'bout you?" They spun and pointed to the caf doors, which swung open as the whispered "Oooh...do it" opening lyrics of the iconic Hustle song from the seventies wafted through the sound system.

Mandy's heart raced as her eyes adjusted to the mostly dark room, the only light coming from a few lava lamps she'd scattered on a few tables for ambiance. Whispering and bubbling laughter echoed around the room.

"This one's for the Queen of Disco," J.T. announced, and suddenly laser lights—where the heck had those come from?—danced and gyrated, illuminating a guy in the middle of the room rocking a white John Travolta suit doing the Hustle dance moves perfectly. A guy who looked just like...

Mandy's mouth opened in shock. "Oh my God," she whispered.

Hoots and cheers filled the room as Caleb danced all by himself...until J.T. joined him, the two of them dancing in perfect rhythm to the song while everyone in the caf clapped in time to the song, laughing and catcalling.

Mandy couldn't breathe.

Cammie appeared next to her, pushing her toward the center of the room. "Go," Cammie whispered. "He's waiting for you."

"B-but I...he..." Mandy stammered.

Cammie giggled in her ear. "Get your ass out there, girl." Cammie shoved her harder this time, and Mandy stumbled into the lights. She thought the cheers got louder, but maybe it was her imagination.

Caleb spun in sync with J.T. and held out his hand toward her. J.T. grinned as she took a step toward them, and she willed herself not to blow it. Not to fall or stumble or wimp out.

Mandy stepped closer and stretched out her hand. Caleb grasped it, his grip warm and strong, pulling her into his arms and spinning her around, and the crowd went wild.

Just like she'd practiced a million times with J.T., she fell into the rhythm, and suddenly Cammie was next to her, then

Jiro and Liam, and they all danced, laughing and hamming it up as they did the grapevine and the eggbeater moves perfectly like they were starring in their own episode of *Soul Train*.

Mandy felt like she'd explode with happiness.

"I didn't know you could dance," Mandy said over the music as she and Caleb did a twisty grapevine move in perfect synch with Cammie and J.T.

Caleb shot her a sexy grin as he leaned in close. "Private lessons from the Blue Ranger. But maybe you can teach me your moves."

She almost lost her rhythm as heat flooded through her, but she kept up, aware that lots of people had joined them, dancing around the caf, some trying to mimic their Hustle moves, some making up their own, everyone laughing and dancing and making Mandy's heart fill to bursting.

"Also," Caleb said, pulling her into his arms, "I need to ask you something." He raised his eyebrows at J.T., who scurried off.

The overhead lights flicked on as Dr. Hairy flew through the door. "What is going on—"

But Mandy tuned her out because they weren't dancing anymore, and someone had lowered the volume on the song, and now Caleb was staring down into her eyes, one of his hands gripping her waist while the other brushed her curls off her face as the crowd, even Dr. Hairy, seemed to hold its collective breath.

"I'm assuming you're not going to homecoming with Gus anymore," he said softly. She shook her head, smiling into his dark eyes. "Good." He turned their bodies so they faced J.T., who held an enormous lime-green poster, decorated in glittering, psychedelic swirling colors, just like something straight out of the seventies.

Attached to the poster were packets of Pop Rocks

candies, pictures of disco balls, people dancing in disco outfits, the book cover from *The Catcher in the Rye,* several plastic Rainbow Ponies and a Power Ranger action figure. A red one.

Tonia, Amber, and Leticia lined up in front of them, arms outstretched toward Mandy, and launched into a full-volume chant.

"You're stuck in the seventies but he's stuck on you!"

They pirouetted in synchrony and pointed at Caleb. "You think he wears too much black, so he dressed in white for you!"

The crowd roared and cheered, especially when the cheerleaders jumped on one of the tables. Mandy saw Reg peek around a group of stoners to watch. He shook his head in mock disgust, but he grinned and gave her a thumbs-up.

Mandy was shaking now—with laughter and embarrassment and giddiness and just...she glanced up at Caleb, and his eyes sparked with mischief as he pulled her closer, then draped a disco ball necklace around her neck.

"It's not too late to get a date!" the girls cheered from the tabletop, legs kicking, arms pumping toward the ceiling. "Come on, Disco, don't say no! You know how much you want to go!"

Mandy collapsed against his chest, giggling, wondering if her heart was glowing through her shirt like Iron Man. "I thought you wanted to write *serious* literature...not cheers."

He laughed into her hair. "Yeah, well. I had help. And some guys will do anything to get what they want." His hand cupped her chin, and he tilted her face toward his. Mandy swallowed, no longer laughing.

"This isn't fake, right? I mean, you wouldn't go through this insanity just to get rid of a st—"

"It was never fake with us, Disco. *Never.*" Then his mouth crushed hers as his arms wrapped around her, molding him to her, while everyone whistled and clapped, and the cheerleaders belted out one last cheer.

"Three more days to bust a move! Get your asses ready to groove! If Caleb Torrs can do the Hustle, just think what he'll do with all those muscles!"

She pulled away, laughing against his lips. "Wow. Nice ego, dude."

Frustration streaked across his face, but he bit back a smile. "Okay, I did *not* write that one. But I know who did." He shot a glare at J.T. and Cammie, who were high-fiving and hugging each other.

"Your posse is insane, you know that, right?" he asked, his finger trailing down her neck and making her shiver.

"*Our* posse. And yeah, I know. That's why I love them."

His arms tightened around her, and she breathed in his amazing Caleb scent. "You know what's funny? I'd decided to ask *you* to the dance. After I KO'd Gus."

His mouth dropped open. "No shit? You mean all this was for nothing?"

She laughed and playfully shoved his chest. "*This* was the best prom-posal ever. I wouldn't have missed it for anything."

"So your answer is yes?"

"On one condition—you have to wear this suit."

His smile—his beautiful, open, Caleb smile—lit her up like a million firecrackers. "Anything for you, babe." He bent to kiss her, his lips lighting her up even more than his smile.

She pulled back just enough to whisper against his lips. "I was lying before, when I said your kisses didn't, um, do anything for me." She felt her cheeks heat up, but she didn't care—she had to tell him. *No more lies.* Somewhere, she knew the universe was applauding.

He cupped her head and drew her in close, whispering in her ear. "Oh, I know, Disco. I definitely know *that*."

And then he was kissing her again, a kiss full of shenanigans that violated every PDA rule and then some.

Someone cranked up the music again and Cammie's camera flashed and all around them people laughed and danced and cheered…

…even Dr. Hairy, who'd apparently decided to forget her "no PDA" rule, just this once.

Chapter Twenty-Five
I Melt with You

Homecoming, October 8

As Caleb stood on Mandy's porch, working up the nerve to ring the doorbell, his phone pinged with a text from his dad.

Have a good time tonight. Maybe bring your date by the house sometime.

He sighed, but a small smile tugged at his lips. *Thanks*, he texted. *I will.*

Maybe he would—some night when Helen stuck around, so it wouldn't be so awkward. With Mandy around, he and his dad might even pull off an actual conversation. But right now he needed to focus. He shoved his phone back in his pocket.

He took a breath, one of Mandy's calming ones, and pressed the doorbell. The door swung open and he came face-to-face with Reg, who stepped back to let him inside.

"And the cavalry arrives," Reg said, his expression something between a grimace and a smile. "I was worried I'd have to take her there myself."

Caleb hesitated, but fortunately the tiny white-haired lady sitting in the recliner came to his rescue.

"Come in, Caleb Torrs," she demanded. "Come closer so I can inspect you with my old lady eyes."

Embarrassed heat burned Caleb's neck as he stepped into the living room.

"She's harmless," Reg whispered. "But a little weird." Then Reg straightened and put his asshole face back on, shaking his head in disgust. "What's that piece of crap you're wearing, dude? You look like a—"

"Caleb?"

Mandy appeared, framed like a portrait in the door to the living room, her green dress hugging her body in ways Caleb definitely appreciated, her red hair twisted up in some fancy style that showed off her neck, and her electrifying smile aimed at him. Just him.

Damn. The crazy prom-posal, the fake drama, the stalker…all of it had been worth it for just this moment.

"Did I hear the doorbell?" A huge red-haired guy lumbered in from the kitchen. Her dad, had to be. He stopped when he saw Caleb. "And who's this?"

"Mandy's boyfriend," Gran said matter-of-factly from her chair, smiling impishly. "Isn't he adorable? A bit devilish, but we like them like that, don't we, dear? A real badass, that Caleb." Gran tilted her head back to wink at Mandy, whose face flushed as red as he imagined his was.

Mandy's dad groaned and scrubbed a hand down his face. "Mom, please. If you don't stop with the swearing…" He sighed, shaking his head, then crossed the room to shake Caleb's hand. "I'm Mandy's dad. You must be her date for the dance."

Every eye in the room zeroed in on him, and Caleb started to sweat. He wasn't used to this type of scrutiny, and he'd never done this whole dance-date thing before. He cleared his throat as he shook Mr. Pennington's hand.

"I'm Caleb Torrs. Nice to meet you, sir."

Reg snorted at the "sir," and Caleb made a mental note to beat the crap out of him later. Or maybe not, since he *was* Mandy's stupid brother.

Mandy's dad released his hand and sized him up, grinning. "That's a helluva suit, Caleb. You find it in a thrift store or what?"

"It reminds me of what you wore to prom, Herb," Mandy's gran said to her dad. "Those ridiculous lapels."

"It's the Travolta suit," Mandy said proudly. "From *Saturday Night Fever*."

"We should take pictures," her dad said. "Caleb, you go stand next to Mandy. Reg, take some pictures on your phone."

"Those two are so ugly they'll crack my screen," Reg joked.

Mr. Pennington thumped Reg on the back of his head, rolling his eyes in exasperation. "Shut up and take the pictures." He glanced at Caleb, who hadn't moved. "Go on, son."

Caleb exhaled a long breath and crossed the room to Mandy, then suddenly remembered the box he held in his hand. "This is for you." He opened the plastic box and removed the wrist corsage, hating that his hands were shaking. "I remembered you said your dress was green so I—"

She put her hand on his, and he looked up to meet her gaze. "It's beautiful, Caleb."

He searched her eyes, overwhelmed by what he saw, which was everything he'd dared to hope he might see someday from her, for him.

"Somebody turn up my oxygen," Gran said from her chair. "I'm getting dizzy. This is better than the *Gilmore Girls*."

• • •

The Silk Lamp was busy, but only one table was full of people dressed for homecoming. Mandy surveyed her friends, so full of happiness she didn't know if she could stand it.

Liam and J.T. wore matching powder-blue tuxes with ridiculous ruffled shirts, and matching rhinestone Elton John glasses. Cammie wore a vintage Gunne Sax dress—a torrent of lace ruffles she'd found in her aunt's closet. She'd added a magenta streak to her dark hair for the occasion. Jiro wore a silly green shiny leisure suit that he'd scored at a thrift shop.

Mandy swooned every time she glanced at her wrist corsage, and her mood ring, which was deep purple, for love. And every time she looked at Caleb, because he rocked that Travolta suit like nobody's business. While the other guys looked silly, he just looked…edible. His shiny dark hair gleamed in the soft lights, and his hand rested on her knee, occasionally giving her a squeeze that made her tingle.

She'd given him a boutonniere, which was pinned to his Travolta jacket, and something else, too—a stuffed bear she'd made at Build-a-Buddy that morning. The fuzzy bear wore tiny jeans and a tiny fake-leather jacket, with a red satin heart sewn inside, but she was keeping the heart a secret—for now. The bear was perched on the dashboard of his car, as their mascot for the evening.

As her friends laughed and chattered, she met his dark, intense gaze.

"Having a good night, Disco?"

"Having a *great* night, TDB."

He smirked and moved his hand to her neck, twining his fingers through a few stray strands from her uptwist, making her forget to breathe. "I know what that stands for now."

"Because you were eavesdropping."

He shrugged, smiling wickedly. He'd been all smug and

cocky ever since he'd figured out the Tall, Dark, and Broody nickname earlier tonight, when he'd overheard her whispering to Cammie.

"You know I'm going to make you dance all night, right?"

He lifted her disco ball necklace and spun it in his fingers. "Of course." He slanted her a smile that told her he'd dance with her as much as she wanted.

Their waitress delivered water and sodas, then rushed away, promising to be back soon to take their orders.

"Oh, hey," J.T. said, "we forgot to ask her to light the candle. Where's the *ambiance*?"

"Got it handled, Blue Ranger," Caleb said, rolling his eyes but reaching into the pocket of the leather jacket draped over the back of his chair. He pulled out his brother's lighter, pausing before holding it to the candle wick since everyone was staring at him openmouthed.

"What? You guys *seriously* thought I could light it with my finger?" He scowled at them, perfecting his stormy glare, but his lips quirked, remembering something Mandy had said a while back. "Let me guess? Like Warren Peace in *Sky High*?"

Cammie's gaze darted to Mandy, and they both collapsed into giggles.

"We were sort of hoping," Mandy said through her laughter as he held the lighter to the wick and the flame burst to life.

He leaned back in his chair, smirking at them. "Sorry to disappoint, posse of insanity, but I'm not a superhero."

"Oh, I disagree," Mandy said, turning in her chair to face him. "You're definitely *my* hero."

Everyone laughed and groaned. J.T. made fake gagging noises and Cammie tossed a balled-up napkin at them, but Mandy didn't care. She leaned into him, trailing a finger down his shiny black disco shirt.

His eyes widened and he swallowed, his smirk slipping. "Am I really?" he asked, his voice soft.

"Yeah," she said, her lips brushing his. "You, Caleb Torrs, are magnificent. And don't you forget it."

And suddenly they were kissing...*again*...and Mandy didn't care if they got kicked out of her favorite restaurant because she'd finally figured out who the villain was...and who the hero was...even if he couldn't shoot fire from his fingers.

And she was never breaking up with him again.

For real.

Acknowledgments

This book was inspired by *Sky High*, one of my favorite movies, so I send major fangirl love to everyone who brought that movie to life. It's a fabulous story—except I always thought Warren and Layla were destined for each other, which is why I created Caleb and Mandy.

I have many superheroes to thank for helping me turn this vague idea into a book:

Brilliant critique partners Pamela Mingle and Laura K. Deal, amazing beta readers Katie Robinson and Alexis Johnson, superagent Nicole Resciniti, and my fantastic editor Liz Pelletier, who doesn't let me sneak anything in that doesn't belong, no matter how hard I try.

As always, my deepest love and gratitude to my family for supporting my dreams, feeding me when I'm in a writing trance, and always making me laugh.

About the Author

Lisa Brown Roberts still hasn't recovered from the teenage trauma of nearly tweezing off both eyebrows and having to pencil them in for an entire school year. This and other angst-filled memories inspire her to write YA books about navigating life's painful and funny dramas, and falling in love along the way. She lives in Colorado in a house full of books, boys, four-legged prima donnas, and lots of laughter. Twitter @LBrownRoberts or visit her at her website, www.lisabrownroberts.com.

Discover more of Entangled Teen Crush's books...

DEFYING GRAVITY
a *Finding Perfect* novel by Kendra C. Highley

Zoey Miller lives for her holidays in Aspen. Her time up on the mountain with the Madison brothers, Parker and Luke, is everything. But for the first time, it's not enough. Now she's determined to win one of the brothers' hearts. The brother she has in mind is a renowned player, with hordes of snow-bunnies following him around Snowmass resort. And the other...well, he's her best friend and knows she deserves better. Namely him. And *he's* going to win *her* heart.

THE SECRET LIFE OF A DREAM GIRL
a *Creative HeArts* novel by Tracy Deebs

Dahlia Greene—aka international pop superstar Cherry—is undercover as a normal high school student. Playing a little matchmaker for Keegan Matthews seems like the perfect opportunity to live a real life. What she doesn't know is that the girl Keegan's been secretly crushing on is her. Keegan figures he'll play along with Dahlia's plan to help him woo someone else, then make his move. But with so many secrets, their romance is doomed from the start...

Also by Lisa Brown Roberts...

PLAYING THE PLAYER

HOW (NOT) TO FALL IN LOVE

THE REPLACEMENT CRUSH